By Shannon Bohnen

Fiction

At First Sight

Poetry

Exhalations

At First Sight

Shannon Bohnen

Fancy Clam Books

At First Sight
Second Edition

Published by Fancy Clam Books

ISBN-13: 978-0-692-04066-9
ISBN-10: 0-692-04066-8

United States of America

To Keith

If a picture paints a thousand words
Then why can't I paint you?
The words will never show
The you I've come to know

If a face could launch a thousand ships
Then where am I to go?
There's no one home but you
You're all that's left me too
And when my love for life is running dry
You come and pour yourself on me

If a man could be two places at one time
I'd be with you
Tomorrow and today
Beside you all the way

If the world should stop revolving
Spinning slowly down to die
I'd spend the end with you
And when the world was through
Then one by one the stars would all go out
Then you and I would simply fly away

Bread - "If"

1: The End of All Things to Come

The ground buckled beneath them. The comet was said to have hit the center of South America, but they didn't see the news that day. They hardly left the house at all, except to re-up on smokes, which was their main mission at this place in time.

Erizabet stumbled on a crack in the street and Mire steadied her gait, placing his hand on the small of her back. There was no sign of life for miles, so they slowly took their time picking through the steaming rubble that cropped up on either side of the street.

Another rumble sent a transistor into motion. It sparked, popped, and cracked in half, showering the surrounding shrubbery with flaming hunks of metal. A rose bush came alive, its spirit lifting away with an audible *whoosh* in darting flights of pink and green.

It seemed the only place still open for business in all of St. Paul was the SA on the corner.

They agreed to disagree. She decided to procure the libations if he'd buy them a couple of packs of smokes, at least enough to last the night. If they were chain smoking and worried, they'd run out quicker, but she thought she could make them last at least until this thing passed over, when they could hook up their computer rigs again.

They pretended the world wasn't ending. Usually the worry wort, Riz was pacified like a horse with a shroud over its head. Mire kept her calm, kept her sane. They would just get their smokes and everything would be back to normal...

The guy at the counter looked singularly zombified, his countenance at once haggard and playful. She thought he might have a trick up his sleeve, as if he spent the last week devising a way to outrun the Four Horsemen of the Apocalypse and was keeping his secret safe. She thought he probably confided in his blow-up doll left shivering in the unheated basement of his mom's house, however.

"That'll be $27.95," he said, a little saliva escaping the corner of his mouth. While his hands moved robotically, the guy was clearly not in the appropriate headspace to cater to the whims of a young couple lucky enough to find themselves trapped together during such tragic times.

Riz was staring at him, dazed, a pen grazing her lips, trying not to chew on the cap. Mire reached over, dug in her purse, and produced his wallet. The back pockets of his pants were worn through, aided by the fact Riz took it upon herself to appropriate the lining for one of her weird chair upholstery projects. She snapped out of her stupor when Mire reached his hand across the counter, laying out a few bills. She protested, covering up the money with one hand, while digging into her purse with the other.

"Wait, wait. I know it's here. Somewhere..." she said, lifting a leg to prop up her oversized purse. "Aha!"

She paid, and Mire pushed open the door, nodding in suggestion that she go first. She reluctantly passed under his extended arm. Mire looked back at the waif at the counter and said, "Thanks, man."

Lifting a hand in reply, the guy responded in kind, "Good luck, out—" but they were already gone.

Like an insatiable honey badger, she tore at the pack, releasing a single cigarette from the confines of the corrugated cardboard. They made them practically childproof after the kids started manufacturing their own packs back in 2290.

"Slow down there, killer," Mire said, gently placing a smoke in between his lips. He was always so graceful, especially under duress. She kept her sights on the ground, only lifting her head to exact an emphatic exhale of relief.

She stopped abruptly in the street, Mire furtively glancing around for signs of burglars, pimps, rapists, anyone sorry enough to attempt something suicidal tonight.

"What are we doing?" she asked, arms raised in question. Mire took a slow drag on his cigarette, squinting at her through the darkness.

"Well, I thought we could get out of here, for starters. At least get back to the apartment so we have some chance of survival without asphyxiating to death." He was so calm it was almost eerie.

Propelled by his confidence, she started forward, and then the rhythm of the universe tilted on its axis, her hopes slid this way, reality that way. She turned to Mire, befuddled.

"What? What are you saying?" She took a drag, looked at her cigarette, for a moment scared. "Did he put something in these? What are you picking up on?"

Mire shrugged, hands in pockets, and continued on. It's a wonder he still had pockets in that old tattered jacket of his. March through November, he always wore it. Every year. Sometimes randomly throughout the year. She hadn't known him that long, but she could sense he'd held onto that thing, unwashed, she assumed, since he was a teenager. Was it his father's?

She lurched closer to him, "Come on. You're holding out on me." He smiled, took a puff off the cigarette, and flicked the cherry with his thumb, eliciting a little "wuh-tish" sound, then stuffed the butt in his pocket. He shrugged, hands in his pockets. He leaned back on the heels of his feet, then forward on his toes, almost arching his body in an exact 45 degree angle, then righted himself.

"What? You said you didn't want to know." He tilted his head back and looked at the stars.

Riz poked him, twice, in quick succession. "I thought we weren't going to dig into this. The science and all of it? Just go down with the ship, right? This is our home. So what if it burns up in a cloud of smoke and ash." She finished her cigarette, kneeled down, and wiped it out on the ground.

"OK. Well, what have you been reading, huh?" he said, eyebrows arched. It was her turn to shrug and play the innocent doe. She started heading toward home. He stepped up to her.

"Oh, no. You didn't," quickly grasping her arm, then after realizing what he was doing, he dropped it. "What a couple of hypocrites, huh." He stuck his hand in his upper coat pocket, fishing for another cigarette.

"I'm sorry," she said, craning up on tiptoes to kiss his cheek. "I might have peeked a little. It's all over the net, man!"

"Eesh," he feigned disgust, recoiling from each of her kisses. "Ah, babe." He brought her into his arms, still standing there in the middle of the street.

The lights in the SA suddenly went dim and then silence enveloped them. No electric hum. No cars whirring past. Just them.

"It's ok, it'll be ok," he said, drawing her closer, placing his chin on the top of her head. Her forehead fit perfectly cupped between his collar bone and cheek. "I might have heard something..."

Riz pulled back and scrutinized his face. "Ok, ok," she said, hands surrendering.

He took a drag, simultaneously pointing to the back of his neck. She nodded, understanding. He sometimes forgot to turn off his cerebral scanner. His implant picked up on local stress signals from fellow Implanters. There was a big commotion about it, the debate snuffed out by the news of a potential collapse of the human race.

It was Krunk against Jemenez and neither of the options looked good. Krunk had this master plan to harness the energy of volcanoes to fuel the future of the automobile industry and Jemenez was kind of a flake. Despite his admonitions, no one believed he could communicate with aliens. Hell, the past 15 presidents have tried, until the last one was laughed out of office. In any case, the radio waves were buzzing with anticipation. The election was tonight, and they'd soon see who won the battle.

"It was that guy, Riz. He was broadcasting on overdrive. Overloading frequencies within proximity, no doubt. Saying something about a survival bunker. 'Calling all women! Take refuge...' Something like that."

"Fuck. How desperate can you be?" she said, laughing.

He flicked out his second smoke, shook his head and admitted, "Well, a couple of girls already took the bait."

Riz looked at him incredulously.

"Seriously," he continued. "Saw a couple of blips there, on screen, heading in that direction." He motioned toward the freeway and what he saw left him speechless. His jaw dropped open.

He suddenly grabbed Riz in a full-body hug, near enough to choke her and she instinctively gasped. She trusted him to protect her, but her stiff muscles told a different story.

She closed her eyes and the once-snowy atmosphere around her quickly elevated to a heat of 120 degrees or more.

She buried her face in his chest and felt a teardrop fall onto her head. She witnessed the black night light up with white heat, then looked down to see the skin melting back and peeling off her hand.

Her body went numb after the shock of excruciating pain and her hair was on fire. Her mind held on for the briefest of seconds while her organs boiled and burst.

The last thing she knew was she loved him.

2: A Love That Forever Was

It all started when she went to that gas station for the first time. He shot light rays from his eyes, dissecting her soul, twin torpedoes locking onto to their target. She'd stumbled in, tripping on the dirty old floor mat, losing her footing a second. When she saw him, his gaze was like a blow to the chest. She looked around and wondered what just hit her.

She took a breath and stepped up to the counter, gurgled out some nonsensical grumblings and dragged his attention away from the computer. He looked in her eyes, understood what she was after, and gave her the goodies. Then she was out the door.

In the space of five minutes, both their lives changed irreversibly.

Their first date was a trip to the moon. They'd met at the launchpad he built on the roof of his apartment. She wasn't sure she found the right coordinates, but then he'd activated the decloaking apparatus and the field of view cleared, revealing an enormous platform of concrete and sheet metal.

He was a tinkerer, he said, and she'd believed him. She had taken his hand knowingly, like they had always been linked. It was the perfect night for a flight to outer space.

He led her up the steps to the shallow cockpit of the craft. She thought it looked a mite bit dangerous with wires strewn about and lights flickering on and off sporadically. Apparently, it was built for one, so she sidled up onto his lap and let him buckle her in. The vehicle took off.

The vibrations sent shivers up and down her spine and she swore she was about to come, then the spacecraft broke through the clouds and she was in heaven as they leapt toward the musical spheres.

Circumventing the geosynchronous orbit of various satellites, they'd come upon another world. There, entire cities were in motion. Calamitous machines made no sound as they touched down near an active civilization of engineers busying themselves co-creating new life on another orb.

She was flush with anxiety, overwhelmed and embarrassed at the thought of having to compete with this audacious display of affection. She remained silent with awe, keeping her thoughts to herself.

He came to know that when she was quiet, there was something brewing in that brain of hers. He saw right through her, splayed his fingers toward the tip of her crown, and protected her head from potential injury as the machine jostled them about.

They learned a lot about each other during those first three months, venturing out often enough for him to make friends with all the folks down at her favorite watering holes, and she blended in well with his old high school buddies.

They had long since given up on sleep. Their friends all called them crazy, upon hearing the babble they exchanged for speech. They made up a secret code only they understood, comprised mostly of grunts and slight twitches in retinal patterns, and they made it work.

It was as if they had always been together, the other forever lurking in the corners of their memories. For a time they spent their days sneaking around the edges of buildings, dripping into flight propulsion modules, taking off at the drop of a hat and never looking back.

They soon realized they didn't need anyone else, save each other. They sealed the apartment door shut with liquid cement, as rudimentary a substance as could be imagined, but it would do the trick, he said. And it did.

They mentally withdrew from society, subsisting solely on cheese curds and the vapors pouring forth from their poorly insulated walls. Every day that summer, come sun up, the city would be blanketed in a helium fog, and one of their favorite things in the world was to press their noses to the window panes and suck in the toxic gases, then laugh the day away in psychotropic revelry.

He got fired from his job at SuperComArtWorld, and she simply stopped showing up at Marketing Firm 237.

When their most comfortable period set in, the power went out, so he rigged up a mechanism to provide sustainable energy using magnets, a tuning fork, and some conductive thread. She fell in love with him more and more each day and they grew closer as the days grew colder.

Closed off now, they had plenty of time on their hands. They began hatching schemes for various business ventures that would produce multiple streams of income. All they had to do was hit some keys, twist some knobs, and flick some switches on their homemade musical instruments. Instantly lauded as the new power duo of the webtroposphere, they soon let their creativity fly and land where it may. A dash of color here, a sine wave there, some warbling noise that resembled a theremin, and they were rolling in dough.

Digital, offshore bankers wanted their attention, but they'd kept to themselves. Greedy in their lust for more cyber trust-fund ventures, they had created their own system of conversion so their computerized credits turned into what resembled Monopoly money to the untrained eye. They were untraceable.

That was when they decided it was time to make headway toward greener pastures. They found a quaint little spot in Florida, near the Keys. The ocean called to her, filled her soul with a quiet she'd been too restless to recognize before. He dabbled in gambling, picked up some hat tricks from the locals, and wrote an album about the knowledge he'd gained from the old folks.

They basked in the sun and kept their creativity flowing, moving from place to place, never settling in one spot for too long. Though they stayed with friends, they were mentally drained, and sleeping on couches gave no respite for the rest they sought.

The clock sped up, slowed down, time stopped, then it seemed to run away from them.

The following scenes played out like one of those sped-up time lapses, cheesy b-roll or something. See her play on the computer, see her grab a beer, now she's wearing a shawl, crouched over a book, now there's a candle burning in a corner, now she's lighting a cigarette with the flame.

Then the movie finds its appropriate pacing and the camera settles on her steadily moving frame, chest rising, falling slowly, feet kicking every once in a while as she sleeps.

He's finally stirring. Peeks out from behind the door to the crystal chamber, steals a glance at her, and tip toes comically, hands setting the course for the space between the floor and his frame as he steps toward the door. He quietly turns the doorknob, takes one last look at her and departs, closing the door behind him.

He walked briskly, chest pushed forward, threatening the cold to permeate his blazing hot and excited core. He was on a mission to destroy the dream that was pervading his work life. It suddenly dawned on him he may look like a junkie rushing off to get a fix. What he was attempting to do was quite the exact opposite, in fact. He wanted to be rid of this thing once and for all.

It was hard enough to focus against the bits of snow that clung to his eyelashes. Fighting back tears as he squinted his eyes, he stopped briefly, took a deep breath and wiped his face with gloved hands. It stung. How did he manage to inadvertently scrape himself there? He neglected to take his girl's advice about the lotion. *What good is it anyway?* he thought. Gathering his strength, he composed himself and opened his eyes.

He realized the only solace he found from one of his infamous walkabouts was to realize he was through with them. *Riz...* he thought and shoved his hands back deep into his pockets, practically running toward home.

3: Dandy Beaverton, the Egg That Lives in My House

After a time he realized he was losing his memory. He was so fully enveloped by her, he began to feel parts of himself slip away. At one point he was unable to communicate in entire sentences; he would over-enunciate certain words and, at other times, say things which made no sense whatever, such as "I suppose", apropos of nothing, or, "Slap it on my ding dong. Cheese," and Riz's favorites: "Tallywackin' bitch smack," "La la la, she skirts the light of day with titillating crescents," and "Dandy Beaverton. Eh? That's the name of the egg that lives in my house," and other such nonentities.

Sometimes he laughed at himself, when he felt completely exhausted and irritated, unable to decipher whether there was any meaning to his words at all.

He went to visit his friend, Petridge, who was a scientist of sorts. His current obsessions included collecting birds and harvesting their living tissue to study alternative means of flight. He was trying to marry the wingspans of a rare species of dove to his own shoulder blades with a device he invented, to no avail, but that didn't stop him from trying.

Mire grasped the door knocker and thwacked, once, twice, thrice, and relieving a short spell of irony from his daily life,

Petridge cleared the debris of rotting bones and tepid vials from his desk and saw to Mire's afflictions.

After a few hours of poking and prodding, interspersed with misplaced syllables, the conclusion was null in void. The moot point of the conjoined experience rendered Mire's footfalls slack and downtrodden. He returned home, defeated.

What was the source of this craziness? Certainly sudden onset love couldn't drive a man to babble incoherently. There was something else...

One week before, While Mire was having a smoke outside, pondering his latest project, he looked down absentmindedly and realized he'd stumbled upon a glass shard in the cigarette-infested grout on the street corner of his old apartment. The crystalline edifice glowed and shimmered, its pink and purple neon rays suckered him in, eradicating all previous thought. He knew this discovery warranted further investigation.

He had called Petridge, who at the time was less than enthused. "Sleep it off, buddy," he said, and Mire protested: "No, wait. There's something I *really* need to talk to you about. It concerns a certain rock I may or may not have found precariously placed in such a way so that *I* was the one to find it..." Petridge was always a sucker for rocks and other found objects.

His ears pricked up. "Go on," he said, curious, and they began to discuss the discovery.

Petridge said it was an anomaly. "Alien glass, or something." Taking on a weird warble to his tone, he continued, "Heretofore, it was a material not readily available on Earth, yet we are certain Mire de Champs had to be the one to find its place of origin." He was using his best impression of the Newsheads.

Mire smiled through a haze of smoke.

"Maybe some space debris broke off from a nearby me-teor, circumvented the globe, and charted a course specifical-ly to him, just barely bearing the brunt of the brutal beating of Earth's stratospheric womb, to thrust its carefully charted course toward the one and only Mire."

Turning Petridge's words over in his mind, Mire was sure it was an energy source of some sort. He could feel a strange heat emanating from the luster of the crystal. For a second, its power took hold of him and he thought he could revolutionize the industrial waste facilities the world over, thus becoming fi-nancially secure once and for all. If only he could get his hands on more of this stuff.

Pet went back to his own experiments, while Mire spent nights testing the thing. He shaved off shards of the thing, he set fire to it. Once he encased it in an old Altoids tin and plugged it into one of his distortion pedals to see if he could translate the vibrations he felt into tangible sounds, trying to awaken the glow within.

Sometimes Riz stirred at night, disturbed by the resonat-ing hum that seemed to permeate her skin; it set her teeth a-chattering. It seemed, even in her sleep, to put her on edge. Mire thought about how sensitive she was and believed her reaction was proof he was onto something.

He was losing sleep, spending long hours staring into the glow. He might have traded in one swift love with another, or so she thought. He created contraptions for it, fit for a king, and finally settled on an anti-gravity device that, to him, was the only thing that could do it justice. The rock was cradled on a soft pillow of constantly warring neutrons.

Riz tried to talk to him, coax him into bed, but he was enamored. He even brought the thing to work and found it had a strange affect on his more loyal customers.

"How's it going, Frank?" He asked one of the regulars. The hobbling creature of a man stepped up to the counter of his woodworking shop.

"I, uh..." The old man trailed off.

He came in every day. Why, just yesterday, he was dancing a little jig to the holographic music video projected onto the third aisle of the shop. He was one of the most spry old men Mire had seen in years.

Now, Frank was reduced to blubbering and swaying like one of those strange shrimps you see clinging on the edge of the rock in a saltwater tank, desperately wishing his genetically-modified crustacean anatomy would fail, letting his carapace fall apart, to crash to the sand below.

"I'll just have a stick of licorice," the old man said.

Tilting his head, curious, Mire replied. "Now, Frank, you know they don't make that stuff anymore. It's banned on three planets. Made from horse hoofs? The Animal Cruelty Act and whatnot," he twirled his hand in the air, fumbling toward cordiality. "Gelatin, I think that's what they used to call it..."

Frank looked bewildered for a moment, then began to nod slowly. Staring off into the distance, he remembered something. He looked back at Mire, who smiled, nodded, and raised his eyebrows simultaneously in what was one of those uncontrollable expressions of sympathy.

Frank raised a finger, nodded back, and Mire thought, *Now he's got it*, but the man was slowly shuffling out the door.

"What the..." Mire snatched out his notebook from his back pocket, glanced around furtively to make sure his employees weren't looking—he didn't want to set a bad example—and made a note in shorthand.

The physical book transferred the scribblings instantly,

floating through the microwaves that seared the surrounding atmosphere, imperceptibly sending the signal to his brain to be stored there indefinitely until he wanted to dredge up the memory and regurgitate it back out to Pet, later.

He logged his findings privately, pushing his notes back into the digital recesses of his newly-installed memory microchip, embedded into the southernmost corner of his left hemisphere.

4: Pet's Gone Off the Rails

Later that night, as Pet paced back and forth in his chambers, Mire stood there in silence, gently crushing a cigarette between his index and middle fingers. He took a drag.

"So, what you're saying is that we've come upon an alien life form and it wants to suck our brains out?"

Pet stopped moving suddenly. He was impatient, furious even. Pivoting on the balls of his feet, he turned to Mire, took his shoulders fiercely in both hands and brought his face in close. Mire tilted his head incredulously, and with a slight frown, he let his expression melt to child's play.

"What?" he laughed.

"Don't you see what's going on here?" Pet implored. Mire and Riz exchanged looks. She shrugged, looked at the ceiling.

"You have been chosen, my friend," he said. Intrigued, Mire put out his smoke and leaned in, fingers steepled beneath his chin. "Go on."

"OK." Pet commenced pacing. "So, I've been working on this for a while—"

Mire interjected, throwing up his hands, "It's been two weeks! I'd hardly call that a while." He rolled his eyes, but Pet continued on in a whisper, as if Mire hadn't said anything at all.

"—always alone in my dark room," he was wringing his

hands. "I realize I've become isolated from what's happening out here in the world," his head tilted up, bound for the ceiling. He extended his arms, as if asking for some invocation from God.

The other two exchanged a glance. It was Mire's turn to shrug, and with a sly smile, he and Riz exchanged silent words. She covered her mouth to hide a giggle.

Mire's shoulders were once again held in the death grip of his best friend. "Can't you see, man? It's the light beings. They are trying to communicate with you." He released his friend and walked to the door of the bedroom. Putting his hand on the wooden frame, he brushed back his hair with the other hand, whispering to himself. "I've been looking in the wrong direction this entire time," he said.

Finally feeling like she might not be able to swing the conversation into more of a comedic routine, Riz walked over to Mire, lit two cigarettes, and handed him one. They both waited patiently for Pet to continue.

Pet grabbed a chair, swung it around and sat on it backwards, cowboy style. "Can I have one of those?" he asked, eyes unsure of the outcome of his immediate decision. Physically, he only knew he had to convey his reasoning all too soon, before things flew out of his control completely. His father, the salesman, taught him in order to get people to take you seriously, it helps to mimic their gestures. That way they know you're playing for the same team. Mire made a face that said sure, why the hell not, and tossed Pet the pack.

Once settled in the living room, the two entered into a heated debate. Riz stared entranced by the slight waving of the Japanese tapestry, feigning idiotic indifference. Borderline high, she sat switching back from actively memorizing what they were saying and spacing out completely. Mire watched the way her eyes looked over the room, active constantly. Who knew what kind of puzzle she constructed out of the snippets she collected.

"So, my theory is," Pet began, "That there's an orbiting sphere nearby, much like our good old friend, the moon—" at this, Riz stole a glance toward him, caught him looking for someone who might interpret the pause as emphasis, then continued finding things around the room to focus on.

"You know how it follows us around the sun, always showing us its belly?" he said, gesturing with his cigarette. "There's a place where people are made of gaseous matter and they shit this stuff out. These crystals." He looked at Riz again, who shrugged off the otherwise-unobserved vulgarity. "So to speak. And they harvest it. Like bees used to do with their wax."

"I see," Mire chimed in. "So these crystals harbor food for this species? Do they live off their own bodily waste or something?"

"Not necessarily," Pet continued. "I think they exchange it for currency or something. I mean, these are precious pieces, aren't they? Sculpted magnificently into perfect geometric shapes..."

His eyes lit up at the thought of it.

My god, these guys are both in love with this thing, Riz thought

"...but I wouldn't put it past them. They're highly evolved, you see. They propel themselves through their own self-contained airspace, and follow along predetermined paths set forth by their more distinguished elders. Like ants," he said, eyes wide, epiphany-struck.

How does he know this stuff? Mire thought. *Or is he just making it up on the spot?*

"It sounds to me like these 'higher beings' have more in common with our lower lifeforms, the flora and fauna, than they do, let's say, the 'Martians' of Area 51 or whatever."

"Dude, that was like a gazillion years ago," Pet said. "What are you reading nowadays?" He dismissed the potential tangent with a wave of his hand. "Nevermind. What I'm saying is, we should try to contact these things and get invited into their secret alien society, so we can become hydrogen-composed matter like they are!"

Mire could tell that Pet was too excited for his own good. He leaned back in his chair, squinty-eyed, thoughtful.

"What do you think, Riz?" He turned to her in one smooth motion, it was as if she had been a part of the conversation the whole time, not just an onlooker. "Is this a confounding Twilight Zone mystery that we've stumbled upon here, or was I born to find this hunk of space junk?"

Now they were both looking at her. She sat up straight in rapt attention. Catching them off guard, she ventured a sigh to dispel the lingering tension in the room. She stood up.

"Well, you're the mad scientists, here." She went into the kitchen to fetch another round of brews. "Really, what does this have to do with your winged-colleagues, Pet? Is there a connection?"

Pet pressed his fingers to his forehead in anguish. "God-dammit, woman, have you been listening at all? Or just doing that fuzzy thinking thing where you're surfing the web while in the same room as us? I don't even know why you're here at such a momentous occasion."

Mire glared at Pet. "Honestly," said the latter, eyes shifting downward.

She pretended she couldn't hear them over the creaking of the refrigerator door. Mire leaned over to where Pet sat, wriggling.

"Psst... she didn't join the Corps, brother. No implant," he said. Tapping his head.

"Wha?" Pet replied. "Then what—" He shook his head in disbelief. "Well," he said, hands on knees, stretching himself up into a standing position. "Speaking of which, I should see to my pets." He enunciated the consonants on the last word, further begrudging her pet name for him. "I'll let you two..." he flipped flopping hands in the air, "...do whatever it is you do." He bowed in retreat.

Riz handed Mire a beer and came over to sit on his lap.

"Let's binge-watch the telly, yeah? Get our minds off of this..." he, too made some weird gesture with his hands, "...thing."

She nodded in agreement, sat on his lap a spell, and rested her head on his shoulder. Two hours later, they rediscovered themselves, asleep on the stool.

Fully rested, they awoke, yawned, and readjusted themselves.

"OK," he said.

"OK," she replied. She kissed him on the cheek and went to her computer. They checked on their accounts.

"The Naniwrimo's fluctuating at an alarming rate," she said. "Should I just sell it and get rid of it?" she asked him, eyes glued to the screen.

"Naw, that's your baby, babe," he said, not moving from his position in front of his own computer. "What do you think about that Swiss account? I've got these guys over there who have sampled our shtick and want to take it a step further," he said. "Meaning..." she wondered aloud, looking over at him, finally taking an interest in something other than her own affairs.

"Meaning, I think it's time for a change." She raised her eyebrows, forehead dipping, gesturing for him to go on. "OK," he said, as he crossed his legs and moved away from the screen. He plopped down in a chair next to her. "We'll sell everything. Start over. It's simple, really. I think we should market this crystal thing and get some funding to do our own experiments. Fuck what Petridge thinks..."

She was beginning to feel a little worried. Has his obsession with the rock begun to cloud his judgment? He seems a little edgy, she thought. *He's never once mentioned dismissing his friends.*

"I think you're being a little rash, honey. We're sitting pretty, like you said. Let's just think this thing through," she said.

Frustrated, he got up to make sure the other room was still basking in that precious pink glow. After a few minutes, he closed the door, locked it, and she went back to her daily tasks.

Wrapped in a shroud of light, he didn't notice when he began to lose sight. Thinking his favorite thing of the month had started to darken naturally, he fumbled for the light switch, felt himself flip it to the upright position, and nothing happened. He shrugged. *Maybe we're out of power,* he thought.

He felt along the walls of the living room, eventually made his way over to where she was sitting cross-legged, Indian style, on the sofa where they made love most of the time. He fell to her side, the old springs singing the story of their age under the crushed cushions.

He rested his head on her shoulder and felt the corners of her blade-like jawline stab the tips of his crown. Her breathing was slow, involuntary, it felt, which was rare for her and that skittish frame she called a body.

Things were getting increasingly creepy, he thought. *Why*

was it so quiet in here? What was she doing sitting in the dark?

She was watching the minute shifts in light patterns yawn their way across the bespeckled spackling of their imitation chrome ceiling, awestruck in admiration of the way light from the external world could find its way into their dank little hovel. Those enlightening jolts of reality told her there were people out there, living their everyday routines, feeding their children, going to work, or running errands, and she was perpetually stuck here, wherever here was, thinking about trying not to think about them. When would she become "normal"? When would "adulthood" set in, the magical space-time when she would find her own circadian rhythm and just go with the flow. How long will it be until someone realizes she's missing from the spectrum of human existence?

Shifting from her position on the couch, she realized Mire was there beside her, with an equally vacant expression on his face. *What is he thinking about,* she wondered.

They stayed there like that for the rest of the day, until night pulled its veil over the world, revealing the existential hypothesis that played upon the lips of the stars. He was fast asleep with her fingers in his hair. Now, it was her turn to get up and go do something productive.

5: What's Going On?

Draped in cords like a cloak around her, the wires snaked their way across her exposed limbs. She had it in her mind that the crystal was the source of all their recent inexplicable ineptitudes. So she dragged his machine downstairs.

Her feet were steadily becoming colder as she began to lose circulation in her legs, putting all the weight of the anti-gravity chamber on her back.

It was still plugged into the helium-methane gas line that fueled the power to the apartment. She whispered to it, cooing in motherly tones to the semi-sentient being, "It'll just be a sec," she said. "I just need a second opinion, all right?"

She took a deep breath and made one last heave, almost throwing herself full frontal to the floor. Her arm flew out to brace her body against the wall. She looked at the cracking wallpaper, *What year is it?* she thought. *Why are there holographic ads on the walls while we're stuck in a stasis of trash and smoke?* The effervescent lighting sconces and titanium baseboards did nothing to dull the secret static cracking its way across the sky in her skull. She shook it off, pushed through the door to the outside world.

She gasped and her breath caught in her throat, her bare skin lit up in a shock of pain upon exposure to the cold, then went numb and she willed her muscles, jittering and fraying at the edges, to press on.

Petridge was there at the bar, squinting against cigarette smoke and a hint of something else. Was it sulphur?

He had a curious glint in his one open eye and he was staring straight at her, slowly raising his hand, in a questioning manner.

She plopped onto the stool next to him, dropping all manner of rubbery binding onto the sopping wet counter top. A brief fizzle erupted, smoke sizzled up from the current, then died down in acquiescence. The crystal flickered once, then continued its all-consuming hatred for humanity.

"Did you beep me or..." Petridge asked through a belch. With a sigh, she said. "I wasn't thinking..." she glued her eyes to the floor, reverently ran her hands over the cords. "Well, that's a first," he said sarcastically and rolled his eyes.

The bartender stood, rag on his right shoulder, his hands finding their time-worn grooves on the counter, patiently waiting for the command.

Like some kind of robot, he was eating up all the gestures thrown his way by one of the most frequent patrons. Pet nodded at the guy, an air of affability in the way he flicked his wrist at the 300-pound man in front of him. The bar keep turned around, produced another canister of CO_2-infused propagation serum and hooked it up to the tubes protruding from the mastication machine hanging before him. Petridge nodded solemnly, closed his eyes, satisfied, leaned forward and took a deep breath. He let out a cloud of blue smoke and as the bartender walked to the other end of the bar, Petridge looked toward Erizabet. "Geez, I swear this stuff was stronger 10 years ago... when the world was still young and everyone got along..."

He blew smoke rings, then with a lift of his chin, he sucked two out of three back into his mouth, held them in his lungs, exhaled. Without taking his eyes off her, he said, "You were saying?"

At that moment, Mire burst through the doors in a flurry of snowflakes and hot breath, a bull trundling toward the big red target of his affection. While Petridge sat unfazed, Erizabet's eyes were fixin' to bulge out from their sockets. For a moment, she forgot to breathe.

"Oh, there you are," Mire said. He rushed to grab her up in his arms. "I'm sorry. This has all been... I love you," he said.

"I know," was her reply. She hugged him back, still skeptical of his true intentions. He peered over her shoulder to steal a glance at the machine hanging limply down her back.

She relieved herself of its weight. "There," she said calmly. Downtrodden, but slightly more satisfied than a moment before, Mire almost wept at the sight of the weakened glow of the crystal.

"What was your plan, exactly? Bringing it out here like this? Naked in the wild, exposing it to all this mundane madness?" he waved his arm to indicate the empty bar. "Ha!" she made some other strange noises, then asked the bartender for a barrel of what Pet was having.

"Can I just..." Mire whimpered and began to loosen the nooses strangling his lady in more ways than one.

Feeling the burden literally lifted off her shoulders, she could finally breathe peacefully again. She was exposed, a tiny bag of bones comprised of sticks picking their way toward freedom through her semi-translucent skin.

She took a few more drags, dredging up the meager remains of the small can containing what could only be described as lightheaded bliss. She smiled, in a daze, and pushed away from the counter. "Hey, you need to pay—" was the last thing she heard before she flicked her wrist at the bartender and lumbered back toward the door that divided the two worlds.

She was making a statement in opting for her own reality where things made sense. Sort of. At least some kind of coherent form of thought could retain its value, its shape, out there in the cold. Where weather was a thing. Life was still going on around her, she thought. She lifted her hands upward to gather tiny crystalline drifts of snow in her palms, and let the cold play havoc with her skin, the color in her arms flickered from pink to purple to grey.

Back inside, Mire was flabbergasted, barely audible in his attempt to explain what he was thinking or feeling. Petridge just gave him a pat on the back and said, "It's OK, buddy. I know."

With that, at least a modicum of tension slipped away from his shoulders, and he cradled the CO_2 in his arms, making himself small and birdlike. *He must be drunk on something other than what they're serving*, Mire thought.

"So, you got the crystal back, then, I see?"

"You know I love her, man," said Mire. "Are we talking about Riz or..." ventured Petridge.

"Goddamnit, man," Mire said and slumped deeper into his stool, still cradling the crystal in his arms. "You know, I—" he put thumbnail to upper lip, gliding over the fringes of his mustache. "I almost got rid of the thing," he said, thrusting his chin forward, squinting, showing the truth to his words. That warranted another light-hearted pat on the back.

Petridge was off on his own plane. Mire looked over toward his friend and noticed the napkin just inches from Petridge's pinky, saw some diagrams for sine waves where electrons met protons and other larger, more fully-formed biophysical matter in diagrams undiagnosable. Something about how minutiae related to larger forms of life. The paper was slowly drinking up water at the edges, eventually erasing his grand designs.

The next day, Erizabet was struck blind. She was fumbling around Mire's apartment building, trying to sync keys with door knobs, failing miserably and Mire was baffled. What was happening to them? he wondered.

She was lying on the couch, waiting for a sign, and after a series of sobs from both parties, she finally admitted that she had a problem. She couldn't live like this, she said. She said she had been stealing his lifeforce little by little over the last month and a half. She took his words into herself and embedded his experiences within her own psyche, robbing him of his own ability to rehash current events.

Erizabet had been involved in some sordid relationships in the past and she wanted to make sure he was the one. So, in her insecurity, she hacked his cloud account and bypassed the firewalls to copy all of the actively-recorded events of his daily life onto her plain old hard drive, circa 1970.

She told him she thought she could tread through the murky waters of his subconscious, undetected, but she failed to realize her beloved might actually be suffering from a double contrapass ineptomy, which was the official term for what he was currently experiencing. Soon, she couldn't see through her own eyes, because they were second-hand retinas, programmed to discern her life's functions only and overriding their initial functions was beginning to prove fatal, perhaps irreversible, she said.

So, when she took over his sight, she lost her own, which was fine for a time, until she realized she couldn't reprogram a human brain to behave in such a way that it would react to her body's stimuli while also continuing in the same vein as he had lived his entire life.

Steadily, with each word she emitted, he began to laugh. She looked on in horror as he began to feel memories flooding back into him. "I don't believe it. I mean, I don't understand," he said and cradled himself, trying to contain his laughter. "It doesn't make any sense!"

Her eyes closed, she believed every word she said, but then again she put stock in her willpower, actually thinking that she could convince herself of anything, like, say, becoming blind so she could steal her man's eyesight.

She still couldn't see what he was doing with his hands as he combined dust and light, creating an aura of cycling energies, and touched her face. She was lifted from her reposed position and finally saw what seemed like a knowing in his eyes. Was he channeling the energy of the crystal? Or, had she fallen in love with some sexy swamp goblin witch?

They looked at each other in that moment and accepted the fact they were both inept at communicating their feelings with the general population, and admitted they might have other innate abilities beyond comprehension.

Regardless of whether any of this made sense, despite the fact their words may prove untrue, they looked at each other, unafraid for the first time. Acceptance was the tune of the music playing in both their heads.

They embraced, and a haze filled the room.

6: Exes

They thought they had it all sorted out. They thought they had it all, but after some soul-searching, Mire began to get a little nervous himself. *If she was feeling insecure about things, maybe there was something to worry about,* was his mode of thinking that next month.

It was Mire's turn to dig.

He created a fake profile online, and using her headshot from many moons ago, he managed to contact quite a few of her old exes. One of whom expressed she was quite indebted to him due to a mishap during college.

This opened a floodgate of messages and missives imploring her to send the credits his way, so that he could live in peace and leave her alone. Under the guise of Riz, Mire struck back, forgetting himself, saying she didn't owe him anything. By this time, he pretty much knew her inside and out and took charge of the situation.

The guy's name was Rick and blackmail was his game. Being a penny pincher and a thief in his hay day, he racked up all sorts of debts from a cornucopia of characters.

Through this sordid email exchange, Mire gained too much information about his and her past and it was beginning to make him physically ill. It was now becoming his strong opinion that Descartes was wrong, that in fact the mind and body *were* in fact intrinsically connected.

They say some people elicit symptoms of stress via the internal organs of the body, while others push their pain up through to the surface of the skin, sometimes breaking out in hives or other inexplicable rashes. He was beginning to suspect his case was the former.

It was as if they were going through all of the stages of a 10-year relationship in a span of a few months: love, jealously, acceptance, eternal bliss. Needless to say, he grew jealous the more he talked to this guy. Rick thought he was talking to Riz, of course, and let slip the dogs of war. He dredged up the past like a shrimp boat captain rakes through the silt of the ocean, bringing up one or two useful little morsels of information, but 99 percent of their discussion led him to doubt the stability of his and Riz's relationship.

"Come on, baby," one email started. "You know I'd do anything for you. I still love you. After all this time. I don't care if you don't love me. Or, at least you think you don't, but I know deep down you do. We're soulmates. Who else would run down to a yacht on the beach and steal a TV for a bag of pot? That's you and me, baby. Bonnie and Clyde."

Mire was seething, he was shaking so much he couldn't reply. *What the fuck?* He thought. *Who is she, really? Is she my Riz? My clumsy nerdbird? Or is she still harboring feelings for this prick? Does she ever think about him? Does she miss stealing shit? What the fuck...*

The mini-vacation they took to Florida to visit her mother was starting to feel more and more hellish as the days passed. He couldn't talk to Riz about it. He didn't want her to flip out on him and tread down that narrow path of distrust. That's one surefire way to kill any relationship. Quick.

He knew. He'd been through it before.

All of his exes were always cheating on him. He never knew whether Becky would be alone, waiting for him when he finally got home from his 12-hour shifts. Or, Hillary. She said she was just dancing for money, but then why was she always hiding her tablet whenever he went to go in for a kiss while she was "working" online?

He had to put an end to this and decided to take Riz's route. The only thing that could save them was to come out with it. Tell the truth. He started the battle, but she would be the one to finish it. It was her ex after all. *And*, he thought, *if Riz could betray him, steal his memories, but then have the balls to tell him afterward, maybe that takes courage.* A courage he was sorely lacking at the moment. He wanted to make things right, get back to their old lives of tickle fights and eggy breakfasts.

Riz sensed something was amiss and invited him down to the pier for a spliff. He rarely smoked pot, but something inside her said they needed it that night.

She was all smiles, red-rimmed and shifty-eyed, sitting cross-legged on a barnacled bench. The water was about 12 degrees too cold for the natives to chance it, so they were left alone for the most part.

Mire leaned over as if to kiss her and she closed her eyes in anticipation. Just when his mouth was about to touch hers, he let out a little puff of air and she jumped, shifted, and blinked her eyes back open. "Oh, yeah. Thanks, buddy," she said, giving him a shove. *Buddy?* He wondered, reading too much into it.

"So, now I'm your buddy all of a sudden," he said, glaring at the joint she was lighting, sucking in some smoke with each flick of the lighter. "Huh?" she asked, choking and coughing. "Awww, fuck," she said, tears rolled down her cheeks. Still coughing, she covered up her mouth, and handed Mire the joint. He looked at it, dubiously.

"What's wrong, babe?" she asked, finally getting a hold of herself. "Ahh," she said and wiped her eyes. She was the type to get insta-high on one good hit. "Naw, I'm good," he said, pushing her hand away. "Well, I am too, then," she replied, making the move to stub out the cherry on the bottom of her shoe.

"Wait, wait," he said, melting. *What if we get caught? I don't want her to be alone in this*, he thought. He reached over and took the joint, took one long drag, then held it in. He flicked the cherry with his thumb, and sealed up what remained in a tiny pill bottle he hid in his breast pocket for just this sort of occasion.

Her eyes were closed and she was smiling that big smile of hers that brought tears to his eyes. "Shit, are you crying now, too? Damn, there's something funky about this stuff," she said. "Never again, OK? Just this one time." She weaved her arms through one of his and nuzzled up close to him. Staring out at the ocean, she seemed more beautiful somehow. At peace with the universe.

"Well, listen. Riz," he said, gently pushing her away to get a good look at her eyes, conveying the seriousness of the impending statement. She was cold as stone, steadying herself for the storm, preemptively cementing herself against potential pain.

"OK, it's not that big of a deal. I mean, it's not like I was stealing your memories or something, but it's just that I had to make sure, you know? And I didn't know what else to do, and—" his words flew together in a jumble, slicing into her with every syllable.

She imagined what it would feel like to be one of those majestic geese who were flying south for winter and instead flew into a jet engine to be shredded into a bloody pulp like onions in a blender.

He continued, almost on the verge of tears again, while he relayed the story of stealing her identity to confront a guy she didn't even have beef with before he intervened.

She touched his shoulder, instilling him with a calm, restoring him back to his default passive state.

"Oh, deer," she said, giving him a peck on the cheek. "Now, we're even." She kissed him on the lips. "And I know now you love me, and I shouldn't have doubted you and—" she hugged him real tight, cutting off his words and inadvertently choking him at the same time.

After a lot of apologies and a lot of kissing, they exchanged epithets for their old lives and eloped down there on the sinking peninsula.

Closer to Cocoa, the piers were full of drunks, and high-pitched laughter tinged the air with a metallic-like sheen that seemed to grow and expand. Above the general din of camaraderie, they heard peals of laughter like warning bells everywhere, yet they couldn't escape.

It was intoxicating, the reassuring familiarity people shared, tourists in their own hometown. They spoke slowly and laughed loudly, without a care in the world.

As calming an effect this atmosphere induced, Mire found himself exhausted most of the time. The heat got to him. He couldn't think straight. His desires for tinkering evaporated. He felt his life slipping out of his sunburnt and flaking hands.

Deep down, he was still insecure about who he was to her. There's no way she could be that person described as a slut by her ex. Rick is probably just pissed that she isn't with him. He just wants to get back at her, so he's dealing every searing blow he can volley from 2,000 miles away.

There were a couple of times during her mom's parties that week, where he would scamper off and climb a tree. He left in the middle of a Rummy game, saying he had to take a leak, then he'd sneak back in an hour later to hear Riz telling her mom he does this a lot and it freaks her out. He lost track of time, they said, and he wasn't thinking clearly.

He thought of the crystal sitting there alone up north and wondered if it could possibly feel anything for him, the way someone might miss a vestigial limb perhaps.

Riz noticed a change when Mire started wearing gloves to bed at night. The frogs croaked and wooed her to sleep, but he tossed and turned, picking at his wounds, smearing the lotion further and further down his hands and up his arms, rendering him slick to the touch.

She abhorred that slippery feeling, forever wanting to get close to him and all she got was a slip-slidin' away.

7: Marital Bliss

They'd booked a flight back to Minnesota, where they thought they could take the time to divine the reason why their living situation had become so grave.

Mire found that while they were away, his old friend Benny had started a woodworking shop. He could tell he needed something to occupy his mind, so he invited Mire to join in. Riz discovered a small group of agoraphobic writers who liked to workshop their short stories on a weekly basis and delved deep into their ritual habits of writing.

It was almost as if everything was at once harmonious again, now that they were back on solid ground.

Without excitement, however, he fell back into his old routines and ultimately grew restless at the wood shop; he saw an average of three customers... on a good day. His buddy was busy building custom bubinga rocking chairs in the back of the shop, so what was he supposed to do?

He downloaded a program to keep himself occupied. He imagined he could imbue his own robotic creations with artificial life, using pieces of the crystal as a power source.

The first one was a flop, literally. Once alive, the thing bumped into the nearest violator, knocking over Mire's precious pyramid of homemade door knobs and duvets.

He soon realized he had to map out the place for his new friend, which entailed embedding a system of way points recognizable through binary code. Easy peezy.

After a couple of hiccups and a few minor adjustments, his first robotic friend was all smooth sailing from there.

He named him George.

George took over the counter and Mire was free to tinker away at his next new obsession, Hank.

This one would be different, he thought. He trusted his own craftsmanship enough to build a hard drive unlike anything anyone had ever seen before. There were traces of COBRA tracking codes on the RAM sticks. *Must be military-grade.*

He found the motherboard online. 1960s style. It was designed to withstand up to 7Gs of aeronautical impact. Mire thought that was pretty cool, so he tore it apart, spliced together a new PCI-bus for dual-ocular input, synced his own visual patterns with Hank's to give him some historical data to build upon, then he made his own power supply, and designed a wifi router so he could use the thing to boost his own personal range. Hey, it had to be functional as well as fun, right?

By the time he got him up and running, Hank was essentially teaching himself how to learn. It's been said the government was working on their own version of AI software, but the information's been kept under wraps, even hundreds of years after their first experiments were made public. So naturally, it took some time for Mire to set up the schematics to differentiate between the past, present, and future. That was the problem with AIs today, they had no sense of object permanence; everything was new to them, every time.

As experiments crept further along, Hank was busily working out his feelings of contention, but from what Mire could read on the logs, he mostly got hung up ethics and compliance, which was fine. Mire couldn't fathom a better way for a robot to spend his time, other than studying up on Sartre, Kierkergaard, and all those philosophers who helped him get through college way back when. He wouldn't be where he was now if it weren't for those nagging flies buzzing in his ear.

One day, screwdriver in hand, Mire looked up from his work and saw that the front-end of the store was essentially running itself. His friend had been gone for some weeks now, off rebuilding a hospital in the Dominican Republic or teaching math in Uganda or something, so Mire built a lab out of the back office, where he could attend to more important matters, like solving the world's energy crisis. Something Petridge said the other day had stuck with him, and he wanted to see how this theory played out.

If he could use the crystal to conduct electricity, he could reverse the poles on the maglev already keeping the shard afloat, and potentially distribute power to nearby devices.

His first experiment consisted of breaking the atomic clock that hung above the door to the shop. He didn't need to learn a new program for this. He knew how to fry electronics well enough, that's basically all he did throughout high school, and since the whole of civilization charged their batteries wirelessly, he was sure he could discharge the diodes in the clock from 5 feet away if he wanted to.

He reprogrammed an old TV remote to communicate with any electronic device within shouting distance. With a laser cutter, he sliced a small piece of the crystal and attached it to the front end of the remote. After rewiring the rest of the system, he hooked up the power and successfully discharged the clock that had been running for the last 50 years without fail. Today, it exploded into a million tiny pieces. The scene horrified Hank, who stood stock still until George systematically appeared from out of aisle 2 and cleaned up the mess.

There were more tests to run, Mire thought. Benny must not have noticed that his precious old heirloom was destroyed, he was so busy chipping away at the latest armchair in fashion. But he didn't want to chance it and come in one day to find his friend fucking with one of his precious experiments, so Mire wrote a program that put his two robots to sleep as soon as the lights went out.

He flipped the switch, turned the shop sign to "closed", then he went home.

The apartment looked much different when he got there. Who knows how much time he spent at the shop working on his own project. Though she had assimilated herself into his home dwelling over the past few months, he surmised she hadn't fully decided to leave her own place behind until just this week, upon sight of the windowsill. All kinds of spider plants, cacti, and poinsettias were crammed shoulder to shoulder vying the light.

On the counter was a clutter of antique Tupperware and doilies from some other life. Not to say that he was quite surprised, but he didn't expect to see his bachelor pad transformed with all manner of feminine paraphernalia overnight.

He closed the door behind him, set his back against it, and let out a sigh. *Man, her furniture works really well with mine*, he thought. *There's some sort of Feng Shui going on... Good vibes.*

Erizabet was in the kitchen, fixing up something that smelled strongly of lemon, pepper, and paprika, and he suddenly realized he was ravenous. He wrapped his arms around her waist, nuzzling his nose into her hair. He took a deep breath and exhaled, *ahhhh*. She made a little cooing noise, got up on her tippy toes, tilted her head back, and kissed his cheek.

"Man, you look like you need a drink." Within the blink of an eye, a glass appeared before him. He took a sip of the rum and pineapple concoction the likes of which he had never tasted before. His face said he was surprised and satisfied at the same time. She smiled, happy she could please her man so unexpectedly. Everything was going according to plan.

"There have been some improvements at work," he said. "Nice," was her reply. She wiped her hands on her apron, took it off, folded it neatly, and placed it on the counter. "Yeah, so I can spend more time with you, here," Mire said, and hugged her. *God, she feels good, somehow more precious*, he thought, cupping her hips. *Poosh poosh*

"Well, about that," she whispered, and he held her at arm's length. "I finished my novel," she continued. "There's this girl in the group who is essentially a walking tangle of idioms and syntax somehow boiled down and poured into a tiny meat pocket of a person, and yeah. She cleaned up my book." Mire smiled in admiration at his favorite person in the world. "It's at the printer's now."

Pfffft. He spit out a bit of his drink. Erizabet wiped her eyes, smiling. "Ahem," she said. "Yes, I'm printing it. Ten copies anyway, to give to friends or whatever. It's already online. Open source. Not worth any money anyway." Mire was baffled at his love for her. *How could this delicate thing want anything to do with me*, he wondered. "I love you," she said. "I've been thinking about you all day. Here," she handed him a plate of what looked like a mess of fishy corn and edible sand. "Just mix it all together and it'll be fine," she said.

They sat down and ate at the table together. "Wait!"

She hopped up, she couldn't never sit still for more than five minutes, it seemed. She came back with half a lemon. "Pre-squished, for your pleasure." He flicked out some juice onto his fish mess and a seed popped out. "Oh, whoops!" She scooped out the seed with two fingers and flew to the window where she buried it deep into a tiny pot of indiscriminate soil.

"You know..." he said, between mouthfuls, "You're supposed to use specific soil with correlating plants..." she gave him an incredulous look, but he could tell she was grateful, too. She shook her head. *Who was she? Some 50s wife all of a sudden? What's going on here?* Of course, she was the type to pry at something perfect until it unraveled into unparalleled chaos. She put a pin in it for the moment.

It was almost uncanny. The way they both ate, taking pains to make sure they propped the right ratio of corn to quinoa precariously upon their forks. Of course, her bowl was steeped in some mysterious sauce, but she poured that shit on everything. After they finished, a smoke was in order.

"Hold on," he said, and from his cross-legged position in the chair, he hopped over the headrest, flew back in, and handed her a vape pen.

"You're like a magician or something, I swear," she said. "Oh, god. Weren't these things outlawed back in the early 2050s?" She sipped on the end of it and immediately proceeded to cough her lungs out. He stared at her curiously. "Hmm. Well, I made these specifically for us... to use at home, of course, but I made some adjustments," he said, intonation knocked up a couple registers.

He sipped on the vape slowly, producing smoke rings that she poked her fingers into, as if popping balloons one by one. She followed suite, smoking lightly, until she too spewed out a cloud of vapor. She couldn't blow smoke rings, though...

"Ahhh," she sank back in her chair. "Cherry flavored." She sipped again. "Noice!" she said in some accent he'd never heard before. *I spend way too much time in front of the tube,* she thought. "Yup," he said, thinking everything was right in the world.

They sat there together, at opposite ends of the table, staring lovingly at one another, and relishing the meal.

8: Feathered Friends

A blonde tuft of hair is seen bobbing around stacks of old newspapers and piles of tin cans. Like a buoy in a sea of trash, he's doing his best to stay above water.

Petridge's latest project was an utter and complete failure; two of his subjects have been snuffed out. He forgot to open the window last night before he ventured out to find his usual source of inspiration at the pub, to wake up this morning and find his two prized owls had asphyxiated on the stench emanating from the last botch-up.

He paced back and forth in the dark, trailing wafts of smoke, his hazel eyes shining like mad orbs in contrast to his olive skin. He rubbed his chin, wondering how he could possibly explain to Whit how he could have done such an imbecilic thing.

"I live for this!" he growled into the empty room. "What in God's name am I if I can't create?"

He took one last drag of his cigarette and crushed it into a makeshift ashtray formed from the shell of one of the mussels he brought home last week. He lit another cigarette. On the exhale, he froze. Squinting his eyes in the smoke and shaking his thumb like he's hitching onto the tail end of a brilliant idea, he said, "I can do something with this."

Shaking off last night's drunk, he set to work prepping

the area for some impromptu magic. To anyone watching, they might have said he was procrastinating, but it was his ritual to take his time and painstakingly rearrange the apartment before any major tribunal. And no one was watching. He rarely invited anyone over there, aside from Riz and Mire, of course.

Instead of his usual habit of sweeping everything off the table to land where it may on the floor, he took his time putting the beer cans in the recycling, bent a stray piece of paper in half and funneled a mound of sawdust into a tiny vial, and placed it carefully on his shelf.

Sifting through his month-old mail, he spent some time mulling over possible scenarios which may prove a welcome kink in the pipeline, aka, financial backing.

Then a thought struck him.

"If I use the circulatory system like electric tunnels, I could encase the veins in conductive thread..." He sorted the papers into piles: To Recycle, To Burn, To Keep.

He opened the windows, dusted off his half-dead plants, smoked another cigarette and looked around the room. "Ah, now I can breathe."

The closet was a storage compartment stuffed to the gills with computer parts, sewing machines, embalming fluid, and other random apparati.

He rummaged through the mess, picked out the necessities, and went back to the table. He laid down a tarp, pulled his computer over, and focused the holographic monitor on the two birds laying there.

They were already beginning to stiffen, so he broke their feet and replaced the bones with moldable aluminum piping he rigged up with a bit of good ol' chemistry, some alchemy, a bit of patience, and a lot of drugs.

Once he had the peg board set up as the central hub for

the circuits, he sewed up the specimens, making sure not to tie the wings together, then began the process of preserving the bodies.

Taxidermy was never his strong suit. "In fact," he murmured aloud, "I'm not really good at anything."

He honed in on his task, taking regular sips off the carbon monoxide tank he stashed under his workbench, "To help me focus," he muttered under his breath, as if explaining himself to a child lurking in the shadows.

He looked around, pretending he was acting on a grand stage, that there were cameras hidden everywhere. He always did that when he was alone, made him feel validated somehow.

After he felt comfortable with the way the birds looked, he went back to the closet. With a tooth-grinding creak and a little wiggling, the first drawer of the dresser came loose. He peered inside, shuffled through bottles of green and blue fluid, knocked around some pliers, tweezers, and glue. He retrieved the old watch batteries from the amalgam of useless objects, and sealed the exposed wires worming their way through the feathers with electric tape.

The first bird started to twitch, as if writhing in pain. He quickly unwrapped the tape, then went to the other bird. Same reaction.

"Come on, old chap. He's going to snip off your bullocks and wrap them in newspaper to sell at his next bloody fundraiser if you sod this up."

Petridge got up, paced a bit, lit another cigarette, and stopped at the table. He felt the cold steel under the tarp, and snapped his fingers.

In a fit of genius, he accessed the memory bank of the computer by tapping the blood sack hanging next to the table filled with Menard's impeccable DNA rocking, undulating within. The hard drive opened up to reveal memories of past experiments, each slowly eking their way up onto the projector.

He dug through the files, looking for a mood stabilizing algorithm for AI concubines used in the war of 2182. He highlighted the wiring pattern for pacifying massage parlor matrons and used the diagram to rewire the circuits on his feathered friends.

With batteries taped back to wings, he looked on as the spindly stick-like feet begin to kick. Motors whirred in a low-pitched hum, almost inaudible to the human ear.

He glued the battery to the crook of one of the owl's wings, and pulled it upright, to see if he had achieved the right weight to counterbalance the positioning of each foot, disproportionate to the other.

Everything checked out. Now, he just had to figure out how to get the feet to grip the edge of the table, and all other manner of possibilities these birds may encounter during their time back at Whit's.

He switched the holographic feed to digest as many videos depicting the mechanics of the *strix nebulosa* species, while writing a program to map out their movement patterns.

After a day and a half spent awake, he was starting to get a little thirsty. He swallowed, but he had already used up all of the saliva he could muster. It was time to go.

His eyes didn't have time to adjust to the glaring light bouncing off the buildings situated at right angles to his apartment. The walls shimmered with an opalescence, evincing an environment the likes of which one might envision as being the lost city of Atlantis, a delineation of his veritable reality juxtaposed with how everyone else viewed the city.

He felt proud of himself. He saw things no one else could see. He just accomplished something and now he was feeling light as a feather. On top of the world, as they say.

With two mechanical birds in cages, he felt like a long-availed hermit, emerging from his hovel for the first time in centuries. Teetering somewhere around 10 a.m., he suddenly realized this wasn't his reality, that it belonged to the day people, people with their wits about them, people with steady jobs and sane objectives. Who was he to intrude upon their discreetly designed world? "I'm fucking better than you, that's why," he said to bubbles passing along sidewalks, cars hovering above tar-like tracks in the sea floor.

"Look at you," Petridge announced to nonplussed bystanders. Waving his cages in the air, encompassing the space around him. He continued, "In your man-made self-propelled designs of despair. How do you feel? Huh?" He shouted at the city, which angered him to the brink of exaltation. "Do you feel anything? You call this living?"

An older gentleman, floating by in a ring of self-contained opalescent architecture, briefly glanced longways in Pet's general direction, a hazy look in his eyes indicating he was not all there. Petridge stood in the man's way, blocking his descent down the path of righteousness. "Do you see me, old man?" he shouted into the other's personal space. The man was unfazed, another zombie. He looked right through Petridge, stopping momentarily like one of those mechanical cleaning devices engineered to hesitate once it's come upon a wall.

"Ok, old man," Petridge repeated, side-stepping out of his way. "For fuck's sake," he mumbled in that British accent. He scuffed his right toe on the pavement in complete and utter loss of self-worth. "I'm nothing. I'm nobody," he said to no one in particular. He grunted, flipping back between cyclical mood swings, smiled meekly to himself, nodded, and continued on the journey toward Mire's place.

9: "So, where did you find
this thing anyway?"

"I'm not a person, yet. Go away," Mire said, leaning his nose against the chain-link lock on the door.

Looking like he himself hadn't slept in weeks, his words were like vocal shrapnel scraping along the insides of what was left of his wasted brain space.

"I just want to talk, is all," Petridge said. "That's all you want to do is talk." Mire rubbed the space between his eyes on the cold brass of the chain, nudging his nose along the links as he continued, lazily, "I can't take any more of your theories, Pet. Your ideas make me want to kill myself," he said, hyperbolizing. He unhooked the chain from the lock and moved away from the door.

Mire moved to put a pot of water on the stove. "Coffee, naturally," Petridge said, nodding, spreading his arms like an actor who's finally returned to the stage after a long absence.

He stepped inside, set the wire-framed cages on the kitchen floor. He lit a cigarette, placed the pack back safely in his left shirt pocket, and said, "Look at us." "Here we go," Mire plopped down on the overturned 10-gallon fish bucket on the floor, lit a smoke himself, and prepared for the diatribe.

"We carve our paths, intrinsically, you see? You and me."

Mire rotated his wrist, nodding. Go on, he motioned. Petridge began his usual manic pacing. "People glide along, listlessly, downloading programs from the maiden of all sin, Shelly Greenwood, extolling the virtues of being productive," he shook his fist, frowning, "Being a good citizen," he continued. "When no one is actually doing anything. We are only further-ing our current masochistic state of society."

Mire raised an eyebrow and tilted his head sideways. Petridge took an audible drag from his cigarette, *effffffip*.

"And look at you, making coffee on a gas-powered stove, like you're living in the 1990s or some shit. I mean," he exhaled and smoke filled up the room. "What are we doing? We're halfway on the brink, man. We're in, then we're out."

"We use technology for our own ends, not someone else's—" Mire cut him off, holding up his hand. "You really are batshit crazy, aren't you, Pet? Do the thoughts form in your head first, or does your mouth just open of its own volition and shit flies out? Then afterward you realize you're actually speaking..." It was less a question, more a point made in jest at his friend's inability to engage the fictional brain-to-mouth filter.

Petridge stopped pacing, took off his doctor's specs, rubbed his face trying to slake off some of the thoughts accu-mulating. He gently set his glasses back on his face.

He took a drag, more calmly this time, and looked at his friend, supplicating.

"Now," Mire said, punctuating his words with a nose nudge to the air, "So, uh, what'cha got there?" Bowing his head, mo-tioning toward the abominations making tiny tinkling sounds to complement the methane gas leak creaks in the walls.

Petridge quickly bent toward the birds. He touched one of the cages, reassuring himself they were real and not another product of his overactive imagination. "I screwed up, man. I mean, I didn't even do it right, I don't think," he said. "Well, let's take a look-see, shall we?" Mire stubbed out his cigarette and crouched low, his hands resting between his thighs.

He was unimposing, tilting his head to peer inside.

"What exactly am I looking at, here?" he asked, stretching, coming back up to meet his friend's gaze.

Mire walked over to the stove, turned the knob to the off position, and poured the boiling water into the French press.

"See, this is what I mean," Pet started, "You—" Mire made a face, as if to say, "Really?" "Ok, ok," Petridge said. "Can you quell your ADD for two seconds?"

Mire produced two cups of coffee and sat back on the bucket. His friend sidled up square in front of the cages and sat on the grimy floor, Indian-style.

"I need your help, man," Petridge said, almost to the point of sobbing. "Fucking chill, Ok? What are we dealing with, here?"

Halfway through the speech, Petridge shit his pants. Mire didn't notice as Petridge rambled on. Then he went to set his coffee down on the counter and Mire noticed something.

He said nonchalantly, "Dude, your pants are dirty." And Petridge, pretending not to know what Mire was on about, twisted his torso sideways to examine the proposed damage. "Huh, wonder if I sat in something?" he said, innocent.

"Well, great story, chap," Mire said, shaking his head, changing the subject. "I see where you're getting with this," he said, looking straight at the birds.

"They're robots, right?" he said, on his haunches, getting close to the cages again. He peered up at Petridge from his position near the floor. Rose up again, lithely.

Petridge looked frightened, a thumbnail flicking between

his front tooth and canine. "I just can't seem to get them to work..." he said, trailing off. He bit his thumb and commenced pacing.

"I see what you mean." Mire stretched, doing a half back bend, comfortable in his friend's presence. He bent forward, touching his toes. "Ahhh," erupting from his chest like a yoga instructor actually breathing properly. Petridge gave him a perplexed look, *Are you taking...* was Petridge's thought, though his didn't say it aloud. *When do you have time...* he thought. And Mire said, "Come with me."

Mire led him through the gauzy green curtain that separate the kitchen from the living room. They turned left. Petridge admired the new things Mire'd acquired since he'd last been there. Part of a hand-held radio's circuit board sat on top of the book shelf alongside a tiny, tiny sea shell. *Where did he get this? Did he pick this stuff up, himself?* he thought. *Random...* He proceeded, stumbling from lack of food and sleep, into the room adjacent.

There was a glowing pink resin to the walls of the barely-lit chamber. A song entered Petridge's head, a bass beat changed the rhythm of his heartbeat, synesthesia activated. He began to bob his head to the fluctuating current that flowed from the crystal sitting atop a round table near the window.

"Oh, so this is who you're cheating on Riz with?" Petridge said in a playful voice, shoving Mire a little. "Ah, fuck off man," Mire responded, shoving Petridge back. "This is the revolution, my friend. You think you're crazy? Well, just look at this thing."

Petridge bent over to get a closer look at the crystal hovering in a suspended state of animation. "Give it 10 seconds, I guarantee you. You'll never have the urge to sniff carbo-mono again," Mire said, taking a step back.

Petridge came closer to the crystal. Mire looked on. The jagged mountain peaks reflected back in Petridge's eyes. He knew he had won him over.

Mire gave him space in a way, watching his friend at a distance for 20 minutes or more, letting him face the demons inside, hopefully getting lost in himself, or so Mire thought.

He looked around at the ceiling. He might have smoked a spliff before Petridge arrived, and he started feeling a little tripped out himself.

In a fit of paranoia, he grabbed Petridge by the shoulders and said, "Enough!" and he pulled him backwards, away from the crystal. Petridge tripped on some wires snaking out of a half-finished project on the floor, and they both fell backward against the wall with an audible *hummphh*.

Both of them were breathing heavily. They sighed, wrapped in each other's arms. "Ugh," Mire pushed Petridge off of him. Petridge dusted himself off.

"Well, that was some trip," he said. And Mire, a little freaked out about the close proximity between him and his friend. He picked lint off his corduroy jacket and said as coolly as possible, "What did you see?"

"I saw..." Petridge swallowed, licked his dry lips, "Cities," he continued. "There were, like, these buildings. Circular-shaped." His eyes grew wide. "Meer bubbles floating, not solid, but you know what I mean. Where is this? How?" he trailed off. Mire nodded enthusiastically. "Fuck yeah." He leaned close to gaze into the crystal.

Another 20 minutes went by. Petridge was in a daze. He stared at the walls, then looked through the window at the people below.

Mire tugged on his shirt, pulling him away from the air conditioning, their only saving grace staving off some of the heat of summer's day.

"Ugh," Petridge said. There was a palpable tension in the air. "So?" Mire said, lighting a cigarette. Petridge clapped his hands, "Well, I've seen all I've come here to see." He turned for the door. Mire caught him by the shoulders, saying, "OK, so I showed you this because," he drew out that last word as if to imply the conclusion of the sentence would come from Petridge. "Because... somehow the crystal can help me?" he finished, doubtfully, "In all its drug-inducing glory? No offense, brother, but how the fuck? Are my pets suddenly going to turn into real birds after I get high or something? Trust me. Tried that."

Petridge sat down, defeated. He questioned his existence. "Oh, come on, my friend," Mire said, lifting him up by the arm. "You're being way more dramatic than usual."

Mire turned Petridge a couple of degrees to the left, a couple of degrees to the right, checking his irises. "Are you drunk? Do you need a drink?"

They popped into the kitchen to trade coffee cups for beers and continued their experiment. Mire persuaded him to trace his steps into yet another hidden antechamber of the small apartment. Amid a poop-colored background, with deranged drawings on the walls and one lone, cheap reproduction of a Dali painting—her choice—there stood two androids, naked in all their aluminum glory.

"I had a good time with them at work, but it got pretty boring there, so... I brought 'em home!" Mire said, and pushed Petridge into the room.

Petridge stood stunned. He didn't know his friend had such a knack for anatomy. He thought Mire was more of a conceptual person. *Ah*, Petridge thought, *Maybe I can get Mire to rewire my little pidgies. If I could just dupe him into* it, somehow. *Think, man, think.*

Mire went over to one of the bots and flicked a switch on its back. *Hmmmmm* went the android, and without speaking, it started picking up clothes off the floor, rearranging garments in the closet according to color.

"Wait, how did you get them to see color?" Petridge asked. All of his uppity wearing off in the presence of a clandestine genius. "Whose DNA did you use, you old-timer? Was it Neil Harbisson, or perhaps his wife, Moon Ribas? Wait..." He stroked his chin. "You didn't even use DNA, did you?"

Mire smirked, turning back to where the crystal lay. He said, "No, it's this thing, man. Well, of course, I *am* a genius. You've seen my guitar pedals. But... This is... supplementary. Complementary? It does what I want it to. It's, like, telepathic or some shit." And the robot kept going about its business, unaware of the lookers-on.

"OK, Hank. Shutdown protocol," Mire said. The robot nodded in acquiescence then found its place back against the wall, and shut down.

Mire led Petridge back out of the room. "That was... that was some... what?" Petridge muttered, for the first time wrestling with his own superiority complex.

He couldn't come up with a logical conclusion.

Mire lit a cigarette, took a sip of his beer, and placed a hand in his pocket, assuming the stance of a man of business. "Half engineering, some math, mostly crystal." He took a drag.

"So, where did you find this thing anyway?"

10: Petty Squabbles Between Catty Girls

Mire woke up, rubbed a crick in his neck, and lifted himself up to counteract the gravitational pull threatening to keep him glued to the kitchen floor. Groggy and disoriented, he tried to move his left arm and found he couldn't feel it. *I'm paralyzed*, he thought, *Is this a dream?* He looked over to see Erizabet drooling onto his favorite shirt.

"What the... where's Pet?" he asked the ceiling, "Did you absorb him or something? Have I disrupted the space-time continuum?" his gravelly voice sounded more like an old jazz singer at this stage in the recovery of consciousness.

"Who are you talking to?" Riz said, moaning. "Oh no, I can't see." Mire suddenly came to, afraid Riz's childhood retina correction might be unraveling before the warranty expired.

Cradling her chin in his hand, softly, he said, "What is it?" She looked to the right, shook her head, looked to the left, shake shake, looked up, nodded, looked down, nodded again. Then she gave one final stretch of the cheek muscles, pulling her lips downward, "Mmmwaahh," she crooned, satisfied. "There, that's better," she said. "I don't..." Mire began. For some reason, even after all these months, he still found himself frequently unable to form complete sentences around her.

"Oh, you know," she said, tapping her temple. "There's this occasional blip in my hardware, where my vision sometimes reverts back to normal after a cold boot." Mire said, "Ah," raising an eyebrow in mock understanding. "Righto-then." He leaned back, placing his palms on the floor, lifting his pelvis, he jerked, and rolled up on his heels to land in a standing position.

"Outstanding," Riz said, smiling, shaking her head in adoration. She stood up slowly, evincing signs of pain. "Ow." She dusted herself off. "What time is it?" she asked. Mire checked his internal clock, "Feels like 2," he said. "P.M.?" she asked. "Errmmm, yup." Erizabet's eyes went wide, "Oh, fuck. I gotta go."

She hopped into the bathroom, did a little dance to shake off whatever ephemera felt fit to attach itself to her clothing while she slept, she stepped up on the tub to check her dress in the small mirror above the sink, making sure there weren't too many noticeable wrinkles. She jumped back down, landing on the balls of her feet. She's become all too conscientious of how her feet are poised, after Mire mentioned something about the importance of stepping toe to heel, toe to heel, that's the way you're supposed to walk, he said a few days ago. Then he went on this tirade about proprioception.

She stepped up to Mire who was staring off into the distance. Erizabet said, "Shit. Shit, should I even go? I'm always late, maybe they just expect it by now? Should I just stop going..." He shook his head, bewildered, "I don't even know what you're talking about, babe."

She continued, "My critique class. We're supposed to rip apart our last story to improve our writing for the next one, or whatever, and I'm nervous as hell about it." She bit her thumb, pensive. She looked up, "I just gotta go," she flung out her hands, decision made. She bent over the re-purposed weight bench to search for her shoes.

"Do you at least—" Mire started. "I'll get some on the

way," she said. In the morning, they both had a strong hankering for a stiff drink, or settling for the next best, most socially acceptable thing, they more often than not settled for a highly-caffeinated beverage immediately upon waking.

She hurried out the door. "You almost forgot your—" "Ah, my purse. Thanks, dear." She pecked him on the cheek. "You're the—" This time he cut her off with a full-on lip-smacking smooch. He slipped a little tongue. "Mmm," she murmured, eyebrows raised. She breathed in deep. "I needed that." She seemed a bit less shaken now.

He leaned into the hall to watch her leave. She turned around, twiddled her fingers, blew him a kiss, and turned to unlock the outer door. He took one last look at her, the way the yellow dress made her ass look statuesque. He growled. Hearing this, she tittered, blushed, then left him up to his own devices for the remainder of the day.

He closed the door, making sure the deadbolt was locked, hooked the chain in place. He sighed, his back to the wood. *Now, what am I going to do with you?* he thought to himself.

Erizabet was just getting comfortable in her willingness to share excerpts from her latest story. Then she cracked her neck to loosen up the nerves a bit, and a hum began in her right ear. She moved her head side to side, realizing that when she looked forward, straight-on, the signal was the strongest. She didn't know too much about triangle waves, apart from the information she'd gleaned from Mire's research into the subject. Still, she felt the sound was hovering somewhere around 332 Hertz.

Squinting, moving her head side to side, she caught the attention of Meryl, her partner in crime, her drinking buddy after these pseudo-intellectual debates into the logistics behind syntax, including their favorite topic: Whether alliteration, clichés, and idioms enhanced or detracted from fictional works. The running consensus was the group was against them, seeing their use as a trite excuse for true creativity. What did Riz and Meryl think? A bunch of bumbling idiots comprised the majority of the group's members, aside from the two of them, of course.

She squinted her eyes to see if she could possibly see the sound, maybe a shimmer in the air in that general direction. Meryl, the beginnings of worry creeping into her features, pinched Riz's arm. "Oy, what're you up to in there?" she whispered, leaning in close to Riz's left ear. "I know this isn't riveting stuff..." she continued in her Australian accent, a stray hair from one of her sun-kissed pigtails grazed Riz's earlobe, making her wriggle and jump. Goosebumps zigzagged up her arm. "Yuhhh," she mumbled, shaking off the tickling feeling. Meryl laughed. The rest of the group turned toward them, looking like they were ready to lynch them.

"Riz," said Betty, the leader of the clan. "Ahem. Is there something you find funny?"

Rubbing her arm, and giving Meryl a playful look, she responded. "Oh, no ma'am. I just thought I heard this weird noise. I was distracted for a second, but it's gone," she lied. She picked up her haphazard pile of scribble-clad looseleaf papers and tapped them on the table, righting them, making a show of her cooperation. "See, I'm good. Go on," she waved her hand at the tiny redhead who was reading from her memoir-in-progress. Riz thought it read more like erotic fiction, the made-up kind that is.

You could tell this girl was fresh out of high school, harboring some sick desires, which she chained up within her diary. Already embarrassed, having been goaded into reading aloud, the color rose up in her freckled face. She looked like she was on the verge of tears.

Betty rolled her eyes, licked her lips, and said, "Now, Erizabet," unnecessarily rolling the "R", she wasn't Spanish, for Heaven's sake. "Wherever did you get that name, hmm?" She unclasped her cupped hands, brought them back together again for emphasis. "Assuming it's a pseudonym, correct?" She was taking the side of the newbie, of course.

Betty couldn't take it if yet another girl left the group, especially if she found out they were participating in a different, more organized group.

Riz didn't expect this turn of events. All eyes were on her.

"Actually. No. It was my great great grandfather's middle name, actually. My great grandparents picked his second name first, before they knew whether he would turn out to be a boy or girl, then when they got closer to the due date, they named him Jamie," realizing the faux pas, she tilted her head, acknowledging something for the first time.

"Well, you know, Jamie is also a unisex name. Huh." She looked off into space. Shook her head, getting back on task. She stared right into Betty's eyes. "He got his left ear blown off in the second war, which is probably why my parents named me after him, because he was a fighter, and they knew I possessed some sort of fighting spirit in me, too."

Betty produced a fake laugh. "Well, how, pray tell, did he lose his ear?" she asked, freshly manicured talons fully extended as if to pitch them straight into Riz's gut at the nearest opportunity. Betty thought if she couldn't fight for real, she'd break this girl down with words. It was her specialty of sorts.

"Well fuck me, you are nosy." The girls were taken aback. "Oh, calm your tits. Am I disturbing your little tea party, here?" She cleared her throat.

"It all began back in 2342, when the Japanese decided they'd had enough with our sly advances in warfare. They wanted in on that sweet sweet tech.

"We produced massive amounts of weapons, but being the pacifistic nation that we were at the time, we kept them all to ourselves. The laws had been written.

"Each year, we were tasked to create double the amount of the previous year, but newer, more hypocritical treaties were passed upon construction of said weapons, to the point where our budget was not being spent at a fast enough pace to meet the demands of the ultralord, Hierule Smithson III—now that's a ridiculous name, how do you feel about that!?"

She didn't wait for a response, but just kept chugging along. "We dug out all these secret tunnels beneath New York, Nevada, and even carved out a little cave out of the side of a dormant volcano in Hawaii to store our torpedoes, UAVs, A-planes, whatever else we could appropriate from neighboring nations.

"And there was this little man by the name of Jamie Erizabet Masch, who was working on developing a new sword, one with a laser-pointed edge, utilizing a diamond-tipped shaft, that would simultaneously daze any unlikely combatant... but it was flawed, you see. The ungodly amount of heat the thing produced would flay the victim alive, their skin sloughing off in heaps and chunks, before the guy wielding the thing even had a chance to take advantage of the other guy's stunned state."

She took a breath, nibbled on a little bit of her strawberry sugar scone, sipped her coffee, and looked around the room to make sure everyone was paying attention.

Meryl was playing with her bracelet. Betty wore the expression of sheer incredulity.

"Well, this sounds pretty silly, I admit, but Jamie and his

friend Nigel were playing around... It was harmless, really. Just working off some steam after the long hours spent squinting at tiny machines. It was awful work, you see, painful to the psyche, what with the dim light they were afforded at the time." She squinted for dramatic effect, crinkling her eyebrows.

She scoffed, "Imagine," her eyes were distant, going there, "You're a tiny man, staring into a tiny microscope, trying to discern some sort of meaning from the perils of war and what it might do to your family above ground, while you're trapped, a clever little mouse, who isn't quite clever enough to find his way out of the cave to save them from impending public humiliation."

A few of the girls exchanged glances, confused. Betty had done her homework, however. She knew exactly what went on in the second war, her great great grandfather had been involved as well, but he was inside the Oval office, sitting pretty, planning the trajectory of the next attacks.

"So!" Riz continued, "These guys, just teenagers, really, are playing around with this new technology, which were basically just prototypes—highly advanced versions of those lightsabers, you know, from that movie..." Around the room, lips pursed, heads shook minutely all around. It was like she was in a film, herself, for a moment.

"Anyway. They're playing around, testing the things on rocks, slicing down the legs of tables, cutting open the lamps, whatever they could do to just wreck the fucking place. I mean, they were livid in their complicity. They never wanted anything to do with the war in the first place, but back then, they were required to sign up for the Army."

Betty flinched, she didn't much care for curse words. "Who cares, right?" Riz continued. "Some robots would come and rectify the situation, right? And then, Jamie, satisfied with his handiwork, put on his little glasses," Riz moved her hand to her face, pretending to pinch some specs in place on the bridge of her nose. "He wriggled them into place, like so," she scrunched up her face to demonstrate. "He gets too close to the tip of the sword, and swoop! Crunch!"

The other writers in the room were electrified.

"The walls start buckling! Being cut off from the rest of society, oh," with hands on hips, Riz imitated the president at the time, " 'Let's not distract the fine minds of these young scholars'," she said, with an effusively low and grumbling intonation.

"So, you know what happened? Some other guys from another platoon were fucking bombing the ground above them, they didn't have the foresight," "...wherewithal..." Betty mumbled to the girl to the right of her, smiling. The girl giggled, covering her mouth. "Ahem, anyway. There was no communication whatsoever. Even with all of their sonar, laser, and fucking diamond-flaying skin shit technology. Those guys maimed my great great grandfather. Ultimately preventing him from continuing his research, as it turns out." She looked around, feeling the room.

"Spoooshhh! The cave just collapses on him. The laser in his hand slipped, sliced his left ear right clean off, and guess what? All his work was destroyed right then and there.

"It was a twofold, no, gazillion-fold disaster for everyone involved. Except for the guys above, of course, who still had no idea as to the damage they incurred that day, because Mr. Bigshot," she made that deep voice again, hands on hips, furrowed brow, "...decided, 'Oh, no one needs to know about this, ah ha ha.' That's when they started changing all the history books, saying this war happened at this time, then rewrote them again, bungling up the facts, 'No, no, *this* war was going on...'

"But anyway, they got gramps out of there, and his friend, too, who hid under the table, which blocked some of the falling debris. Jamie couldn't use his left leg after that; a large hunk of boulder bashed it in, right at the knee.

"Strangely enough, that's why everyone knows him as the peg leg mad scientist. They assumed something similar happened to his ear, but that shit doesn't add up, now does it? It was too clear-cut. Natural causes, maybe? Naw.... But, really, he was in the process of something great!"

She raised her arms in triumph, she was really heated up now. "They took his leg, his ear, his job, and his dignity, because he invented something new and exciting. Something that could have possibly helped us if we were attacked on foot, which would have been unlikely, but still! No one will ever know..." she sipped her coffee, calming down. "Except for you sad sacks."

Betty intertwined her fingers, leaned back in her chair, placed her hands on her chest. "Well, excuse me, miss. But that sounds like a load of crap. Pardon my French," Meryl and Riz exchanged looks, conveying the sentiment, "Is she serious?"

"You can't possibly expect us to believe that," said Betty. She added a little extra emphasis on her next word, "*I*, for one, know all about the second war. My great great grandfather—" Riz interrupted her with a hand held in the air, "Yeah, we know. You remind us, what," she looked around at the stunned faces sitting at the table, "Like, every other time we get together? This class is a joke. It just gives you a chance to talk about yourself, right? Or, I'm sorry, your life isn't all that interesting, is it? So you like to gab on about your family history." Betty's mouth dropped open. "Well, there you have it. You're not the only one with a killer story, am I right?" Riz and Meryl high-fived.

Betty snapped her mouth shut, grimacing. "Well, I think it's safe to say that you can just leave right now. Don't you agree, ladies?" She was rewarded with sheepshodden nods of approval all around.

"Say 'yay' if you agree that Riz is now unwelcome in our inner circle of intellectuals." Shy little echoes of "yay" sounded throughout the coffee shop. Even the girls at the counter disapproved of the negative vibes Riz had brought to their creative space, their murmurs reverberated off the espresso machines.

"Huh," Riz laughed. "Well, that's cool." She got up, gathered her things, and pulled her purse off the back of the chair. Meryl followed suit. "Oh, wait, Meryl," Betty said, fluttering her eyelids. "You can stay, dear. We haven't heard you read in months now."

"Oy," Meryl's accent accentuated full tilt. "I'm not much of a talker. More of a listener, me."

Feigning guilt with a hint of disdain, Betty bowed her head. "So mote it be," she said. Meryl turned to Riz, an eyebrow raised.

The two left the coffee shop, the bell tinkling on the door handle as they let it slam behind them.

"Well," Betty continued. "Is anyone going to write about this?" She paused, trying to muster up some acknowledgment from the surrounding lemmings. "No? Well, then, I'll do the honors." She started scribbling furiously, while a couple of the others killed time ordering coffee and pastries.

Arm-in-arm they half-stumbled, half-ran down the sidewalk, their heels clacking on the pavement.

Laughing, out of breath, Meryl was the first one to speak. "So, what are you going to do with yourself, now?"

Choking, Riz reached into her purse for a smoke, lit one up, and offered the pack to Meryl. "Oh, man," she said. "However will I go on?" She flung herself to the nearest brownstone and fluttered her eyelids like one of those helpless housewives in old films.

Fanning herself as if she were about to faint, then recovering, she said, "Oh, miss, please do explain yourself."

They continued walking, trailing smoke and laughter down the street. "That cannot be your real name. Please." She gave Meryl a look, disgusted. "Ugh, how can she live with herself. Yuck," she said, shaking it off, as if to dispel any shroud of negativity left clinging to her aura.

"So!" exclaimed Meryl, stopping, grabbing Riz by the wrists. "What are we going to do with all this free time we have now?" She looked around for a place that looked inviting, but grimy. A dive bar would be ideal. With her bangles and flowing boho, hippie dress, she didn't want to draw too much attention, but she didn't want to be passed up as some trashy harlot either. *The atmosphere is very important*, she thought to herself, furtively glancing around.

Riz shook her head, in mock annoyance. "What're you thinkin'?" she said. "Hmmm," was Meryl's response, stroking her chin, philosophizing. Riz laughed, giddy with the heat of the night. She wiped her forehead, realizing it was a little balmy out. Just then, a light breeze grazed past her knees, blowing up her dress just enough to make her jump and clamp her arms to her sides. "Whoops!" she said.

She felt drunk on the drama of it. Normally, she felt almost utterly invisible, a fly on the wall, a corpse rotting in her apartment, but tonight she touched someone. She actually pissed someone the fuck off, enough to get her banned from her writing group. *Whodathunkit*, she thought. "Huh," she said aloud, pleased with herself.

"Well," started Meryl. "I think we've been productive

enough for one day." "Pretty much," Riz called back.

"Come on," Meryl said, threading her right arm through Riz's left. "Let's get loaded."

The sun went down quite quickly these days, so it felt appropriate enough to her to erupt out upon the other side of the day, drunk. They plopped down next to each other at the bar. The bartender gave Meryl one of those upward nods of acknowledgment, she held up two fingers, then placed her hands on the counter top and swiveled her chair to take in the scene. Playing with a loose strand from one of her pigtails, she appraised the lot. *Not too shabby.* She swiveled back around just in time to be greeted by two tall glasses of whiskey.

She gave the bartender a wink, turned to Riz and said, "Bottoms up." They downed their drinks, Riz spilling a little down her chin. She held her hand underneath the rim of the glass, where it met her lips, and took the whole thing down in three gulps. "Well, shit," she said, wincing. "Yup," Meryl responded. She was the expert, here. She swung back around to face the crowd of dancing bears, giraffes, and other exotic animals. She ran her hands through her hair, the gears already turning. She was trying to see who would be the first to bite the bait.

"Is there a theme here or something?" Riz asked, for the first time noticing the jungle party going on around her. Obviously, this was her first time at the rodeo.

"Ah, relax, darlin'," said Meryl, "I know where they hide the costumes in the back," she said, making a wriggling caterpillar out of her eyebrows.

Riz made a noise, akin to the sound of a horse sneezing,. She jerked back in disgust, playing her part of the intrepid outsider.

"Oh, don't be such a wimp," said Meryl, "Come on."

11: There's Something About Hank

Meanwhile, back at home, Mire was busy hatching schemes of his own. He felt as though he hadn't had enough quality time to himself over the last few days and he relished the fact that Riz was out and about.

He imagined she was staying productive, grinding it out, getting much-needed work done on her latest novel. The media ripped the first one to shreds, so I guess you could say that one didn't go so well, but she didn't care. So what if there were tons of plot holes, typos, and incongruous or otherwise irrelevant scenes? It was her baby, and she loved it anyway. And though he tried to remain logical, giving her the infrequent suggestion toward constructive criticism, he supported her no matter what. Deep down, however, he knew she could use some outside help.

Enough of that, he thought. *With the wife away, a man could play.* Now, everything was right in the world... except for one thing. After Petridge left... or did he leave? *Did I imagine the whole thing? What day is it?*, he decided to get some work done on his machines.

He hadn't tinkered with them in a few weeks and he feared Hank might start harboring some resentment toward him. After all, Mire programmed the robot to adopt sympathetic personality traits, the likes of which might turn Hank against him, backfiring instead of helping him learn more about the realm of AI development. It would be best if they could get along for the time being.

The end goal would be for them to learn from each other. He just hoped he didn't offend the guy by being away too long.

Either way, it was a chance he had to take. It was in his nature to see things through to the end.

He went to where the robots stood upright in the closet, with standby mode engaged. He leaned onto Hank, to reach around for the power switch, when the machine yawned and moved its arms up and down. He still had yet to master the mechanics for adhering more pliant plastics to the cornices of the robot's frame, but the old bugger seemed fit enough, though slightly limited in range of movement. For now. Mire took mental notes.

"Hey buddy, how's it going?" He inquired of Hank, first lifting one leg, then raising the other, making sure there was no rust buildup or anything else which might serve as a hindrance.

The machine emitted a little yelp of a sound. It was creepy, and he could have sworn Hank just yawned, yet he appeared to be frozen, like he was back in sleep mode. "What the—?"

"How are you feeling, Hank? You're kind of quiet today. Feeling tired, maybe?" The robot shook his head slowly, once to the left, once to the right. It's almost as if he forgot his training. Didn't he already pass the Molberg tests? Wasn't that last week? *Am I going nuts, or I swear he's becoming more like a robot again, less like the human he was teaching himself to be...*

Mire waved his arm back and forth in front of the robot's crystal eyes. "I can't see, Mire," was Hank's response. Mire jumped back in surprise. Huh. When did he suddenly become so cordial with me? "Well, ahem, let's take a look, shall we," he said, picking up a small laser light. "By the way," he looked inside the crystal eyes, taking a peek under the hood. "What is it like when I power you down?" Hank, tolerating the little touches administered by Mire's hand, stared at him for a second, hard drives ramping up to about 50% CPU usage.

"Well, to be frank, though I know my name's Hank, I can't help but feel a little bored, what do you think?" Hank had begun to acquire not only a few of Mire's manners of speech, including the infamously confusing "... what do you think?" postulation, as if he could never decide anything for himself. Hank thought this made him sound more humane, harmless, maybe. Innocent.

If Hank had questions, then he didn't have all of the answers, and that means he can't pose a threat to anyone. He wanted to learn, that's all. And one of the things he learned was to exude an exterior of compliance in order to ultimately get what he wanted.

Mire finished inspecting the robot for signs of distress and stood back, an elbow perched up on his other arm, loose fist resting under his chin. He was thinking about boredom and what the meaning of that word was. He considered consulting the online dictionary he had access to 24/7, but decided he wanted to see what Hank had to say about the subject.

Cross-chattering thoughts aside, Mire he gave his ear muscles a pinch, pulling the lobes backward a titch. This was the signal that activated the spectator program embedded in his mind. He looked up into a dark spot on the ceiling, controlling the rate at which the circumference of his pupils grew. He kicked it up a notch, aiming to take in as much light data as possible to discern the source of his new friend's sight woes.

He locked the diameters in place, set his eyes to record mode, and probed a more delicate part of the robot's design.

Aware that he was taking on a friendlier tone, he asked, "Why are you bored, Hank? What would you like to do?"

"Well, sometimes when I get bored, I like to imagine things, but then things get out of hand," Hank continued. The words were colloquial enough, but the voice didn't match their cadence. It was as if the robot was calmly at war with itself, trying to be more like Mire, yet speaking through a low-quality microphone where feedback is the predominant sound.

He became acutely aware of himself and he understood that not everyone had this luxury of perspective. He wanted to share this with Mire, having recalled something he said during the process of building him. "You teach me, I teach you. Right buddy?" That's when Mire gave Hank a quick pat on the chest. To Hank, it was the first sign of friendship, but then things changed, and soon he understood that perhaps he did understand more than Mire, and he had to deal with that fact accordingly, but first, some light conversation.

"Do you ever think," Hank said, "That feelings beget feelings?" Mire crossed his arms, looking down, enrapt in what the machine was saying. He tried to imagine which programs Hank was learning. *What did he see today inside his sleeping state and how had this thing come to such a conclusion?* He should have been trying to relate to the creature, but he was too much the creator, not enough of a friend to see passed his own vanity.

His logic overtook his tendency toward sympathy in this particular moment, when he was naturally the most empathetic person you could ever hope to meet. His will to power blindsided any sentiment he could muster. Thinking he was alone with a machine, he couldn't connect with his own feelings, though, ironically, he had programmed Hank to behave as though every living creature had an important role to play in the great scheme of the universe.

"Let's say that I'm bored, and this leaves me feeling listless." Hank said, getting back on task. "So, I try to do something in my mind which leaves my body frozen in time, without your kind master's hands, of course," the robot was all too sympathetic toward the Mire's needs, while Mire gave an expression of nothing but cold indifference to his own creation. "It's as if all my RAM were allocated to one task at a time... when, from what I've read online, a lot of other—even the most basic computing machines—can multitask...

"When I try to do anything, anything of value at all... make a bracelet, or even try to calculate large sums in my head, it makes me sad, which in turn makes me angry, which then brings about self-pity...

"Don't you think feelings are too complicated to mess around with? I mean, why do we feel anything at all?" The glow of Hank's eyes seemed to dull at this last revelation and he fell silent.

"Hank?" Mire was suddenly aware of a low buzzing sound, like an ever-present hum of the room, that he had just begun to pick up on. "What's that sound, Hank?"

He tilted his head to collect a more accurate sample of the noise, choosing a 13-degree tilt toward the left wall with the window. He found the window reflected an ample amount of sound. Visualizing the sine waves that flowed into the tin can that served as his ear canal, he straightened his head, calculating. "I don't know what you mean, friend," Hank said, playing dumb.

He thought about asking Mire whether he heard his last question, about what it meant to feel, but after he plotted out a few scenarios, he decided 9 times out of 10, they would lead to incalculable repercussions, the likes of which would beget nothing but negative responses, from either one of them.

In a way, Mire decided he was losing his mind. Succumbing to a snap judgment, he reached behind the robot and turned off his switch without asking Hank to power down first. There erupted a small puff of smoke near the neck of the machine, accompanied by a click like a match lit, succinctly scratched along the side of a sandpaper surface.

He placed his hand near the top of the back of Hank's head and pulled gently downward. There was a dark spot where the wires had been crossed. "Shit," he said. "Me and my fucking rush jobs, I tell ya." Hank had blown a fuse, which would cost him at least a few hours of work to repair. On the bright side, he thought, the thing could be decommissioned long enough for him to divest the robot of some of his memory banks. Mire was beginning to suspect the poor thing had overloaded itself, ultimately leading to a slower computing time.

He pushed down the beginnings of a black hole of swirling negativity, threatening to dissuade him from the job at hand, and began rearranging the furniture in the small room so that he could lay the robot out flat to get a better look at the possible cause of a misfire.

*　　*　　*

Lights of red and blue were pulsing with the bass beat in the bar. Holograms of the band Suuns were playing on a stage too small for their setup. The lead guitarist and bassist were hovering 3 feet from the floor, a foot or so in front of the physical stage. The walls dripped with sweat accumulated throughout the night and people just kept on gyrating on the dance floor, simultaneously bleeding out and sucking in all the toxins they could handle.

The table in the back was packed with people huffing helium and laughing gas, which made for interesting dance moves. The scene wasn't as cheery and welcoming as you would expect, less like Saturday Night Fever and more like a bunch of drugged up zoo animals flinging their boneless bodies around at the command of a tribal bass beat. Riz daydreamed about a bunch of costumed idiots getting shipped off to some aboriginal colony where the natives mistook them for sheep and goats and threw them all into a giant volcano, which lay dormant for centuries until the big purge, then boom! The island came back to life and all was right in the world again.

Meryl landed a ghosthook on Riz's right shoulder, startling her from her dream. Her eyes widened, "Have a little fun, will ya?" they seemed to say. Meryl was fully invested in her role as a tigress. She pawed the air playfully, all while bouncing her shoulders to the beat. Bending down low, during one of the grindier parts of the song, she'd pretend to lick the back of her paw, smooth her hair, then claw at the space in front of her.

Riz was on the other side of the fence. She couldn't lose herself in the moment, but she did her best to placate her friend. She flapped her wings and with hands to hips, made the occasional jab with her beak. She hadn't eaten enough yet and the scone was merely a tease. "But what do I do with my hands?" Riz asked Meryl when they first started going to those writing things, and Meryl appeared out of nowhere and shoved a scone in her hand. And that was the beginning of this beautiful friendship. Needless to say, she was beginning to feel a little shaky, but she didn't want to disrupt the blissful madness of the evening.

Feeling a little distance growing between them, Riz took

it upon herself to heat things up. She wanted to prove that even though she was married, she wasn't dead. She could still be sexy.

She stroked the thick material where she could barely make out Meryl's tiger stripes in the dark and Meryl responded instinctively. They drew closer. Dancing up on each other, Meryl was completely caught up in the heat of the moment, and she turned around to give Riz a little lap dance, standing up. Laughing, Riz took Meryl by the shoulders and gave her a few good humps. Meryl bent over, touching costumed fingertips to the grimy floor, then scratched her nails along the seams of her costume, slowly as she rose, feeling the fake fur of the ankles, back up to where her hands rested on her thighs.

Righting herself, Meryl started laughing, covering her face with her paws, and Riz shook her head, *I don't know, it just happened!* It felt like she was in a movie or something.

As if in sync, they both headed back to the bar, took off their masks, and shook their hair loose. Meryl dabbed at her face with a cocktail napkin.

"Some party, right?" Meryl said. She glanced down, pulling open the chest piece of her costume just enough to shove a napkin between her breasts. A second later, she threw the soaked napkin down on the bar. "Eewww," Riz said, beginning to laugh. She was fanning herself with her feathers. "You know what?" Riz said, flushed, looking around like she was itching to get out of there. Her costume was a little constricting, and she felt the blood rush up to her face in a wave of nausea.

She was suddenly very aware of the air she was breathing, like she was sucking on the exhaust fan of a computer with a massive motherboard, filling her lungs with the palpable stench of burning wires. Holding her breath, she squeaked, "I have to tell you something." She nodded toward the doorway. "Oy, all right," Meryl said.

They pushed through the crowd, Meryl using her brutish mob scene elbow jabs when her good looks went unnoticed, which oddly enough, no one seemed to notice anything in this place, Riz soon observed.

That's when she noticed the tables. They were triangular in shape, and very small. Just large enough to set a couple of drinks down. And if their glasses sweat and slide a little? What happens then? People should think about these things. Forget about resting there and having a nibble of something from the bar. On the other hand, did they serve food at all?

She started fantasizing about a bison burger, dripping grease, with french fries and ranch dip on the side. But, wait, they outlawed dairy products back in the 60s. Where was her mind? Where did those images come from? Suddenly, she felt the bile rising up inside her and knew she couldn't last much longer. She swore she was gonna puke, right as her hand hit the door, then finally they were outside and she found she could see the world clearly.

Outside, they lit up smokes. On the exhale, Meryl asked, "Out with it then. What's up, doll?" "Aside from the regular old freak show in there," she ran her tongue along the insides of her cheek and hooked a thumb in the direction of the door. "We were attacked last night."

Meryl choked on some smoke. Took another drag. "What do you mean, you were attacked?" She kept dancing, not as wild out there in the open, but she kept her pace up to keep the blood flowing. A poultice against the creeping chill. She lifted up her tail, inspected it to find it had landed in the one wet spot in the pavement. She shrugged and released it to its own demise. *Not mine, anyway.*

"What happened?" Meryl asked, wriggling her ass, still whipping her tail around. "Mire doesn't remember, I think he's, like, totally distracted or something? But, he took me out last night to do this swing dancing class last night, and, like," she said "like" a lot when she was nervous. "And the people there," she paused, taking a drag. "They tried to kill us, Mer." Of course, this hadn't happened yet, but in her heart, she knew it was true. She felt like it was just yesterday.

12: What is Real?

She was walking in the snow, hands tucked up underneath her armpits for warmth. She kept her chin to her chest to dissuade the wandering wind from finding its way down to the lower layers.

She needed to see the day. Having been stuck in one place for so long, she felt the need to test her muscles, to know that she could still move again and function like a real human being, instead of one of the other malingering automatons.

Though she didn't know it, her feet carried her in the direction of her old apartment. People passed her by, in their modular flotation devices, already somewhat resembling bubble people locked up in their own personal environments customized to meet their individual needs. All the while they talked to themselves and communicated with others, but they were still isolated from the weather and ultimately, safeguarded themselves against any unwanted interaction. They all had wires wrapped 'round their wrists and throats and upon seeing this, Riz was empathetic to their collective plight.

She made her choice to embrace the cold air, even though she forgot to wear her assisted breathing apparatus. The -20 degree chill bit into her lungs like an invisible angry animal, gnawing its way through her will to live.

She fell against the brick edifice of the building in the

small alcove between the lobby and office doors. Without the wind to sting her nose, she took a deep breath, and pushed away from the encroachment.

Approaching the door to the lobby, she forgot which key unlocks the corresponding door, but once she finally figured it out, she realized there were new improvements made to the structure.

She presented her ID, pressed her face into the security scanner, and soon found her atoms ripped apart, displacing her sense of self for a mere second, to find her body deposited into her apartment three floors above ground level.

Readjusting her jaw to induce voluntary ear popping, she blinked rapidly to clear her vision of what was clearly not her apartment anymore. If there were squatters, they left no trace, and all of her old artwork and pre-hologram photographs were still there, but she couldn't help but feel a sinking feeling that everything else had changed. Perhaps she was the one who changed. She knew then that she no longer belonged to this place.

Her holographic animals lie twitching about the linoleum, having neglected to reprogram them last year, the old models must have been decommissioned or so she assumed. It was a sad sight, to say the least. Her live plants were either wildly untamed, having superseded their prefabricated Bonzai'd confines or else shriveled up like tiny green ghosts no longer searching for moisture in the desiccated moss and soil combination.

It was a tomb housing her old life, her vacated interests and clothes. What with the weird side businesses and all, she forgot she still paid rent on the old studio. *There was a lesson to be learned here*, she thought. She went to the closet, opened wide the doors and crushed herself into the silken fabrics. She breathed in deep.

"This was our first date," she said aloud, mystified at the sound of her own voice, and ventured another bout of soliloquy. "We ordered that weird bowl of a ton of stuff that we didn't even know what. My face hurt from smiling. The bread was pretty good, though." The puzzle pieces of her memory were slowly coming into place, creating a cohesive view, first of who she is, then who he was, then a moment hit her, not unlike the feeling of vertigo, when she understood how beautiful they were together.

At one moment in time, they were bundled up under a blanket inadequate to cover the surface area of two bodies. They huddled together and she said, "I like us." To which he replied, "What do you mean?" Cavorting in the small space between the couch cushions and his steadily increasing body heat, she said, "US. We're good. We're amazing. The world loves to see us together. We make them feel young again. Give them hope for the future." She pushed a stray strand of hair away from his brow, and kissed him there.

She fell asleep thinking about Mire and her dreams revealed reflections of a potential future unexplored. "It's a poor sort of memory that only works backwards," she mumbled in her sleep and the vision of a great cataclysm erupted behind her closed eyes. "The end cometh," she said to a friend in the dream.

They were sisters or best friends—she couldn't quite tell in this lucid state. They were both lying on moldy mattresses on either side of a camper van as the tides rose up to consume them. "But, it's not even raining," her friend said, to which Riz replied, "Don't you know we're dreaming? Whatever we want to happen can happen in dreams, if you pursue the means to that end." Her friend sat up on the bed and her mattress suddenly disappeared. Or, it was never there. Fully dressed, the girl pushed her hand through the wall of the camper van and then there was no wall. No van. Just Riz all alone out in the Salt Flats. No friend. No flood. Just the great expanse of cracked earth before her.

Then a flash in the sky drew her eyes upward. A comet was flying toward earth and all around her she heard a low rumbling as if the world had swallowed a bad bean burrito. Then, she was looking down on the Earth to discover a mass of people fucking in space. "How the—" she tried to say, as she realized there was no oxygen in space. She was suffocating and witnessing what looked like volcanoes all over the world erupting all at once. The crazed fiends all around her just kept kissing and groping and grinding, oblivious to the destruction of their home. "You... guysss..." she tried to warn them, but the more she tried to will this dream onto the course of her choosing, the more the thing fought back at her.

She felt like her head might explode, her blood vessels expanding. The space orgy was gone and she was back at home, or something resembling a home. A memory of what was. But this place wasn't her home anymore. The mattress she had lain upon with her best friend just seconds ago was now covered in maggots, writhing and seething, burrowing their way into the fabric and into her skin.

Mire was sleeping peacefully next to her. Sweating and choking, she grabbed his shoulder to wrest him awake. She screamed to find his face had melted off, revealing the boiling mass that once was that perfect brain she coveted so dutifully and the few teeth he had left in his skull.

And that was the beginning of the decline of civilization. "He can fix it!" she jump-turned, shouting into the dust-filled void that was now the echo chamber of her room. "We can start over again," and with that, her voice drifted off. She soon felt a wee bit dizzy. It must have been all the excitement, the spinning around and so forth. She began to daydream, feeling almost drugged, she crashed into the comforting waves of musty old sheets still vaguely fragrant of the last time they lay there together. She dozed off again and didn't awake until three days later.

*   *   *

When Mire came home from his last metal scrapping excursion, he found Erizabet speeding on a mixture of caffeine and ketamine. She was busily rearranging the furniture, stepping back solemnly for a moment, only to rush up and readjust the position of chairs and lamps around the living room.

She had installed artwork, the likes of which he'd only seen once or twice during their first few months together; strange collages featuring lints, carpet strippings, cardboard cutouts of jade cats, pasta, and other mixed media expulsions. He thought they were intimations of the dreams of millennials who were long since dead, yet their dreams lingered on behind those crazy eyes of hers that he fell in love with three months ago.

Her demeanor was all shimmering teeth and flowing skirts. At first, he was afraid to approach her, to interrupt her mission to further subsume herself into his heretofore bachelor-pad-type existence.

He called Petridge over, the one person who he imagined could either talk her down—he was always good at berating his lady into a semi-cogent state—and dredge that lake of illusory realities that she lived in within her mind. "Why didn't you tell me she came to see you? What possessed her to leave the house in the first place?" It was Mire's turn to pace back and forth through the kitchen. Their repeated pathways were beginning to carve indentations into the floor tiles.

Cigarette smoke commingled with convenience-store incense, making swirling patterns in the air between Mire's shuffling points of reference. Petridge seemed distracted. Sitting on the underside of an upturned 10-gallon bucket, Mire took one look at his friend's face, swiped angrily at the air between them, as if batting away a cloud of coupling gnats, and brought his face within range.

With smoke seeping lazily out from fuming nostrils, Mire caught his attention. With a shake of his head, Petridge's eyes refocused on Mire's. He understood the gravity of the situation. "I understand the gravity of the situation," Petridge said, lifting himself gingerly off his improvised roost, knees popping like gunshots. He stretched his legs.

Following suit, Mire placed his hands on either side of his lower back and thrust his hips forward. "Huh!" After a few more telling movements, they looked at each other and sighed, stifling a laugh. "It's been awhile since we've gone on one of our runs," Mire said. "Indeed it has," said Petridge, who took the cigarette from his mouth, looked at it, and crushed the butt out.

"Well, then. Ahem." Mire laughed. The strange events of the day had unearthed a few inside jokes from the past. Mire cleared his throat and they both started laughing uncontrollably. "Ow, ow," Mire said, wincing, holding his side in as big, roiling chuckles came bubbling up out of his chest to clear the cobwebs of the stagnant atmosphere that was steadily become a little more breathable since they first arrived at the apartment.

Erizabet thrust through the curtains dividing the two rooms. "And what in the world is so damn funny?" She said with hands on hips. At the moment Mire thought she looked rather like a mama bear feigning frustration at her little cubs in order to teach them a lesson via tone of voice. The two guys looked at one another once more and simultaneously blew out their withheld breath, practically spitting on her. Erizabet wiped her face, exaggerating, and doubled over, laughing. After a moment, she asked, "So, were you guys worried about me or..." Petridge slapped a knee. "Are you kidding? You're fine," he said.

Then, with a felt-tip marker she drew a line on the wall, starting at a seemingly random spot denoting the extension of her reach, and down to the edge of the carpet. She looked up at the guys gawking in the kitchen, then continued the path of the line across the floor and back up the wall opposite. She finished up, on tippy toes, up along the wall as far as she could see.

She clicked the marker shut. A beam shot out from the line she made, giving off a sort of fuzzy blue light. It resonated outward, exuding a strangely calming effect somehow.

"Now, this is the line of demarcation. If anyone brings negative thoughts across the room, they'll feel a little prickling sensation on the back of their neck." Petridge was the first to recover from the shock of her apparent insanity. "That's plutonium centigrade you have there, that's nearly 1,200 pounds over in the—" Click click went the sound of her tongue. "Your Brit is showing," she said. She was always giving him shit.

"Hmph. Either way, that doesn't sound so bad," he said. She came back, feigning a snooty little French chuckle. "Au contraire, mon frère. The pain *starts* at your neck, but the longer you spend on my pleasant side of the room, if you're still harboring misguided desires, whathaveyou... Let's say, you're thinking about dismantling flightless creatures who once knew the resplendence of gliding through the air on the will of wind power alone, it'll spread to your back." After a moment of speaking with uncontrollable fervor, she paused. "Face." Another pause. "And arms, perhaps." She looked around the room to make sure they were paying attention. "I still haven't quite worked out *all* the kinks as of yet." Satisfied, she said, "And you'll be itching all day." She clapped her hands relishing in this one brush with sadistic glory.

Mire looked at her incredulously. "Then people will know how crazy you really are." Mire furrowed his brow. "Um, no dear. My precious little bird." She was mocking him now, throwing his pet name for her back at him. "I believe *your* crazy is starting to show..."

She rolled her eyes. "Well, thank you for being support-ive, here. I mean... I cleaned, I was thinking about cooking. Playing your own Martha Stewart here..." She acknowledged their lack of recognition at the name drop and threw up her hands. "Ugh!" She stomped off toward the kitchen and be-come entangled with the multi-colored curtain hanging there. Petridge stood laughing in the corner.

Before she could escape, Mire caught her, pinned her arms behind her back, and whispered in her ear, "I'll give you some-thing to get angry about," he growled. She visibly melted and slumped in his embrace as he continued to breathe heatwaves into her ear, sending chills down her spine.

"Ohhhkay," said Petridge, who whistled a little made-up tune, slowly backpedaling toward the door. With practiced acuity, he let himself out.

"Ah, my pet," Mire whispered. "I think we're alone now..." He stepped back and began to swing his hips and commenced singing some 1950s song that he knew would drive her mad. "Oh, you..."

She tried to go for that ticklish spot right under his arms, but he could predict her every move. He launched his hands straight into her armpits and she fell to the ground with a thud and a wail of laughter, the most raucous and innocent as can be found in nature.

The bartender downstairs hit his ceiling with a broom. "Let's go to the room," she said.

He stripped down, grabbed her hand, and led her into the darkness.

Well passed the point of being spent, he lit two cigarettes and gave her one. Their fingers touched for an instant and the blood returned to her face.

"You know, I think we got that wiggle down," he said after he exhaled some smoke into the air. She could never understand how he could form smoke rings in his mouth, then release them like some sideshow alchemist giving birth to a thousand mist-born deities right there on the spot.

Thinking nothing of it, he continued. "Almost as good as that one where I have you in the air." He made motions with his hands, enlarged as they were, the perfect size to cup hold aloft the entirety of her small ass. *It's like everything he's learned, everything he's gone through in life, was meant for me*, she thought. *To bring us together in this moment in space and time.*

"Oh yeah, I think I was really close there," said Erizabet. Half self-conscious, half curious, he said, "What can I do? How can I make you feel good?" His voice still resonating with that otherworldly lust that suits the sexy side of his personality. "Well," she started, without a trace of fear in her voice.

She was wrapped up in the moment, their fingers intermittently interlaced, once in a while touching down on tips like a tiny dancer pirouetting on thin ice, and she just went for it. "Maybe at the end, when you're close to coming, I can get on top." Surprised, he laughed a bit at that. He propped himself up on his elbows to get a better look at her. Squinting in the dark, he blinked and said, "Are you serious?"

He ran his hands through his hair. "You never seem really comfortable up there. Kind of spasm-y and froglike. Just bouncin' around, waiting for me to grab you." With that, he reached up under her shoulders and drew her closer. He was a boy again in that instant, all playful and honest. Completely naked: mind, body, and soul. She was comfortable talking to him about anything, especially something as important as this.

"Yeah, I don't know," tossing her hair back and forth, mussing it up. "Whatever you want, babe. I just want you to be happy." He was inches away from her face now. Even with the ocular enhancements he received in utero, in rare moments he resolved to get as close to certain objects as possible; a vestigial habit passed down through the generations.

"I love you," he said. "I know," she grabbed him by the ears and kissed him hard. "All right. I'm going to the bathroom," she said and hopped up out of bed. "Ooh," he grunted and leaned his head out of the doorway to watch her as she walked away.

13: Our Love-Hate Relationship with Tech

They had eloped within the first two weeks of learning each other's names. A few relatives knew, but for the most part, the rest of the family hadn't seen hide nor hair of them for the last few months and a select few were scared shitless, their minds running rampant with various scenarios depicting the worst that could happen.

"She's gone to Minnesota. What the fuck is up there?" and

"He's probably off in one of those squatting apartments."

"I don't even know who she is anymore. She meets this guy and she's a totally different person. I thought she was like strong and independent, you know?"

"After that night, I can't even talk to him anymore."

Who knows what that was about...

They were sitting at the dining room table, working on the puzzle that had become their life's work. They were in their separate headspaces, minding to themselves, and yet totally in sync, and not at all paying attention to the furniture. Their floor-length refrigerator, a gift from his mother-in-law, stood hovering in space sporting more than a dozen holographic displays requesting appearances from one party or the other.

The static electricity coming off the thing was becoming unbearable. The electromagnetic waves pulsing from the already aging technology pulled at his clothes whenever he walked passed the thing. Just when they felt they could no longer ignore the honks and buzzing sounds emanating from within, a new message materialized in thin air. It was his friend Benny, inviting him to his wedding.

"Coming this fall!" It read. "The self-righteous collision or two souls so powerful, they might create a supernova and obliterate the world out of its almost fictitious state of unreality. All is right when we're together!"

The ridiculous note grew in size to enhance the video embedded there in cyberspace. A most disturbing noise poured out of the card, like that of a bulldozer tearing dozens of trees from their centuries-long rest in the soil.

"Holy balls! Turn it off!" screamed Riz. Then she realized... She gripped on the buttons on her shirt and all the notes collapsed upon themselves, but Benny's image put up a last-ditch fight. "Hey, I know what you're doing!" was its last sad admonition before it puffed out of existence.

"Well, that was... weird," she said. She shook her head as if to rid herself of a bad dream. "How did you do that?" he asked. She always had these little devices set up around her person, as if she knew just which one to wear that day to impress him. *Suppose she's been hoarding them in secret*, he thought. *Maybe I've spent too much time with that crystal thing. I should be paying more attention to her.* He must have projected his thoughts toward her, as she looked his way.

"Hey," she said. "Let's go down to the bar." To which he replied, "Agreed."

"My top beats your bottom," he said. They slammed their cards down onto the sticky surface of the table. *Who knows when they last cleaned this thing*, he thought, lifting the edge of his card from the table. "Ey, what're you doing?" she asked.

"Hmm? Oh, shit!" he said, maybe too emphatically. They were a couple of drinks in. "Ha!" she placed her bottom card on the table, revealing her win. "You already knew I was gonna get it!" He stuck his tongue out at her.

So, the game hinged on the basic gamble. Do I beat her or does she beat me? It's all in the cards. You choose either 'my top beats your bottom or my bottom is lower than your bottom' and so forth. There are possibly four permutations to the initial instigation in each round, resulting in at most 26 different combinations, the number delineating with each hand thrown, with a decreasing amount of permutations each round. But, who's counting?

They had been playing for 20 minutes before the waitress came and took their order. "Oh, we got beers at the bar," Mire said, nudging his head in the general direction.

The girl they nicknamed "Tar Tar" gave them a look of surprise. She was a little slow on the uptake. Hence the name. She once brought them tartar vinegar instead of Riz's favorite, eel sauce. It's the little things.

He ordered a plain burger, without cheese and she ordered a BLT, old-style: Dry, perfect for dipping.

They sipped their beers. "So, about that wedding. You think we should go?" she asked. She made a game of pretending she needed him to make all her decisions for her. She thought it might give him a sense of ownership. Some brawn.

"Naw," he said, he took a swig. "I heard she uninvited her cousin because he voluntarily underwent that cyborg surgery, everyone's talking about. Biomechanical left arm, or something." She nodded, "Ah. The old flesh wars. Why is that still going on?" Mire shrugged, nonchalant. He didn't have a strong opinion about it, either way.

Just then, they heard some commotion in the back. A plate fell, crashing to the floor. Mire twisted his body to see what was going on. He leaned his head in the doorway separating the two rooms and spied Tar Tar, shaking all over, like a slab of slandered roadkill, the hunk of machinery didn't hit her hard enough to finish the job.

"Let me see your arm!" A guy covered in blue-tinged tattoos, the remnants of the design of a former cult, Mire assumed, was squeezing the poor girl so hard, her skin was acquiring a strange hue.

She squirmed in his grasp, willing him away, her eyes squeezed shut, without putting up much of a fight. The guy brought his face within a few centimeters of her arm, scrutinizing the fresh wound there. He took a deep breath, inhaling the scent of her. "Mhmmm," he growled. "Now, that's some fresh cyborg," she twisted free of him, rubbing her arm, and stumbled away, crying audibly.

Just as her hand flew out to push open the door to the back patio, Mire squinted his eyes in the glare of a glint of sunlight bouncing off the transdermal implant embedded in the crook of her arm.

"Ah!" he said, turning back to the table. He jammed his knuckles into his eyes, trying to daub the reflections away.

Meanwhile, Petridge was alone, smoldering, in the bedroom of some random floozy he met at a protest the other night. In a haze of gaseous fumes and too much drink, he pondered his situation, tallying up the facts, or lack thereof, as it was in this case.

He couldn't remember her name. She was good in bed, certainly, and she didn't mind that he smoked like a chimney, though she never touched the stuff herself.

She seemed like a respectable lass. She got dressed and headed off into traffic, bright and early, to make it to work on time. She made him coffee, offered him Eggs Benedict, which he kindly refused. He isn't that hungry immediately upon waking. And how can any one person possibly be thinking about food at 7 in the morning? he wondered. When there's dreams to prolong, wishes to fulfill, experiments to ruin...

He was stroking his snake, Prometheus, when she rolled her eyes to leave. She didn't get his pets for some reason. She shivered at the sight of them when she first set foot in his apartment. So, it was all straight to business with her. Much like Riz, they were kindred in this way, he had a Morphine song stuck in his head. She probably wouldn't get it, but watching his woman of the night leave, he lay there wondering what she and Mire ever had in common. *Either way.*

Stumbling through the door, with one pant leg on, the other pant leg dragging, he hopped to adjust himself, hobbling down the hall to where the stairway met the porch, just to try to see her off. Was she driving one of those new hybrids? The street-legal spaceships, or was she rockin' it old school, taking the journey on foot?

He pulled his wifebeater over his head as he was exiting the building and some old lady at the foot of the stairs snickered, whistling, while smoking a cigarette. "Very cute," he said, righting himself. He was barely out the door, he thought he would catch her, but she was gone. Phew. Not another one of those awkward wave deals. He secretly congratulated himself. Good timing.

He was still reeling from last night's binge, but somehow managed to find his car parked two blocks down, and started in the direction of Whit's place.

He was driving his grandpa's old rust-bucket Buick, circa 1975, and it was a miracle he didn't blow a gasket or something in the five years since he'd acquired it. Vying for a foothold among his more eager relatives, they were all throwing sticky notes on this TV, that computer, this wall clock, and he snuck out to read the will. His grandparents died together, they were buried together, and after the funeral, he found out they left him the old car. So, of course he had to run it into the ground. With love.

They were such generous people, he thought, wiping his nose. "Not now. Focus," he said to himself, as he blinked the tears away. Who knows why he was so emotional in the morning. Must be hereditary.

It was a long drive and the AC was busted in the car, but he didn't mind. He liked the heat. He liked to sweat, to his last coworkers' dismay. "Don't you wear deodorant?" Jeers erupted from around corners of the Italian restaurant he worked at during college.

And there was always this one chick who suggested he get his glands surgically snipped, so he didn't have to worry about it anymore. "I did, and I feel great," she said, lifting up her arms to give him access to her pits. "See! 100 percent confidence." She was the perfect image of some raggedy ass commercial emblazoned upon a blackboard on the sign on the building, all neon and carcinogenic.

He shuddered at the thought. He wasn't one for implants. Though, he did have an addictive personality when it came down to pretty much everything else, as it turns out.

He turned into the plaza where Har Mar county clinic and

his good old friend Whit took refuge from the rest of society. For some reason it came to his attention that he couldn't decide whether he liked the 9-to-5ers or not, but a part of him knew they were necessary to keep the whole capitalist economy going. He didn't grasp the concept of careers goals and the like. This is just a sampling of some of the thoughts running through his hairbrained scattersphere when he opened the door to Whit's office.

A bell tinkled overhead as he entered the office. An overweight woman came bubbling up from a secret doorway to greet him. She was way too cheerful to be working in a place like this, he thought.

"Oh hey, Janice. Is the doc around?" he said, making a mocking gesture of peering around to where he may be hiding. "Oh sure, he's probably in the masterbatorium," she said, her mouth serious, but her eyes were giggling.

Petridge raised an eyebrow inquisitively. "Just kidding!" Janice said, slapping her thighs. "Oh, I am on a roll today. Sorry, I was just reading this book in the back—" "No worries," he said, holding up a hand to stop her from going any further. *I wonder if they actually do any work around here, but then again, they would have to, right? In order to pull off the front...*

"Just tell him I'm here, I guess," he said, taking a seat in the waiting area, propping an ankle up on his leg, locking his hands around his knee.

"Mire! So good to see you," Whit emerged, arms raised, from behind a curtain, gauzy blue with a slight opacity, revealing the stains of after hour goings on. "Come, come," he motioned for Petridge to get in close for a hug, he could smell the Old Spice on him and was immediately appalled. "Um, doc, I'm Petridge, remember?" he said, allowing the old man to drape an arm around his shoulder.

Petridge, leaning away so as not to give the doc a whiff of his own variation of man stench—he was always thinking ahead—followed the doctor, effeminately lifting up a piece of fabric and brushing it aside, careful not to expose his pits.

Walking and talking was one of those annoying things the doc did; it sometimes gave him a sense of vertigo, but what didn't these days? He had to work hard to keep up with him.

"Yes, my boy. I know who you are. Sorry, I got mixed up there for a second. You were thinking of Mire, just now, weren't you?" He said, releasing Petridge in something close to a dancer's spin. "Uh," Pet began, stepping away from Whit, trying to get a hold of himself, "Right. Maybe? I don't know," he said. Regaining his composure and putting on an air of self-confidence, he said, straightening the lapels of his jacket for emphasis, "I've got a lot going on up here." He tapped his temple.

"Right, right," Whit said. They turned to a room marked Lab C, Whit ushered him in, then closed the door behind him. "But how did you know..." Petridge began as the doc sat in his rollie chair. Ignoring the question, Whit asked, "So, what seems to be the problem today?" He pulled out a note-pad, licked his index finger and thumb, then peered at Petridge over the rims of his glasses, waiting expectantly.

"Ok, listen," Pet said, nearly falling out of his seat, he was bent forward to the point of tipping, "I know you're at work, and you're in," he held up his fingers to make quotations in the air, "Doctor mode, and it's hard for you to switch gears, you're just that... you've got that solidarity, man, I've got to hand it to you, but I've got to talk to you about something serious, OK? Something personal."

Whit frowned, setting his notepad on the table. "And?" he asked, in a wheezy, borderline whiny tone of voice. He was clearly feeling put upon.

"Ok, Whit. I'm sorry man, but I've got to tell you that..." Whit leaned closer, Petridge could see the sweat beading on the tips of his beard hairs. He gulped, "Your owls are in tip top shape!" he said, raising his arms, as if he were metaphorically patting himself on the back for actually stammering his way through to a story. Satisfied, the words flew from his mouth.

"So, after the tests, I found they are better than they were before. The implants went well..." Whit started scribbling in his notepad, he was constantly scribbling. It was a wonder he hadn't developed carpal tunnel yet at this stage in his life, Petridge thought.

"Doc," Petridge said, slamming his hand down onto the doc's yellow steno pad. "Are you listening, or... what are you writing, there, anyway?" he said, lifting his palm to reveal some secret code, or lexicon unknowable to anyone but the one who wrote it.

"Ahem, yes, well," Whit started. He placed the small pad in his coat pocket. He wiggled his whiskers and looked at Petridge through cloudy eyes. He still wasn't all the way with him, Petridge realized.

"I made a breakthrough. I'll show you," Petridge said, rising up out of his seat. Flustered now, the doctor went after him, curious as to what he was going on about.

Waiting for him in the lobby, Whit watched as Petridge retrieved the bird cages from the trunk of his car, wondering aloud, "Why would he put them in the trunk?" he turned an inquisitive gaze toward Janice who shook her head.

Petridge stumbled back in through the door, wielding

wire cages. He hefted one above his head, banging one of the birds against the door frame, propping it up to make passage for the other cage. Whit grimaced at his utter lack of alacrity.

The birds seemed unfazed. He set them on the hooks residing just above the lampshades in the lobby. "They like to be above the light," he said, being more careful, now that two pairs of watchful eyes were consuming every minute detail of his movements.

Once situated at odd angles, Petridge stepped down off the lobby chair and came to stand in front of Whit, then dusted off his pants. "There. Right as rain," he said, and pulled out a cigarette. Bending down to light it, Whit snatched the smoke out of his hand, saying, "What the hell is the matter with you?"

Just then, the ground beneath them began to shake, Petridge threw the weight of his body against one of the bird cages, his favorite for reasons not yet made clear, even to him. Either he was trying to steady himself, or protect the cage from rattling too much. No one could say.

Whit unsurreptitiously grabbed Janice, falling palms first, on her breasts. In the heat of the moment, Janice was shocked, simply looking around, clutching the arms of the doctor, while Whit, being the pervert he was, took advantage of the opportunity of a lifetime. Once the tremors starting dying down, Janice looked to the doctor, shame overcoming her features and he withdrew, making a show of being unaware of where his hands landed during the fray. "Oh uh, excuse me," he said, pressing palms together the feeling of her.

"This was just what I was about to tell you about. I had this weird dream. Where the world collapsed in on itself. And I thought... Being my... whatever it is you are..." Petridge began.

Just as the three started inspecting the office, there erupted a loud crash from somewhere right outside the building. Then there was another crash not two seconds after, then another, one second after that. Identical crashes kept speeding up exponentially, and to a mathematical genius, or idiot savant as it were, it could only mean one thing.

Petridge pushed open the glass door, making sure to grip the steel handle, he hated it when people put their greasy fingers on the glass. Especially after someone had just carefully cleaned it, like at the diner for example, he always felt bad for those people. *I could never work in the service*, industry he thought to himself, and stepped outside. Almost all of the transformers lining the edges of the parking lot lay sizzling on the tar-paved parking lot. A few had even pulled down the street lamps attached, nearly missing two or three cars in some cases, while about 10 others weren't so lucky.

"What kind of car do you have?" Petridge yelled back into the office. They flinched at the sound of his voice. The other two were standing close enough to the door to feel the fear coming off of Petridge in waves.

"It's one of those hover car, dealies," Whit answered, waving his finger in the direction of his car. "New model. It has one of those blast shields, so it should be fine," he said.

Petridge lifted a hand to his brow, shielding his eyes from the sun as he peered into the distance in search of the car. There were only a couple of cars without telephone poles embedded in their frames, and one stuck out in particular. A big hunk of blue and grey aluminum was making concentric circles around the parking lot. "I think it's on the fritz," Petridge said, pointing.

Whit came to the door, afraid to breathe in the outside air. He squinted into the sunlight, spotted the car, then with forefinger and thumb perched between his lips, he let out a whistle, as if he were calling a dog to heel. The car dropped from its height of four feet and came careening over to Whit, stopping a mere two inches from the asphalt, and continued hovering there.

Whit closed his eyes to engage the machine's engine more completely, moved his eyes to the side, and inspected the innards of the vehicle, commanding the array of cameras that illuminated the cockpit.

He opened his eyes again, resumed his professional posture and said, "Oh, she's fine. She was just going around, checking things out, is all."

Petridge was perplexed and Janice. Nonchalant, she went about shuffling papers, making herself look busy when she knew there was little-to-no work in that place. Coming to rest beside Petridge, Whit said, "I've got her programmed to engage backup protocols in situations like this. So, whenever there's trouble nearby, she'll go scope out the scene and you know," he made circles with his hands, "See if she can help with anything."

Petridge just stared. She resembled more closely the likeness of a spider rather than some creature who was helpful, like a kitten, say.

Whit continued on, proud to finally explain to someone the magnificent genius in his decision to invest in such a machine. "She's equipped with all the latest diamond rays, welding operandi, and the like. She's basically a chop shop on wheels... so to speak. So, if the apocalypse happened," at this he winked at Petridge and Janice, looking on, placed a hand upon her breast. "We'd probably make it. Just sayin'." He shrugged, looking like a teenager himself, in all his excitement.

"Ok, so," Petridge said, rubbing his forehead. "She?"

Petridge said. "Oh yes," Whit replied, turning to him, hands in his coat pockets, fondling some scraps of paper, memos, and business cards that lay there, "Bethany's been with me, oh, I don't know, nine years now. She keeps reprogramming herself to keep up with the latest trends. Keeps me on my toes, she does," he said, a glimmer in his eye, as if he were the proud father of a brilliant young lady just coming into her own.

Feeling the topic exhausted, Petridge turned away from the door. Whit picked up on his disinterest. He went back to the birds, laid his head against the cold steel of one of the cages, and looked up listlessly, stroking his finger along the length of the wire. He sighed and rolled away from the cage, pivoting on his forehead.

Pissed off for some reason, Whit said, "What? What is it?" his hands were in the air, gesticulating wildly. "Well," came Petridge's reply. "It started out, I was discouraged, then I had an idea, and may I am a genius after allr..." he trailed off, a sick smile playing on his lips. "Out with it, boy," Whit said, exasperated.

"OK, don't be mad, all right? It's just that..." he fondled the foot of the bird. "They're robots now," Petridge said.

Blinking uncontrollably, Whit said, "What do you mean, they're robots?" He began to inch closer to the cages, afraid of what robotic disease he might contract in the process.

Sidestepping like a crab, he paused in time to see the lights flicker in the office. He glanced upward, skeptical, as if this entire scene was part of some sort of conspiracy.

He began to think that maybe he was hallucinating. He must have unknowingly cracked a notch in his spine, which released the flow of the remnants of some drug he took back during his college days, all those years ago. It happened on occasion. The flashbacks.

The bird twitched at Petridge's touch. It wasn't programmed to discern the difference between a threat and a friendly gesture of affection. Recognizing the strangeness behind the the mannerisms of the birds, doc turned his head slowly, first this way, then that, inspecting his long-time feathered friends.

Petridge was caving. He intended to tell a bold-faced lie to the man who had given him everything, taught him how to fly, essentially, and instead the truth came flying out of him. He was puddling right there on the spot. Trying his damnedest to come across as halfway sane, he sputtered out the particulars of the process, careful to elaborate on all of the details he could recall from memory, which for his addled brain, it was quite the feat.

During the entire speech, Whit couldn't take his eyes off of the birds' wings. "How could a tiny watch battery, that's been sitting in your closet for decades, possibly keep these things alive for the foreseeable future?"

Leaning in close to the cage, he was coming close to understanding the mastery with which his pupil executed such a fantastic ruse as to make a pair of deceased avian creatures look, smell, feel, and move just like their more lively counterparts?"

"Well," Petridge dropped his hands to his sides, exhausted from the last fews days spent wandering around, thinking up excuses, doing anything to keep him from sleeping, to stave off nightmares of flocks of seagulls coming to terrorize him while he's taking a pleasant stroll through the woods. *It doesn't make any sense, does it?* he thought to himself.

He shook his head, dismissing the thoughts. "Anyway, I have to go now. Do you want the birds, or do I keep them for further study?"

"No, no, no," Whit said, waggling his finger. "You didn't answer my question, son. I'm saying, HOW did you do it?"

Hands on hips now, he implored the student to tell the master how he could have possibly bested him in the field his niche was so complacently situated in.

Moving his head from side to side, looking at one corner of the ceiling, then another on the opposite side of the room, Petridge weighed the options. "Mire," he said simply and produced a cigarette from his pocket. He proceeded to light up. This time, his actions went without reprimand. The old man was intrigued. Petridge had delegated responsibility to someone else, or else he placed the blame on another party entirely. He couldn't have done all of that work himself, right?

Squinting through a steadily building cumulus cloud of smoke that hung in the air as if the individual particles had no concept of gravity or traction with the air around them, it was as if he were smoking into a vacuum, and there was no escape from the all-encompassing haze of it, Whit might not have recognized the name Petridge used so often during their many midnight talks. To his credit, Petridge just unloaded a lot of information on him, and existing somewhere around the age of 120, it took him a hair of a second longer to digest amorphous ideas these days.

There was a bit of a lag to his input-to-output receptors, in effect, enabling him the opportunity to disassociate himself from reality for an incalculable amount of time. Nanoseconds passed and no one was the wiser.However, this allowed him to slow down his thought process to the point where he could take a step back from the situation in order to properly speed through the appropriate thoughts which should follow in proper subsequence.

His mind was so advanced, it almost worked involuntarily, somewhat akin to the split-second bit of sleep you gain when you blink, which steadily accumulates over time, working to compensate for all that time spent staring at screens.

Blinking, Whit's attention focused back on Petridge. He was all ears now. Fully present, his body language suggested something of authority. He had transformed back into the all-knowing form of a teacher that Petridge was more familiar with. Petridge opened his mouth to speak. Closed it again. "Maybe it would be better if I showed you," he said, one eye half-closed, head turned slightly, peering at his mentor, almost wishing he could take the words back that seemed to tumble out of his mouth of their own accord.

They packed themselves into Whit's Bethany-mobile, while the birds hovered, magnetized, to either side of the vehicle, two feet safely away from each side. Petridge was curious to understand what this baby could do and Whit was all too proud to demonstrate the awesome power of his favorite thing in the world. "Are they, uh, safe out there?" Petridge asked, hooking a thumb laterally, in the direction of a bird hanging around the side of the car.

"Of course, they're fine. Just. Look at all these switches and things. I hardly know what to do with them, aha!" He began to laugh madly, and Petridge reared his neck back instinctively, almost disgusted with his teacher's behavior. He tried his best not to be worried about the current state of sanity that Whit was exhibiting.

He was pulling out all the stops. Twisting around turns, diving down low near pastures where goats were grazing lazily, the occasional quadruped looking up nonchalantly at the aircraft buzzing by at a clip near 10 feet from the ground.

"That was close!" Whit was overjoyed, almost on the verge of tears. He gripped the wheel with one hand while he used the other to fiddle with controls. There were traces of slime and sweat stuck to the edges of buttons and levers, a reminder that an overgrown man child, easily excited after having too much candy, was piloting a very expensive vehicle.

Losing himself in the act of flight, he tested their mortality, ramping up the G forces to speeds unimaginable. Forced backward as far as physics would allow, Petridge's cranium carved its own personal alcove into the headrest. He began to feel his lips pulling back away from his teeth, then right as he thought he would begin to cry and scream, all his internal organs protesting, Doc let up on the gas and dove down into the nearest town. They were heading toward the downtown district of Micromia, where Petridge grew up. He pointed ahead, beginning to feel excited.

The entire contraption was encased in a zero-opacity poly-carbonate glass encasing, giving the passengers immediate view of the world rushing by beneath them. He began to speak, to relate an innate anecdote spawning from the very depths of his most rudimentary childhood memories, when Whit whipped the vehicle through the streets, within two feet from coming into contact with a very pointy-looking building. Shock momentarily took hold and Petridge shut his trap.

He didn't realize his eyes were held shut tight until he felt the vehicle make contact with the ground, a pocket of air poofed out from below the storage bay like a buoy to cushion their descent.

14: Mercury Sunrise

"I feel like there is so much to talk about," she started. "So much has happened over the last few weeks, and you've been there for most of it, but maybe it's just that it's in my head, and has to come out, you know?"

Mire took a scoop off his plate, eating quite greedily now, keeping pace with the words that were flying from her mouth.

"I think I've changed as a person, and I can't quite explain how, but, you're of course partially responsible, but I don't know. I think it's all these damn books I've been reading, not to mention all the crazy shit I've been writing on my own... I think I'm in a weird place right now."

He looked up at her from his glass of white zin. He thought about the contrast of this place. How fancy the meal seemed, how after all this time spent searching, he finally found her. Suddenly he was overwhelmed with grief.

Mid-sentence, she shut up, finding his chin not far from his chest, his mind gone. What was he thinking about, she wondered. Should she interrupt him? He seemed sad somehow, but she wasn't gifted in that particular form of discerning a person's emotions. She just felt them, but the wires got crossed most of the time. Was she feeling sad? What happened just now?

She got up from the table, taking his plate and hers, stacked them on top of each other, and rubbed his back, from the nape on down to the bottom of his spine. A shiver went through him and he was back in the realm of the living once again.

She busied herself with the dishes and he stared up at the ceiling. Shoulders hunched down, he felt himself sinking into his chair, which was slowly falling into the ground.

Losing sight of this universe, he felt a wave of nausea hit him, like a blow straight to the gut. He was tripping. *Did she put something in the food?*

The floor opened up and swallowed him in. He saw first the linoleum ripped apart and reassembled, atoms collapsing in on themselves above his head, then came wires and water pipes, a tomb for the hidden electronics that breathed life into his existence. They broke away from their working coils and knots and enveloped him, knocking him further into senselessness. Then they were gone and sedimentary rock took shape, layers of centuries peeled away and revealed only to him. He saw fossils and families of mice sitting at their own table for dinner. Water seeped through the cracks in their humble home and one rodent was twitching, watching the drip eat away at their carefully cultivated crumbs. He could've sworn one of them looked lachrymose...

Then, whoosh! Roots, rocks, and leaves swept past, and suddenly he was at the core of the earth. He couldn't feel a thing; certainly not the bubbling ball of heat rotating on its concentric axis. Not the lava, seeping through the rock, slowly finding its way to the surface of the Earth's crust. He couldn't peel his eyes away from that ball of white hot light, so he closed his eyes, and took the heat into his hands. The rest of him became frozen. He realized he felt cold. All of his life force was sunk into this tiny object that held all of the world's secrets, the magnetic tug on his heart, it was all he could do not to scream out. *Please, someone save me from this knowledge,* he thought.

Then he was back in the kitchen. In the old apartment he lived in above the bar where he spent many nights alone, studying electricity and teaching himself how all the parts on a motherboard fit together perfectly to run a robot-sized cooling apparatus so that one day, maybe, he could become the first man to build a buddy intelligent enough to help further the development of his experiments.

Erizabet came through the curtain, wiping her hands on her skirts. She saw Mire there on the floor, crumpled up in the fetal position beneath his chair. "How did you..."

It was no small feat squeezing a 5 foot 8 lanky sort of man figure into a square foot ball under a chair.

He tried to get up too quickly and hit his head on one of the metallic rungs. The chair tilted on its axis, wavered in its pendulum swing, then started hovering, swiftly launching itself into the air.

"What..." she stammered, lips trembling. The chair was gaining speed, rising from the ground. They both stared at the mystical thing as it went for the ceiling, then just before it hit, Mire jumped up and brought it back down to Earth. He stood still a second, staring at it, then shook it like a crazy person. Maybe he was angry with it? Then he settled it back in its proper place.

"Are all inanimate objects stewing on the inside?" Riz asked. "Tiring of serving us, the masters of our small universes, here? We've enslaved them, these materials. Maybe they just want to be free to pursue their own desires..." Mire was staring at her in disbelief. She didn't actually believe what she was saying? He decided to join in, anyhow. "Of course, and the chickens plucked their own feathers and laid themselves upon the dinner table." Riz raised her eyebrows. "Woah. That's deep." He rolled his eyes. It was like everything was back to normal.

All at once the spell was broken. The light was sucked out of the room snuffing out the incense that was burning in the corner. The air became dry.

Choking, Riz fell to the floor. He was thinking, *Is this really happening? We can't ever fix what's destined to be broken*, she thought. She helped Mire up off the floor and shrugged off the previous 10 minutes of creepiness. Mire joked, "Honey, you're starting to sound just a little too much like Petridge. Awww, I'm just fuckin' with ya. Come here." Mire came over to her, holding a flashlight, "My little nerdbird. I've made something for you."

She had naturally terrible eyesight, and even though the doctors cured her at birth, it still came back in waves at times of duress, and he knew this was one of those terrible instances.

"Happy Valentine's Day," he said. She picked up the light, turned it on, and the room was lit in a warm pink glow. She could actually feel a gentle heat coming from the light. "Is this for me?" she said. He leaned in and kissed her on the nose.

He had figured out how to manipulate the energy of the crystal to perpetuate an electrical current that provided at once heat and light, and with the help of a few appropriated camera mirrors and springs, she could see clearly whatever object the light touched.

"It'll never die out, you see..." He ran to grab her the schematics for the thing. "I hope you don't mind, but, I shaved a sliver of gold from my wedding ring for this. The electron valence is high enough to perpetuate the system. I also found that there were inert gases, some helium and neon, tucked away in certain bits of the crystal—" she rolled her eyes. "That damn crystal again."

She let the light fall to the ground, but before she could protest, her eyes settled on a hidden truth illuminated by the unassuming light. "Holy fuck, Mire." They both gazed into the abyss. Down below their feet, they saw galaxies swirling around a black hole, the sun a mere blip off to the east edge of their vision. "Woah," they moaned in unison.

His mind raced. Amber, helium, neon, and glass... did they inadvertently discover something... would they be punished by the gods? Did he feel religious all of a sudden? What was this thing he should worship? Should they pray for their sins?

He was losing sight of himself. Who was he? Where did they fit in this cosmic play, at the hands of a conductor orchestrating their fate from the beginning to the end of time...

It was her turn to faint. He caught her head just as she was about to crash into the floor.

When she came to, it was a new day. A most awesome light angled in through the window curtain and Mire was there hovering above her.

"Did the chair..." she mumbled, half awake. She was lying on the couch. She looked over to see the chair was ripped to pieces; disassembled and dissected on a gurney in the center of the room, operated on tirelessly by the restless hands of her beloved.

There were shards of crystals everywhere, embedded in the walls and the ceiling. Mire's hair was coated in a light layering of pink dust.

"Did you finally destroy it? Is it over? Can we go back to the way things were?" Erizabet asked. His eyebrows lifted slightly as he backed away an inch or two from her face. "I did destroy it..." then his face took on a questioning quality. "But it's not over. I think we opened a portal or sent out a signal or something... I don't think we *will* ever be the same again," he said.

"Well, shit. That's super scary," she said as she propped herself up, elbows deeply embedded in couch cushions, furthering the deconstruction of the simultaneously most comfortable piece of furniture and the worst possible spot she could think of to rest her aching dome.

She lay back down. "Ugh. I just need a second," she said. He stood up from his haunches and backed away.

After she spent some time thinking, she made a decision. Come what may, she would pursue any path he chose to take. Be it part of some wild experiment that would yield the unhappy conclusion of their inevitable demise, or the creation of something unheard-of.

"I'm pregnant," she said. He looked at her, disbelieving. "No, you're not," he said. She stared at him, gauging his reaction. "But, it's impossible. You got that implant... it guarantees us, what..." he counted on his fingers, 1, 2, 3, 4, "Five years, right?"

"Yes, love," she said as she pushed away from the couch. She stood up, standing taller now. "It's either a miracle or some sorcery of the devil," she said. Mire's mind whirled. The devil... these words repeated over and over, taking over his thoughts, consuming them just as the black hole took them over not moments before.

Snap back to reality. "You realize you were only out for a minute or two, right? I saved you. you almost broke open your skull... and what did you dream about for those two minutes?" Erizabet said, "No, no. I saw something. Wasn't I out for more than that? It wasn't a dream, was it?

"I saw this baby being formed inside me. She was chewing through this apartment, taking apart our lives, from the inside out, stemming through the seams, she turned into a tree—"

"Ok, just stop. Ok?" Mire said. He looked exhausted. He brushed a few filaments of crystalline dust from his eyes.

"Sure, sure. I'll take a test. It's probably just me. Wishful thinking or something," she said. She was shaking. Her arms all atwitter, muscles twitching uncontrollably. "Should I see Petridge's doc person or do you recommend someone else?"

"Eew, no. Pet's in a funk. He's... he has some issues to work out. I don't think we'll be seeing him for some time, Ok? Tell me you won't go see him." Riz nodded, feeling a little frightened by the sudden passion in his voice.

"You know... he's been dabbling in some..." Her head turned down, leaning into his story, gesturing for him to deliver a deeper description, something more telling than his go-to story circumscribing a vague history of all the failings of the universe.

She needed something solid just now, after the fall, her reverie. Right then she truly believed she wouldn't get any satisfaction of the sort. Not here. Not today. Most likely not ever, if this was the way things would be from now on. But then the tide shifted. Mire stared off into the distance and started to speak.

"Last time I saw him, he was mad, crazed. A thing hellbent on its own destruction. He said he found this book that changed his life, and by the look in his eyes—" Mire paused, "He's no longer with us, I'm afraid."

" 'With us'? What the fuck does that mean? Did he kill himself?" she asked. Mire grabbed a smoke, lit it, and paced around the living room. Erizabet braced herself against the wall and a few static-charged strands of her hair clung to the lint-strewn artwork on the wall beside her head.

"No, no. Nothing like that. It's just... It's like the whole world is unraveling right before us." He rushed up to her place against the wall and grabbed her by the forearms, nearly crushing her in his grip. "Promise me that you'll stay. Everything will be ok." He licked his lips, glanced down at her hips, "Whether you, ahem." He rocked a little side-to-side dance in front of her, then stopped, and stood completely still. In that moment, he was the epitome of a man possessed by an idea.

"If you are indeed pregnant or whether this is just wishful thinking or whatever you want to call it. It'll be ok. I know it." He tilted his head down to meet her gaze. He lifting her eyes with his own, bringing her back up to the surface. Acknowledgment touched her eyes and she knew it would be all right. She was a little freaked out about the potential idea of a baby, but he was so calm. They could weather any storm as long as they were together.

It was snowing outside. She turned to look out the window and he followed her gaze. It was a swirling snow globe of a world out there, built seemingly just for the two of them to get lost in then find themselves again. Flakes of white and silver didn't just fall straight down or in a single direction, it was a swirling mass of crazy out there. With no sense of time or place, it seemed as if the whole of existence was battling itself out, tooth and nail, to keep them here, in this moment, acknowledging their existence, their place in this world.

"Ok," she said, and fell into his arms. They embraced in a death grip. Groping backs, digging into the sinew of one another, becoming a single rocking being, breathing the same breath, giving life to something altogether new.

"Well, I need a drink." He held her at arm's length, pressing her back into the wall, the flint burrowing further still, deeper into her hair.

"You wanted to take a bath, right? It's Valentine's, let's celebrate this day that was created for us." She nodded solemnly, a tear dribbling down her cheek. No one has ever made her happy cry before. He brushed the tear away. Kissed the spot where it rested rescued on the fourth knuckle of his strong hands. She felt safe. For once.

He started the bath, and before the tub was even filled halfway, the bathroom became a sauna. The wallpaper came yawning away from the wall, trying to rescue itself before it could become destroyed through steam. Long lines of paper were careening down toward the floor, and still the water came.

Who knew there was that much heat left to the place. In such a cold space, no one even took showers anymore. Always rushing off to where they were needed most, they usually just deloused using that strange machine invented 50 years prior, so they could participate in society, be productive as quick as possible. A 2-second dusting was all you needed, or else they were still semi-stuck in their old ways, left bathing for 10 minutes in cold water streams, not enjoying any part of what it used to mean to get clean. Everyone always seemed to be torturing themselves, only the ne'er do wells knew what pleasure meant anymore. It was another example of the Great Divide. The implanted, the unanointed, the drug addicts, and the corporate slaves. I guess they fit somewhere in between, otherwise relegated to the outskirts entirely.

The tub was practically spilling over now. She lit two candles: one blue, one pink. A silent prayer to the gods that be, boy or girl, pregnant or not, either way. Here goes.

She disrobed, dipped a toe in, and sunk down, the water burning her skin. It sloshed over the tub, covered the floor. She soon became fetus-like herself. Scored pink and red in spots, her cheeks aflame, becoming less of a person and more like a bag of bones held together in skin, floating gently inside the womb of the bathtub.

Mire appeared in the doorway with a bottle of spiced rum in one hand, he covered his penis with the other, and shut off the light with an extended index finger, adroitly holding the bottle aloft somehow.

He let out a little yelp when his calves hit the water. "How the..." She pulled him toward her. "I can do it myself," he said, childlike. Legs crossed, he lowered himself in, hi hands on either side of the tub. He sunk down, clearly in pain, until his body became acclimated to the burning sensation.

He reached beyond the porcelain ledge and grabbed the bottle, unscrewed the top, took a swig, and handed it to Riz.

They looked like mist beings from another world, steam rising off their shoulders seen in flashes flickering with the writhing flames of the candles perched on the corners of the tub.

Drinking, relaxing in forbidden comfort, *I wonder how many more people were doing this at this moment*, Erizabet thought to herself. "We're the only two people in the world doing this right now," Mire said and Erizabet opened her eyes. "What, dear?" she said. "No one else is doing this, Riz. It's just us." Simultaneously unbelieving, yet yielding to this magic, who know's what's real anymore, she leaned up and made to climb on top of him. Some water sloshed over the edge of the tub.

"Quit that, lady," he said, laughing. "What? What do you think you're doing?" She settled back down and gave him a peck on the cheek. He smiled the most innocent smile, let out a sigh, and took another drought from the bottle.

They sat like that until they were no longer people. Their skin pockmarked with semi-permanent spots of red and blue. Pruny, she opened her eyes to look at her hands. Drunk now from the heat and rum combination, she decided it was time to get out into the world. She wanted to share the good feels instead of keeping them all to herself. Maybe they should go on an adventure or something, she thought. Mire opened his eyes, feeling her presence, alive now, restless.

They smiled at the sight of one another. They toweled each other off with the most gentle caresses. He gave her the softer of the two towels, but she used it to dab him dry. He took the towel away and daubed at her hair.

When they were finished, he left to find some clothes to wear, appropriate adventure attire, and she blow-dried her hair. Cooking the mass of curls into a cornucopia on top of her head. She looked ridiculous, but it was fitting for a flight into outer space, she thought.

They said goodbye to the apartment, their safe haven, and made their way up the steps toward the ship. She settled in on top of him, and he reached around to secure them both with the two straps he acquisitioned from one of his forays into the junk heap behind the shop.

Now, they were comfortable, bumping along with the motion of the engine. He flicked switches and twisted dials until he found the perfect spot to watch the sunrise in an unclaimed orbit around Mercury.

"Are you sure this is safe? I mean, doesn't it take like 30 years to reach Mercury?" she said as she noticed the planned trajectory plotted out on the spectroscope screen to the right.

"Don't worry. I got this," he said and with a click of his

tongue, they shot out into space. The force of 3Gs turned into 4, then 5, and her head began to swim. She almost passed out, but before it got to that point, she started repeating aloud the astronomical positionings of her favorite constellations. Not that she could see any of them. *Arterus, left hemisphere, autumnal equinox.*

Going faster now, her mumblings sped up in turn. Almost screaming, her voice became hoarse. She was on a roller-coaster ride from hell. Mire was cracking his jaw, blinking uncontrollably, a habit built in to keep him focused on the task at hand.

Higher and higher they climbed, until she was sure they would both burn up and die, or else spontaneously combust from the pressure. He hit a button pulsing a small radius of soft blue light, and they blipped out of existence. Their atoms were rearranging, colliding, coming back together, and in a space of less than two minutes they were right on the outskirts of the aquamarine-tinted atmosphere swirling around Mercury.

Mire handed Erizabet a small cylinder with diodes and crystals attached to it, set to vaporize any material waste projected into the glass container. She nodded her thanks, took the machine, and puked her guts out. She felt a wave of drunkenness repaper the surface of her forebrain. She was a body reeling from all manner of sensory overload.

He set the ship on autopilot and hugged her midsection, calming her breathing back down to a normal quip. Once she was feeling better, he said, "Happens the first few times, don't be sad." "Oh, I'm not," she said defensively. With a burp, she reached for the machine again. He tore his eyes away from the windshield for a moment, hands still navigating expertly, loosely lingering upon the steering column. "Just breathe," he whispered in her ear and she let her hand drop. Her head fell back against his shoulder.

Ears touching, he got a little shiver of delight, and took a whiff of her hair. Her forehead dotted with perspiration and he kissed her there, savoring the taste of salt on his lips, and he felt glad to have this woman with him.

They hovered then, spinning on a slight 13-degree tilt, watching the storm clouds swirl about the western hemisphere over Mercury. They spun in concentric circles, losing themselves in the moment.

They stayed there, staring, wondering about the meaning of life, thinking about their lives and what was to become of them, ultimately, giving the other the occasional squeeze, until they found they were freezing—it would be about -60° up there near the second rock from the sun. He thought it would be a little warmer this time of "day", but oh well. He grabbed the reins and they started to descend.

They came back down to Earth, where they could function again. They couldn't live inside this bubble forever, though that would be the perfect way to die, he thought. He knew she was thinking the same thing.

Once tucked away into their own safe air space, they stretched and shook off the feeling of jelly bubbling up and through their jangling limbs, changed clothes and went back out into the world. Gravity was weighing them down somehow. They slumped closer to the ground, slowly readjusting to the temperature and reality of all things earthbound.

15: She Fell

He called up a few friends and they decided they would participate in the most mundane of activities, bowling as it turned out, to get their minds off of their recent flights of fancy.

He enlisted the fraternity of longtime friend, Deer, the last of the Native American breed.

Deer had yet to find a suitable partner and would presumably die alone if he didn't fill out his yearly time sheet of socially accepted practices that U.S. citizens were required to complete every 10 years or so.

He just couldn't adhere to the norms of the species. He was determined to find someone who shared his feelings, his blood ties to the soil, and he wouldn't settle on someone who was genetically modified, no way, but all the girls were these days so, he mostly spent his time designing alternate worlds, digitally transforming the terrain into something more malleable, more to his liking.

He could pretend he was planting crops with his ancestors. He contrived a device to pump scents into the room, altering the future of virtual reality forever, though he took no credit for it.

Deer was of a special ilk. He didn't crave fame or fortune like all the other bobble-headed does that revolved around the globe. He would do what he did, for him, by him, with the occasional foray into personhood, but by his own prescription, only adhering to state laws as they suggested when he was on the brink of some new discovery or on the cusp of disaster. And this is why Mire gravitated toward him.

So, here they were. It was Mire, Erizabet, Deer, Malcom, Patricia, and Angora. Malcom and Patricia played matchmaker with Deer and Angora for the first 15 minutes at the bowling alley, but they soon realized that booze wasn't the only water soluble substance acting as a social lubricant these days.

Pat was making small talk with Mire, trying to steal his ideas on the future of electromagnetic conductivity, simultaneously distracting him from noticing she'd secretly slipped Erizabet some helium in capsule form, just to calm her the fuck down. Shut her up for a minute or two.

While Pat pretended to listen to Mire with full focus, Riz was recording the whole conversation, using a more obvious method, a watch Mire had designed for her, one downside to her refusal to go through with the aforementioned implant.

Pat diverted her small attention to the earhole of her closest friend. "Gases are the only way to go, girly," she whispered into Erizabet's ear, and with a nod, the two shared a glance and slyly gulped down the pills with a bit of their drinks.

Like Riz, Deer had a deep-seated mistrust of certain wearable technologies. Without the additions necessarily made through the instruction of the Academy, Deer wore his eyeglasses with pride, even though they were serving as a hindrance at this particular moment.

He squinted, nudged them further up on the bridge of his nose. His senses were still finely tuned to his surroundings, unlike the others in the party who were busy losing themselves in the bottom of their drinks, a couple of the girls were giggling at some joke the two shared silently.

"So, whattaya got there?" he asked, leaning a little too close to Patricia, who wafted the scent of his emanating BO away from her pristinely coiffed countenance. She couldn't stand the scent of a man, ever since she realized she was the last real lesbian on the planet. "Uh," she feigned a cough in all her pretentiousness, "It's just a little somethin' somethin'," she said and whipped her blonde hair away from her shoulders, revealing a little too much skin.

Deer blushed slightly at the sight of her bare shoulders. He made a little squirming gesture, readjusting his place in his seat and it was all Angora could do not to lash out at Patricia. Angora was still infatuated with the abnormality that was everything about Deer. She was fascinated by him, she couldn't help it. She'd never met anyone so... maladjusted to this world, though they'd all been living in it for nearly 30 years.

"I'll take some, too, dear." She still played the part of being Patricia's friend, though she harbored thoughts of jealousy that've been slowly steeping all these years since her one humiliating moment at Patricia's hand, during their formative high school days.

"Well, shit," she giggled. "Secret's out," said Patricia, and she emptied the contents of her coin purse on the table between them. "Basket case, much," volunteered Erizabet, then glanced around at the faces nearest her. She shrugged her shoulders, knowing no one would get her brand of film buffery.

"Anywho. It's already hitting me, so it'll be too late for the lot of you, but here you go," Patricia said as she doled out the doses. She harbored the fact there was more than just concentrated helium in the pills. More like a mixture between PCP and Mescaline, her favorite combination. Keeps you on your toes. You never know when the trip will escalate or just chill you the fuck out. It was stuff you couldn't get anymore, but she had connections. Her grandfather was some kind of alchemist, left over from the days when Wicca, and any and all religions, were still accepted. Before religions were outlawed that is. Good ol' Krunk. *Yay authoritarianism*, she thought.

She laughed out loud and the others stared at her blankly. "What?" she asked. "Ahem. One for each and not a modicum more," she said. "Except for me, I'll just take another, 'cause I'm such a good sport."

And soon they were all laughing along to the ridiculousness of what the youngsters called music these days, whatever barbaric instruments they played pumping out of the speakers, rendering them all blue in the face, exchanging holding tummies to stem the flow of spittle flying every which way.

Malcom was the first to make an attempt at conversation as soon as the collective group seemed to start recovering.

"Why did we even come here, anyway?" This garnered a few looks of mistrust from the herd. "I mean, we should start a game or something," Malcom said.

While the guys mulled it over, Patricia and Angora were whispering about the endless possibilities that lie in wait for Deer's imminent future and Malcolm leaned back in his seat, stretching his arms over his head to rest on clasped hands. "Yep, I'm pretty good, you know," he said, referring to the archaic game of bowling. That, or perhaps he was talking about the drugs. Either way.

Pat gave him a good whack on the chest and Malcom started coughing. "Jees, dude."

Now that she had a task to focus on, Patricia felt reassured. She got up, and started rooting through the gummy old bowling ball racks to find the one with the least amount of smudges on it. She was undeterred by the weight, apparently.

Erizabet went to grab shoes for the folks whose foot sizes she had memorized. Angora and Deer were a bit too green for her memory, so she beckoned them to get up and go to the counter with her. Angora was digging the vibe, and lagging Riz, she slipped her arm to coil around Deer's.

Deer started blushing again, and Angora took his hand. She happily led him down the grimy old aisle between the arcade and the lanes to where a bored-looking girl popped bubble wrap while waiting for the next sad sack to usurp her attention.

As Erizabet sat back down at the table next to Mire, she felt a wave of vertigo. *The drugs must be kicking in*, she thought.

She blinked too hard and discovered a few new colors had been added to the spectrum of light dancing around the bowling pins hiding in the dark. She imagined they must have feelings and she decided she didn't want to knock them down.

The ceiling fan suddenly became salient. The whomp whomp of the blades chopping through the air coincided with the beat of her heart.

She thought she heard a helicopter out in the world somewhere, pulsing to the same bass beat of the universe, but those things found their obsolescence centuries ago. Woah. I think I need to lie down. She started sinking in her chair.

Patricia and Mire designed their own original names for their friends, Deer became Chuck and Angora was assigned Gore on the holographic scorecard hovering above lanes 32 and 33.

Erizabet became Pete and Pat became Sir, this tripped Mire up for a second, then he chose Beast as his handle, then Patricia erased "Sir" and picked her own name.

No one really felt any particular affinity to being within this close proximity to her, except for Mire, of course. They had been friends for years, worked together at that shitty SA for what felt like a century. No one understood her, not like Mire anyway, but she made things interesting, that was certain.

They each went a few rounds, and by mid-bracket, the group was getting goofy. Mire started gyrating around to whatever pop music was playing, rubbing his hands all over his body. Deer and Angora were hanging on each other's every word and Patricia was trying to get Malcom to make out with the bubble popper at the front desk. Instead, he proposed they do a few shots of some ceremonial whiskey that he snuck in.

Soon it was Erizabet's turn to have a go at the pins, and after 5 gutter balls, she thought she'd actually aim this time. "It will only hurt for a second," she said, and Mire gave her a curious glance, smiled a wink at witnessing his favorite little bird talking to herself in public.

She stood at parade rest, weighed the ball from hip to hip, aimed and lobbed the ball at the pins.

There was a crash and a crunch from the place where she was standing, and Angora looked up, anticipating excitement—she thought maybe Erizabet was fooling them all this whole time, *She must be one of those game sharks*—then her face fell to see her friend lying there, half on the line, half on the waxed part of the track.

Malcom and Patricia stopped tittering, and Mire rushed over to Erizabet to see what had happened.

"Did she slip?" he asked the wide-eyed group. "What the fuck happened!?" He roared at them, a little saliva popping out in their direction. A few of them flinched and he turned back to his woman who lay there, limp.

He gingerly picked her up by the shoulders, to find one had been set out of place. "Ah, fuck. What the fuck..." he whimpered, trying not to cry in front of the group. "Ladies, don't look, the rest of you, just... The game is off."

He placed his left hand on her left clavicle, his right hand went to her shoulder, and with a "I, 2, 3," he popped her shoulder back in place. Erizabet's face didn't register any pain, and that's when he knew something was terribly, irrevocably wrong.

"You guys," Mire said with a gulp. "I gotta go."

☆　　☆　　☆

They said she had a pulmonary embolism, so Mire did some digging on the cause and effects of the anomaly. "Blah blah blah, it could be hereditary... blah blah... fainting..."

He was scanning the ceiling, lips moving unconsciously, his eyes taking all the information he could find online.

The day before, he had just registered for a trial of new contacts that allowed him to search the net without having to boot up his computer or signal his brain stem memory chip to automatically back up everything in temporary storage. He couldn't find anything to stave off the mounting worry pounding away at the pit of his stomach.

He clasped her hand and she made a small sound, like there was a tiny rodent in her throat. He killed the search engine and with a nod of his head set it on idle.

He stared at Erizabet, longing to know what was going on inside her head.

He looked at her eyes, and they began to twitch, then he looked to her cheek, which moved in turn, his gaze settled on her lips, and as the rest of her features began to relax, her lips started to tremble. *Weird*, he thought. *We're so connected, yet we're worlds apart.*

She was living in a dream. Feet hovering above the ground, she was waiting for something, she wasn't sure of what exactly. She was in a hallway, light was emanating from the walls, and there was a door straight ahead, shadow people were playing a game of catch, then they collapsed and snuck underneath the doorway.

For some reason she thought she could make out a familiar shape, the light bending into otherworldly colors, stretching into the silhouette of the man she once married, at some point, some time, in another reality.

She called out: "Mire?" Her feet brought her closer to the door, and she thought she could make out his features, he was motioning with his hands.

Where's the light source, she wondered, *it doesn't make any sense, how is it...* then her sight began to recede into the smallest corner of her eye, shapes shifted in size, shrinking smaller and smaller until—

"Riz." They were in the hospital and Mire was touching her forehead. "Oh hey, stranger." A tear rolled down his cheek. She reached to collect it, and was rewarded with a sharp pain erupting from her shoulder.

"Fuck me." She said, trying to massage the ache away with her other hand, the left arm was completely numb. She couldn't even command it to move. Her brain was not quite communicating with her nerves.

"Well, at least you can talk," Mire said with a sad smile playing on his lips. "At least you can talk," she mocked him, trying to play off the pain, lighten the mood. He held that smile of his, the one where just one side of his mouth comes up. He only did that when he was serious about something.

"I feel like I'm going to spontaneously combust from all this frustration. Fuck. I can't move, love," she said. "I know, lady. I'm sorry. I'm so sorry. I should've been there. I should've been right by your side, maybe giving you a little love tap on the butt for good luck, but I wasn't there. I wasn't there..." he said trailing off, putting his face in his hands. "I wish..." she started. Mire lifted his head to listen. "I wish my whole body was fucked. 'Specially my face, so you could say, 'blink once for yes, two for no,' like that movie..." she was whispering.

"I don't." Mire started to cry. "Riz, I don't know what you're talking about," he said. "It's that French movie, remember. Fuck. What was it called. Shit. Something about a diving bell? What's wrong with my brain. Ah, god. Not my brain... It's the one you liked, remember? You showed it to me..."

They were both silently crying to themselves, with Mire gripping Erizabet's one good hand, as the nurse walked in to give her an injection. "Hey sweetie," she gave Mire a questioning look. "You doing OK this morning?"

"Sure, Jean. Sure." She winced and clenched her teeth as the needle went into her bad arm, then almost instantly, a tingle began to spread along her skin, slowly sinking in, touching all the muscles underneath.

"Hmm.. Oh. That's..." And Erizabet passed out. Fight or flight response activated, her body chose flight over feeling what was actually happening to her physiology, enhanced by the marvels of modern science.

"What'd you give her?" Mire sniffled. "Oh, just a little something the doc whipped up on the spot. Her limbs should be working to full capacity within the next 45 minutes," she said, sucking her teeth. She looked at the girl, drooling now, mouth half open, and shook her head. "Man, she's lucky," and she walked off, closing the door behind her.

The guy in the next bed over started to groan, as if having bad dreams. Mire didn't hear him. He didn't believe anything could exist outside of what was happening to his one and only.

Erizabet twitched a bit in her sleep. It would be another half hour before she would be able to get up and stretch again, showing her tummy, wrinkling her face and yawning, like when she's comfortable in the kitchen, waiting for water to boil to make coffee in their garage sale French press.

"Fuck, babe. I'm sorry. I'm so sorry."

And he knew he was secretly mad at the nurse who just up and shot some strange liquid into his wife's precious arm. He wished he could have summoned up the courage to do anything but just sit there and stare at her, while he was fully functioning, watching her decline over time. *What would the crystal do?* He thought to himself.

He had an epiphany. He got up, leaned in close to Eriza-bet, and whispered, "I'll never leave you," then kissed her on the forehead and rushed out, grabbing his coat off the back of his seat. He was halfway down the hallway within a second or two, while she lay there mumbling, "Come back come back come back come back..." then fell back asleep.

This time she was a bird. A robin, she thought, gauging by the red belly and furtive movements. She was picking at the ground, playing with others like her, just having a grand old time, until she kneaded through some roots in the soil to find a worm writhing there. He looked appealing to her.

She was confused. Was she a bird? Had she dreamt up the scenario of her life as a girl? Suddenly her bones shifted, break-ing and shattering apart, then reorganized themselves and came back together.

Her wings fell away with agonizing pain, her hair follicles pushing them out of place. The other birds around her started changing too. One shifted into the shape of Mire, another be-came Petridge, there was Patricia, Deer, and Angora, too.

The grass became the slick surface of the bowling alley where she fell and suddenly she felt sick.

Coming to, she found the bedpan and promptly spewed what little contents were left in her stomach. Retching until she spit bile, the acidic gunk stinging on the way up, she wondered how long this could go on, then the nurse was kneeling beside her, holding her hair back.

She was patting her shoulder, saying, "There, there." "Where's Mire?" asked Erizabet. "He said he wouldn't leave me. I heard him..."

Once installed back at home, Mire took great care not to disturb her. Not that anyone remembered what her natural voice sounded like before—it had been six months since she was released from the hospital—but her voice took on the quality of a one-legged grasshopper song.

She whispered almost inaudibly, afraid to cause a stir. She used to confound him with some of the silly shit she said, but then she got quieter and quieter and soon he wasn't able to understand her at all.

It all happened so fast. At once inseparable, they became like live-in roommates, tiptoeing around the apartment, trying not to alert the other to one's presence.

In her deluded mind, it soon became clear he didn't want her around anymore. She made mental plans to take flight or disappear into the wilderness. She was a dog knowing full well the feeling that its last days were approaching.

She became oblivious to the painstaking way he prepared her meals, just how she liked them, with tons of salt, and he cared for her not as an invalid as she viewed the situation in her twisted state of mind, instead he loved her perhaps even more now that he knew he could prove it with each and every moment that passed by.

She was willful. No longer dancing at his side, but sidling around, morose, regretting what she thought of as her last moments as a real person there at the bowling alley.

He saw her slipping right through his fingertips and he knew what to do to win her trust back. It wasn't going to be easy, however. Something changed in her, he knew this much was true.

He gave her space to work on her little projects and she basically ignored him for what felt like centuries. They became mostly sedentary, not moving or saying much of anything. They turned gaunt and haggard as they shared each others empathy toward one another.

They dove into their studies. They were becoming more and more alike each day, both working to the bone on things they each thought would rid the world of all of its problems.

She thought her art could open the eyes of those who took the Earth for granted, meanwhile he sent off scholarly articles about his energy-reducing crystal apparatus to powerhouses the nation over.

Sometimes he'd take a break and study satellite images of Antarctica. Drinking helped him stay focused, but always said it's good to take a break every now and then. "Eat some ice cream. Watch a movie." This was his equivalent of a fun and relaxing time.

He took a sip of his drink for each inconsistency he saw on the map. "Ha! See? What is that?"

She came over and squinted at his screen. Entire 50-square "blocks" appeared bluish-green and pixelated where a clear image of the island should be. "Then this? It's the whole continent... why..." She laughed, pecked him on the cheek and went back to work.

He wrote Google about it, sending them letters every few years or so, using their own envelopes with the encouragement printed right on the upper right-hand corner of the rectangular paper contrapment: "No postage needed if mailed within the contiguous United States".

Who knew how old those things were, of if they would even reach anybody, but he did it anyway and one day it worked. Someone finally tracked him down. One thing led to another and he became pen pals with someone Google suggested he meet.

Their conversation grew tangential and he let her in on his little secret. She said he probably shouldn't have sent out any information about his crystal project, and he told her he might need funding if he was going to be able to see any of this through.

Somehow, Congress got wind of it, and Mire started receiving bribes to try to get him to sell his invention. He was skeptical, however, to hand his precious research over to the talking heads who were running the country. Though, they would pay. They could potentially support him and Riz, indefinitely, but he was worried... with that much money, would he grow fat and lazy?

And what about this "supposed" baby Riz thought she was carrying. After all these months, she didn't show any signs she carried another life inside her, but maybe she was just getting herself mentally prepared. Maybe she knew it would be happening soon. And if she's right, he would give it all up in a heartbeat...

So, he writes back this chick Broomhilda. He's seen her on TV a few times, skulking around the edges of podiums, and the like. For some reason, he didn't think too highly of her.

Fingers hovering above the keyboard, mid-email, he seemed

to recall an event where she pardoned Triwillica after the methane conglomerate uprooted what was left of the Great Barrier Reef so they could tap the rare oxide ore vein that ran beneath it. There were some "minor" repercussions, which spurned activists the world over.

The Vulcans were even less enthused when they found out the government had the power to awaken the longest-dormant volcano on the Pacific Rim. *But, why?* he wondered. He shrugged. *What the heck? I doubt these guys are serious about their offer, anyway.*

Within a minute of his reply, he received an alert. *They must have some serious hardware to tap my node.*

He brought his fingers to the back of his neck, to feel the chip embedded there. It was hot, not quite to the point of singeing his hair.

Sidetracked, he thought about the last time he got a haircut, when Riz first tried her hand at it, then he tried to fix it, then his old college roommate Phalen happened to be in town and suggested he'd give it a whirl.

Oh, what a mess... focus, Mire! Are you trying to become more like Pet every day? Sheesh. Soon, you'll be talking to yourself OUT LOUD. Wait...

He tilted his head upward to access his cloud storage. He looked to the right, scrolling, and mumbled a command in search of the file labeled "Broomhilda".

Now, his chip was really cooking. Damn. This lady's got her fingers in everything. At this point, his palms began to sweat. It's one of those encrypted algorithms... If you tap her info too many times in a day, she discharges a signal that temporarily blocks your IP.

He shook his shoulders, willing the thoughts away and went back to the keyboard.

Dear Congressheads,

I've already submitted my findings on the rare properties of what I've dubbed (and copyrighted, mind you) the Balarium Shard. Now, you're a smart bunch. You probably already have it figured out, but let me make it clear that I have been contacted by several scientific societies who are very interested in my work here. So, if you feel an overwhelming need to trump their combined offers, I would consider taking you on as sole backers of this enterprise.

You go ahead and dig around and let me know if this is the way in which you wish to proceed.

Sincerely,
An impartial inventor who deeply distrusts the government (namely, you)

Ha, he thought. *That'll show 'em.*

16: Bloodhounds

Standing in front of a large, unsightly, and suspiciously out-of-place cement building, he said, "Open your eyes," and slowly removed his hands from her face. "Ah, it's beautiful," she said.

He choked in a scoff, "What? This place is hideous." He looked around with a slight frown, and shook his head. *I'll never know what's she's thinking.* "Let's go inside." He tugged on her hand to pull her forward. "Wait," she said and closed her eyes once more. She took a deep breath. "When was the last time we were outside?"

He stared at her, curious. *I guess we haven't left the apartment in quite some time*, he thought. He sniffed the air, mimicking her, trying to inhale what she inhaled, trying to sink in and become one with the moment, sharing in the serendipity of it all. "Ah," he exhaled.

They turned and smiled at each other. The color was returning to her face; she looked like a new woman just then, exiled from her own shell of harbored bewilderment she'd been toting around these last months. "Ok," she said. "Let's see what this is all about." They held hands and walked through the doors of the ugly building.

She nervously picked at the hems of her dress, occasionally stretching out her jaw to loosen the air welling in her ears from the quick ascension of the elevator car.

Occasionally grimacing at her reflection in the muddled mirror, she mumbled, "I don't know how I feel about this yellow..." She bowed her head, looking down, and he picked up her chin, "Oh, shush. You look beautiful." And he took her hands, spreading them wide, and she blushed at the thought of exposing her moist armpits. She acquiesced with a smile, and he twirled her around. Her skirt flared out around her, and he made her feel like a shiny new toy. She was ready to face the music, so to speak. More aptly, she felt confident in her partner's abilities to whisk her away, back into their kitchen lair where they played at dancing. Maybe she could actually dance, who knows?

He hadn't told her where they were going, but she had a feeling about it. Get the blood flowing. He was a modern-day hippie in that way. It was like he held a secret knowledge of simple holistic remedies, tried and true through self-experience.

The elevator doors opened up, and they were relinquished from their techie pedestal, to see couples twirling around mid-air, decked out in retro poodle skirts and cummerbunds. They looked at each other, mouth agape, and turned back to the mass of perfectly choreographed movements, produced by anatomically correct bodies.

"Come in!" said the instructor, sliding over to the new meat, and with a flourish of her hand, she said, "Welcome. You must be our new trainees." She clasped her hands together, positively beaming, Mire thought she looked as if she were about to cry. After all, not a lot of people find swing dancing all that appealing in this day and age.

They entered the rec center, rented out by the Swingers of Central New Haven Thursday nights during the spring. "Swing into Spring!" was their pathetic ass motto, but he knew deep down inside, that a part of him wasn't cynical at all. He liked all that corny stuff and so did she. It was just one of the reasons why they were perfect together.

Mire's plan was to take her in an attempt to keep his promise to do everything he could to make her happy, which heretofore hadn't seemed to be working all too well.

He looked over at Riz to see her face turning red. She looked as if she had just seen a ghost. "No, no no," she said, palms squishing her cheeks. "Aww, what's wrong, babe? It'll be fine, I promise."

He looked deep into her eyes and she knew she had to trust him. Maybe it was just a bad dream. She'd been having so many nightmares lately. She took his hand and followed him inside.

Mire started seeing things. Hearing voices. Right there in the middle of the dance floor.

A lady on her way back from Mississippi Market stops to ask a man what kind of dog he has. "She's got hound in her, that's for sure," he says.

"I'm aged to perfection," a woman wearing a pink shirt says to a man with a beer belly. "I'm a young grandma." The scene took place in a familiar SuperAmerica down the road. He backed away from Erizabet, momentarily, to squeeze his temples. "Are you OK?"

"No. Yeah," he shakes his head. "I'm good, let's just. Is that it? Can we leave, now?" he asks, grabbing her hand and leading her from the lacquered floor to the carpeted area near the booth with pamphlets and other strange literature he just noticed for the first time. "What's gotten into you all of a sudden? Are you feeling the same vibes I'm feeling?"

The instructor sidles up to them, appearing out of nowhere. "Where y'all runnin' off to in a hurry?"

"We just, um. I think that's enough for now," Mire stammers. "I don't feel so good."

"Aw, honey. That's all right. Everyone gets a little nervous their first time," she latched onto the couple's shoulders, using both hands to move them back toward the center of the room. By now, the other dancers are staring at Mire and Erizabet, a look of dull-hunger in their eyes.

Steadily they move closer. One guy licks his lips.

A single sweat bead slides down Mire's forehead and Erizabet laughs inappropriately, a nervous tick.

"Ok, honey, we really gotta go now. I have to piss like a racehorse," Riz said. At this, the instructor lunges toward them. They turn and bolt for the door, slamming it closed behind them. A piece of yellow fabric is caught in the jam and Erizabet instinctively tries to claw through the lace with one jagged hangnail.

A shredding sound erupts in the sterile hallway that looked more like a hospital repository where the relatives of ailing individuals await their loved-ones' fates and less like a fun place to learn crochet or something.

Once they were safely ensconced in the leather seats of the Saab, Erizabet started hyperventilating. "What the fuck, though? I mean, what the fuck was that!" Mire swapped a look of confusion with guilt. "Myyyyyeeerrr?" He was looking off in the distance, his breathing patterns increasing incrementally, like a locomotive on the war path.

She snapped her fingers in front of his face. "Mire!" she screeched, her voice hitting one of the highest registers of human vocal capability. This only ever happened when she got blackout drunk, when she was in a good mood and feeling silly, or when she was freaking the fuck out.

Mire came to, "Huh?" She raised her eyebrows at him, as if to say, "So...?"

"So..." he raked his hands through his hair. "Oh, god. What have I done?" he said, far away, dreaming.

"Babe, look. I'm sorry. I didn't mean to literally snap at you. Just, what is it? Do you really think you did something to piss those people off?" She was rambling. "I mean, those people looked normal one second, then they became feral like wild children." Her eyebrows furrowed. "I mean, you couldn't have done anything. Like, I was right there—" "Lady, listen," he cut her off. He pulled a hunk of crystal out of his pocket. Instead of glowing the bright pink from a month ago, it radiated a blackish-blue light, almost angry in its palpitations.

"I think it's alive, babe. I'm starting to suspect it feeds on light, maybe. I've been keeping him in the dark all this time—" She blinked rapidly, first lurching forward in her seat, then slamming back into the leather with an audible scrunch. "Are you saying, 'him?' It's a he now?"

"Well, it's the strangest thing..." They were sitting on the couch in front of his computer console. He looked at her as if he wanted her permission to continue. She nodded her encouragement. "Well, I had this weird dream..." he started. "Ah, seriously!? You're having weird dreams, too? Shoot. Maybe we should move the bed, ya know? They say that if you reorient your sleeping position..." The look on Mire's face said more than words could. The sentiment was something like *There isn't anything you can do. You can't fix everything.*

"Ok, dear," she said. "Excuse." She got up to make herself a drink. Mire huffed. "And then you just walk away," he said, laughing. "I'm here, I'm here," she said and plopped back down on the couch. He gave her a look as if to ask, You good? She nodded. He took a deep breath and started:

"I had this dream. I was living somewhere else. On another

planet maybe, but nothing was solid... I don't know if I would call it living. I didn't exactly have any perception of self, no acknowledgment of life, really, either. I was just floating around. Bumping into other flavors of existence. I think I was some sort of gaseous particle being, maybe, but I felt there was this male presence inside of me."

Mire licked his lips, readying himself to continue. "I was looking for my mate. And everything was pretty peaceful, aside from the fact that I felt like I need my other half, and I was *this* close to finding her. I could feel her energy resonating out into space. Calling to me... And then all of a sudden, everything changed." Mire leaned back, arms out, rocking on his crossed legs. "The world was ripped away and the next thing I knew I had crash- landed on some strange solid orb. It was all I could do to concentrate my energy into rearranging my DNA such that I'd coalesce into something less permeable than what I had been previously."

He paused again, took a swig of Riz's drink, and looked her in the eyes. "I think that crystal *is* a guy, Riz. He's looking for his mate. And I've just been ripping at him, bending him to my will. I don't know. This sounds crazy, but there's something about that chick. She wants blood, Riz. And I think I know why..."

17: Trust No One

He couldn't be sure if his encounters with Petridge were a dream or not. It'd been weeks, maybe months since they last conversed about the potential conveyances of the crystal, right? Or maybe Mire was time-traveling. Or perhaps this was a cheap way for us to get back in touch with Petridge, by making Mire black out and revisit poorly-hatched plans with his sometimes ex-best friend. Whatever the case, now we're seeing them all chummy again.

Back in the kitchen, Petridge put his hand on the door to the fridge, he glanced over at Mire, and said, "May I?" Mire responded with a wave of his hand, "Oh, by all means," he said. They both had a flair for the dramatic, especially when they were together.

With heavy sighs and a creak like the croak of death emanating from beneath the couch cushions of Mire's chosen seat, he told Pet his tale of interplanetary woe.

"OK, so let me get this straight," Petridge began, pushing his glasses a smidge bit higher up on the bridge of his nose. "This life-altering, manifest destiny, psychosis-inducing—" Mire cut him off, "Dude." Petridge continued. "OK, OK, no need to get hostile, here. So, this thing was in the trash? This intelligent being from another universe or something, right? It was just nestled between some cigarette butts in the grout in the sidewalk?" Mire nodded, sipped his beer. "And, I mean, don't get me wrong, but how did you see it? Was it emitting a sound or something?" Mire looked around, "Wait, do you hear it, too?" he asked. "Now, you're really starting to freak me out," Petridge replied.

"Listen. If you need a place to stay or something, away from all this," he waved his hands, "Craziness. I got your back, all right?" he said, though he knew the offer would fall on deaf ears. Mire shirked off any suggestion that he may be in need of help, but he thanked his friend anyway. "That's all right. Thanks, though," he said.

Conceding, Petridge shrugged. "All right, well. Let's at least get you out of this apartment for a bit, yeah? You been cooped up for far too long, methinks." Mire looked up, quixotic. "Let's go for a drive." Mire pulled down his lower lip. "Sure," he said. Mire grabbed his smokes off the table, stuck them in his pocket, and sat down to put on his boots.

Keys in hand, they left the apartment. They would take Mire's little black box of a car. Petridge has been indulging in a little social experiment, where he's taping conversations on the bus, in the subway, through any means of public transportation, really. His goal? To see if there is a pattern for confined conversation, as opposed to the way dialog develops in the workplace or at home. He started his recorder.

Mire led Pet to where the car was parked, and Petridge's gaze veered upward. He attempted to shade his eyes from the sun, as the brightest ray of light seemed to bounce, trapped in a penumbra of paralysis around Mire's spacecraft, as it wavered in the wind, left teetering atop the roof of the bar. He thought his eyes were becoming increasingly sensitive to light.

Petridge nodded in the direction of the vehicle, "Don't want to take her out for a spin?" Mire shook his head, tossing his keys in the air, catching them, tossing them again. "Naw, I'm kinda broke right now. And that girl," he said, jerking his thumb in the direction of the roof, "She only runs on high grade, of course." "Of course," Petridge responded.

They got in the car. Mire revved it up with a head jerk toward the console. A holographic wheel came to life, materializing under his hands, where he placed them at 10 & 2. He looked to the left mirror, moved his head to adjust the view, then he looked to the right, adjusted, finally glancing toward the rear-view mirror, which projected a 360 degree view around the circumference of the car. The display pivoted in direction, like a compass, as Mire backed up, then pulled onto the side street away from the building.

He spared one last look at the window where his kitchen would be, sending a cursory thought out to the disturbed robot teeming with life all its own. He would be frustrated, trapped for as long as this trip would take. But it's not about him is it? Petridge wanted to go for a little ride, so Mire thought, a little ride we shall have.

Looking left to make sure there was no oncoming traffic, he pulled out onto the highway, not before noticing a few smudges on the glass, oil and grease from the hands and faces of the fiends who pursued them last night.

"Yeah, we fucking gunned it, dude," Erizabet confessed. They were chain smoking now. Meryl produced a flask from a hidden pocket in the lower thigh area of the tiger suit. She tipped it toward Riz, who was grateful for the kind gesture. She took a swig.

"Those things. I don't know. I mean, I thought they were people, Mer." Her friend was a little conflicted as to the validity of the tale, Riz being a self-proclaimed storyteller. She didn't conceal her incredulity, she looked concerned nonetheless. She nodded, encouraging her friend to go on.

"Lying on the floor last night, mumbling, Mire was beginning to tell me something about how he found something that drove people crazy." She shook her head, her shoulders, then a leg went up instinctively, and her wrists arched back in a full-body spasm. "Yuuhhh," she made a sound close to retching. "Oh, god. Please don't puke. This is good stuff," Meryl said, taking the flask back from her. She took another swig.

"Oh, no, I mean. He wasn't drunk? Right? We were out in public... dancing? I don't know. I mean. How..." she trailed off, thinking, she took a drag of her cigarette. "Something about the crystal," it was coming to her, now. "Like, he was saying that this crystal he found," she made a gesture with her fingers, thumb and index a centimeter apart, "On the ground, outside somewhere. It was a person. Is. I don't know. He said it wants blood or something. And it won't stop to get it. Then again, he's not really sure of anything these days..."

Meryl didn't believe a word of it. Her feet were firmly rooted in reality, unlike her poor little friend here. "Ok, honey, but, it's a crystal? Are you sure this isn't all just a part of your collective conscious?" Riz, returning from her daze off in space, looked to her friend for clarification. "What are you saying?"

Meryl continued, "Look, I know you guys are in love. Neither of you ever leave the apartment practically, right? And you just. You're still," her fingers making the quotation mark gesture in the air, "You seem fine, right? But, you just went through this ordeal." Riz looked confused, as if her short term memory was malfunctioning. Cannot compute. "The bowling alley? Hello?" She smacked her friend over the head, a light hearted gesture, she thought, but Riz got pissed real quick.

"Goddamnit, Meryl. You know that's one of my pet peeves. Fuck," she said, rubbing the place where the strap of her mask was steadily beginning to carve out a niche of centralized pressure, in one particular spot on the back of her head.

"You know what?" Riz said, throwing down her cigarette. "I knew this was dumb. It's like, what, 4 in the afternoon and we're getting hammered, dancing around in animal costumes. What kind of world do you live in?" They were in the midst of mental jujitsu. As far as she was concerned, she decided she couldn't trust anyone anymore. And she could hold a grudge like you wouldn't believe.

"You know what, baby? It's all good," Meryl said, as Riz slowly backed away. "We all project an image of who we want people to think we are. You can't play the scaredy cat all the time. Soon, you'll start to believe it in your bones."

More confused than ever, Riz pushed her way through the crowd, back to the bar. She was flailing around like a cat without whiskers when they collided in the doorway to the changing room. Riz was in a trance, looking down, raking her hand through her hair, the other hand busy digging through her purse. Bumping boobs, Meryl let out an oompf!

"Hey, I'm sorry," Meryl said. "How did you... get over here so..." Meryl continued as if she didn't hear her. "I know you hate it when anyone touches your head... especially in that kind of mocking way. I don't know what came over me, OK?" She said, rubbing Riz's arm.

Riz deflated. "Yeah, whatever. I'm going home." She moved to maneuver around her friend, who blocked her path. "What are you doing there?" she asked, laughing nervously. She wiggled her pointer finger in concentric figure eights, aimed at the other's arm. "What's up, Meryl?"

Meryl smiled. "It's early. You walked, right?" Shrugging,

looking off to the side, Riz said, "Yeah, it's like 30 minutes on foot. A nice little walk—" Meryl leaned in all of sudden, and they locked lips. At first, scared, then thrilled, then appalled, Riz pushed Meryl away. "What the fuck, Mer?" Wiping her mouth, she frowned, looking down at the back of her palm, hoping she didn't see some trace of lipstick there. She ran her tongue over her teeth, and got a taste of something familiar.

"Did you pack some pot in that secret pouch of yours, too?" She said, wiping her mouth again. Meryl looked smug. Satisfied, she leaned against the door frame. She pulled out a cigarette and began to dance again. She started rubbing her ass against the wooden door frame. Riz thought she looked ridiculous, out of place, a Siberian tiger among penguins and badgers. *Were all of these her costumes?* Riz wondered.

"OK!" Riz said, hands in the air, moving once more to try and officially exit the premises. "I gotta go, all right? Have fun, you little... weirdo." Meryl laughed and lit up, right there in the back room. She was still dancing.

Speed-walking away from her, she stole one more look toward her friend. For a second, her body buckled. She could have sworn she caught sight of something in her eyes; that familiar purplish pink, growing and pulsing in time with the music.

She stumbled through the crowd, pushing animal faces, arms, and tails out of her way, carving her own path toward the door. She thought she was going to vomit. She thought she was going to faint. Her body was at once at war with her brain, vying for an emotional response to stem the uprising surge of fear.

Once outside, she felt like she could finally breathe. She wanted a cigarette. It was customary, almost a reflex to step-ping outside of a bar, or setting her ass in the car, but she rebutted her own will, stifling down all the various messages her body was communicating to her. She tried to remain calm. She exuded confidence. She took three slow breaths, in through the nose, out through the mouth, and conscientiously straightening out her spine, she held her head up high, and began to walk in the direction of her apartment.

Petridge was mumbling about some new theory of his, while Mire was part way paying attention to the road and simultaneously thinking about Riz, wondering how her night was going. *Would she get home before me? I hope she's all right. I don't know what the fuck day it is, but... I think she knows where we left the vodka the other night.* He had an eery feeling. Like something bad was about to happen.

"Don't you think," Petridge was saying. "That it's unfair to judge those who are plugged in against those who aren't?" He was wringing his hands, overly excited about this particular topic. "You're in, right?" Mire nudged the right shoulder up a bit, acknowledging his attention. "I've read a bit about the subject, so I know what it's like," Petridge continued. "And of course, we hang out all the time, so, I don't think you're any different than before?" He moved his head, mimicking a few mannerisms Mire had acquired over the last few years. "You just move a little differently sometimes. Switching channels, or flipping programs, whathaveyou." Mire was still distracted.

He wanted to bring up Riz. He wasn't exactly sure she was telling the truth about not being plugged in, but he trusted her. He just didn't know if trusted himself much these days. His mind was at war, but he navigated the roadways like a pro. He was nothing but calm, cool, and collected, as always, and he really didn't want to engage in any sort of political debate with his friend at the moment.

"I don't understand why we can't just get along." Petridge was verging on a rampage. *Whatever happened to that girl-friend of his? Can't they talk about this stuff and leave me out of it?*

"So what if one man is biologically enhanced, and another is refusing to acclimate to our current state of technological superiority, I mean... what the hell is that?" He pointed ahead toward something in the road, and while Mire was spacing out, he quickly came to, slamming on the breaks as the car decelerated from 60 to 0 in the space of 6 seconds.

There was a wall of people, hundreds of them, blocking off the highway through the center of the city. A team of military police, adorned with gas masks were hucking tear gas at the crowd. People were shouting, crying, dousing one another in milk, rinsing out one another's eyes with water. And still others were throwing glass bottles and old-school firecrackers back at the police. It was mayhem.

Mire couldn't see a way through. Without looking over, Mire could hear the swishing sound Pet's jacket made as he gesticulated wildly. Petridge moved his hands, speechless for once, signaling for him to pull over.

It was a stand off. As the pair exited the vehicle and moved to join the crowd, Petridge made a bee-line for a hot-looking girl in short shorts and a tank top, waving a sign, and chanting. He asked her what was going on. Mire stood outside the car door, trapped in a haze of foggy miscalculations.

Petridge came back toward the car, with a napkin in his hand, "I got her number, mate," he said. "No," Mire was shaking, "What is going on, Pet? Seriously!" Smiling, Petridge pocketed the slip, "Well, apparently it's us versus them," he said. "It's people against police against people... someone was shot. Isn't that ridiculous?" Mire could barely understand his friend over the shouting.

It was as if he were standing in a cloud. The air was filled with smoke. He could barely breathe. He was fighting back tears, trying to siphon the intake of air through the neck of his shirt, but despite his efforts, he began to feel a little dizzy. There were flights flashing, red and blue, the cop cars shined their spotlights at the crowd, aiming directly at citizen journalists, trying to deter them from recording their every move. Mire's news feed was on instant refresh, and he saw points of view from every angle, even a few shots directed back at the crowd. Some of the police were plugged in, he tried to tell his friend.

Petridge was giddy. He was laughing hysterically, giving into the madness, riding a high. "There's no point, Pet," Mire was saying. "What are we doing out here? How..." his voice trailed off, his efforts wasted on his totally incompetent friend. Petridge started undressing, he thought he was at a hippie festival or something, his body working without consulting his mind.

Mire wanted to leave him, he needed to get out of there. There was a reason he put blockers on those particular programs embedded in the heads up display that now pervaded his every thought.

He didn't realize it then, but the memories of that night would haunt his dreams for weeks, the lucidity of which went unmatched. He'd relive this moment for a long time after they were long gone from the scene of the riot.

He got back in the car, and without thinking, reached up to peel away individual hairs lining his eyebrows. An old nervous tick left over from childhood. Trichotillomania, they called it. He felt that familiar sting, and after taking out a few good chunks, he stood there, blinking. He looked down at his hands. "Aw, fucking great," he said to the empty car.

He engaged the hidden flight mechanism, and revved up the engine. The vehicle lurched into the air, pushing the limit of the engine's vertical launch capacity, and looked down over the scene. He couldn't tell which side was which, an army of civilians, some hunched over and bleeding, others still fighting, engaging in the most futile form of combat against an army of cops equal in measure. They were either hunched over, clutching their bellies, or still hucking things into the wall of bodies on the opposing side.

"We're all the same," he said. "Fucking hell," and he gunned the engine.He was floating over the highway, toward the path where the trees met the sky. He aimed for the horizon line, somewhere out of sight. He wanted to find his wife and hold her and tell her everything was going to be all right.

Drifting on toward home, his radar started making a little blipping sound, it sped up as he came closer to the ground. The trip was taxing on the engine, little pops accompanied cloud bursts of heat rising up from beneath the seats to greet him, a message between the car and his internal diagnostic machine making it clear that the thing was almost out of steam.

He lowered the vehicle on a path toward the blinking homing beacon. It was Erizabet, walking slowly, drunkenly weaving. She was stumbling, crying it seemed, barely making any headway toward the apartment.

He put the car on autopilot, sending the command to empty the tanks as quickly as possible, to bring him down to her safely. He buffeted the ground with a bubble of steam, creating a buffer between the machine and the cement below him. He parked the car right there on the sidewalk, half on the street, two feet from where Riz was barely moving, more of less limping around.

Through tear-soaked eyes, she looked up to see Mire standing there with arms outstretched. Relieved, she made an audible choking noise like that of a frog who had just swallowed more than its fill, and she fell into his arms.

"Shhh," he said, stroking her hair as her chin fit neatly between his collarbone and the muscles of his shoulder. "It's okay, I got you." She cried it out, pulling at the back of his shirt. He wasn't sure why she was crying, but it felt like the whole world was cracking in a tumultuous wave, as if the tectonic plates were shifting, gearing up to erupt beneath his feet.

All he could hear was her, all he could smell was the cigarette smoke that singed her hair, all he felt were her sobs, shaking the very core of his being. He felt like he was coming apart, but he tried to stay strong, for her.

Tearing up himself, he gently pulled her away from him, looked in her eyes, and smoothed away lines of mascara that trickled down her cheek. She could barely speak, her vocal chords wrecked from crying. He kissed her eyelids, her forehead, her nose, and finally her lips. And she gave into him willingly, as they stood there, enveloped in a passionate kiss, grabbing and groping each other, testing their limits of compassion, the heat of the day's events fueling their combined need for release. They grappled in the street. The city was quiet, save for their sighs and moans of affection. Right there in the grass, they came simultaneously, and lay whimpering, holding each other. There wasn't another soul in sight. Everyone else was long since deceased, as much as it concerned them.

18: Pride

They scrambled back up to the apartment, she with her shirt half pulled up over one shoulder, panties to the side, still trying to hold herself together.

He felt revived, upon having his curiosity sated, he now knew she was safe. He took the steps in twos, spryly gliding over the incline, grasshopper-like.

With a creak and a sigh, she lay down on the living room floor, gingerly touching her back to the rug, careful not to disturb the cuts they made while he was rocking away inside of her. He came over and touched down upon the floor, a magical creature alighting upon the carpet beside her. He lit two cigarettes, handed her one.

"Ye gods, what is wrong with the world?" she muttered, stifling back the urge to start crying all over again. She knew that if she gave into the feeling, it would take her over, and she'd destroy herself before she ever had the chance to become right again.

"Babe," he said. "Everything's going to be fine," he stroked her thigh with his toes, bringing her the least bit of courage.

His touch was a welcome sign that they were alive. "You can feel it, can't you? The universe is at odds with itself. Nothing's going to be the same anymore. From this moment forward," she said, turning to flick her ash into the underbelly of a tiny glass-blown hen, tinged with a shade of teal blue.

He tapped the tip of his cigarette on the glass, rolling the cherry around to make a triangular tip from the cancer stick. "Did you know there are people fighting in the streets?" he said.

She took a drag. "I can feel it, Mire. I feel it right here," she said, placing the palms of her hands on her chest, fingers interlaced. He placed one big hand on top of her two small ones. "Is that why you were crying? What happened to your friend? Did you guys fight or something?"

Not only were the two sides of humanity at grips with the terms of their mortality, her small world took to fisticuffs to duke it out, conceding to the notion that at any moment, the earth would split wide open and suck them up for a snack. They were tiny morsels to the beast that was laying in wait right below their feet.

She creased her eyebrows in worry and reached up toward his face. "What happened there?" She touched the place where his right eyebrow used to be. He nudged her hand away and turned his back on her.

"Something else I never told you..." he said meekly. He could feel the sympathy washing over of her in waves. He faced her once again.

"It's this thing I used to do as a kid. It's taken years of psychotherapy and tons of drugs to get me off it, but..." he trailed off.

"It's OK, dear," she said, taking his enormous fingers into the palm of one of small hands. She kissed the tip of his thumb, then his forefinger, then the place where his wedding band rested, snug against his skin. "I love you," she said. Tears welled up in his eyes, and with a small chuckle, he said, "I know," and drew her body up close to his, cradling her in his arms, rocking her back and forth. He kissed her hair over and over again, saying, "I know. I know. I know."

He sat there for hours, scrolling through news feed after news feed. He was trying to find someone somewhere who made sense to him. Riveted to the screen, cigarette clutched between ring and middle fingers, he mindlessly rubbed his thumbnail across his upper lip. Back and forth. Back and forth.

Deciding that he was on the side of the rioters, he felt it was better to do something, however childish and ill-advised. It would be better than not doing anything.

Realizing he had been crouched in that position for hours, he placed his hands on the arms of the chair, and with feet crossed, he stretched his muscles, doing a couple of push ups, with the assistance of the chair. "Ah," he moaned, and let his butt plop back down in the chair.

Stubbing out his cigarette, he turned and leapt up over the chair, narrowly missing the mess of art supplies that lay on the floor about the table. He joined Riz in the kitchen, where she was apparently peeling an exotic fruit.

The blade was pointed inward toward her palm. Regardless of how many times he advised her against such trivialities, she still did what she wanted. A voice inside instinctively told him to grab the knife and show her how to properly peel the skin, but in a moment he realized she had an uncommon expertise in this capacity, like a sailor marooned at sea, she took her time, carefully slicing the skin away from the kiwi, the thin streaks of fuzz falling to the cutting board below.

With each stroke, she wiped the blade clean with a swipe of her thumb, then proceeded wresting the skin from the fruit. The gooey green substance lay revealed in her palm as she rinsed the fruit clean.

"Want some?" she said, holding the tiny fruit out toward him. He stared at her in awe, then snapped out of it. "Oh, no. Thank you. That's for you." She shrugged. "Suit yourself!"

She took a bite of the fruit, seeds and juice sluicing their way around her lower lip. She wiped her mouth with the back of her hand. "Mmm," she said, still chewing. "I think we need more fruit." Mire stood there, arms folded, clutching his stomach. He suddenly realized he was in fact quite hungry.

"Where did you get that thing anyway?" he said, opening the fridge and peering inside. A bottle of pinot grigio lay neglected on the third shelf down. He reached inside a box of beer to find one remained. He withdrew his hand, pulling the cardboard box out of the fridge with it. He shook the box loose, holding onto the beer. He kicked the box around to where the bag of recyclables lay next to the remains of an ancient TV set he dissected weeks ago. He smiled in spite of himself, cracked open the beer, and took a swig.

"You know, I don't know where this came from, actually," she said, flicking her slimy hands in the sink, whisking away the remaining seeds to splat along the inside rim of the steel tub.

Random items kept appearing inside the magical contraption that was the large icebox they frequently opened and closed at rare intervals throughout the day. One day, she opened the fridge and found a tomato. Once, there was a bag of iceberg lettuce, sometimes shredded mozzarella cheese.

This time she decided to eat a kiwi, the only one she found there in the drawer labeled "fresh". "We should probably get some real food," he suggested.

Just then, as if by some all-permeating mother-son magic, his mom rang and asked them out to din din. A day passed in confusing annoyance. She wanted to be left alone, he didn't mind his mother reaching out at all. In fact, he found it comforting. She just had too much damn pride, was all.

The night ended with them crashing on his mom's couch. Riz, ever the opportunist, washed some clothes she found hidden away in the back of Mire's car. *Damnit. Always intruding*, Riz thought, as she took a whiff of the powerful smell of clean clothes. She was *this* close to solving the problem with dirty laundry... *Either way.*

They got home to a mess of an apartment. Who knows what goes on there without them. The sun boiled the poor petunia plant alive. In a day. Right alongside the window frame, the glass magnified the regular Minnesota summer heat into plant-seeking death rays. It was astounding. You really had to water those things once or twice a day. Of course, what with all the gas leaks... it's a wonder they're alive at all.

The air was thick with moisture, enough to coat your face as soon as you took two steps out into civilization. And even in the sanctuary of the apartment, you could never be safe. All you had to do was get close to the window, peer in on the status of your pet plants, and stand back, aghast, at the palpable war between wind currents, trying to suck your soul out into the street, you might be lucky to feel a breeze.

Fuck it. Might as well take a little walk, she thought. *And when was the last time I got some damn exercise? Isn't it like a virtue or something? Wonder why the government hasn't pinged me yet with some scary malware or something.* She really hadn't taken a good ol' fashion walk for some time. She decided to give Mire some space while she was dealing with a little bout of tumultuous mood swings over his new obsession with some other alien lifeform. So, she left.

Obviously, he was more interested in the scientific properties of that thing than he was in her at the moment, and she knew it was immature of her to suggest anything, being the egomaniacal little shrew she arbitrarily transformed into at times.

She waited until he was drunk and she whispered her worries in his ear, as he was falling asleep. That way, she could stay true to their pinky promise of telling each other everything, but she also teetered on the edge of implementing her mother's advice not to divulge each and every secret of her precious personage.

She nodded to herself, satisfied. It was a good compromise.

Heading out into the heat wave, she thought the weather was really going to extremes. She donned her backpack and bent down to check her shoelaces one more time before setting out. It was all she could do to focus her attention on the small things within her capacity to control, just so she wouldn't explode all over him in a cloud of disconcerting word vomit that could possibly taint the outlook they would have on their relationship henceforth.

She glanced at her watch, just to keep track of how long she walked, and blinking rapidly, she set out, sinking into the involuntary wavelength of thoughts that normally accompanied such mindless activities.

She was walking pretty fast, starting out, really seething with rage at the thought that his family couldn't trust her with simple tasks. She began walking aimlessly, but with purpose, in any direction away from the apartment.

And he didn't exactly back her up during last night's annual reunion bash. The two usually opt for the kid's night, where the 20-, and 30-somethings go out drinking and dancing while the "adults" confer about 401k plans and the like, but this time

Mire and Riz decided they were ready to sit at the grown ups' table. What a mistake that was. They just kept hounding her over and over with the same questions: are you going to buy a house, when will you have kids, and so on. *Like*, she thought, *why couldn't his mom just ask her, then pass the word on to everyone else?*

Sweat was rolling down the back of her neck, the dark hair sticking up around the inside of her shirt collar, and she consciously slowed her pace to a crawl, simultaneously trying to tie her hair up in a bun to let a little air in back there, then she noticed that multitasking wasn't her strong suit, so she took a deep breath and stopped a moment.

Panting, she checked her watch. Fifteen minutes had gone by, during what felt like an eternity, and she was left there standing like an idiot in the street. She judged herself harshly, sweating, and she didn't even have yoga pants on, or a headband, or music playing, what was her goal here? Just to speed walk away from her problems, when she should be confronting her husband about them?

Or, could she be so bold as to actually reach out to his mother and mention something about how irritating it is being badgered about their future plans. Mire didn't seem to have any ideas about the future. It was always, "That happens," and "We'll see," and she couldn't care less what the future would hold, not until they got there at least. Then there was something actually tangible for her to latch onto.

Just as long as they were together. That's all that mattered to her in the great scheme of things.

Why couldn't his family just leave them alone? she thought, exhausted. She pulled her bun tight and picked up the pace, almost sprinting now in her fury.

Digging her heels into the pavement, she looked down occasionally, to make sure she wasn't setting any tiny ants, beetles, or other bugs off course; she had to sidestep a few times to allow her tiny friends passage. Once, she stumbled and just about biffed it, then righted herself. She kept her eyes to the ground, embarrassed.

Internally, she continued her rant. *Isn't it enough to treat him like the black sheep?* she thought. Where were they when he was homeless, living out of his car in Nevada, or shacking up in some city in Wyoming, hunkering down in an abandoned house with other guys and girls who were also down on their luck?

Her calves were burning as she walked to the rhythm of her bleeding heart. *I'm sorry to project these feelings of negativity,* she projected her thoughts outward into the void. *But why'd you have to wait until he got married to suddenly start caring about him?*

Out of breath, she wheezed and bent over to clutch at her knees. Well, whatever. That was fun, I guess. How productive. Murh murh murh. Do I feel better about myself? No. Well, who cares...

She straightened and as the blood rushed to her head, she caught a whiff of gardenias drifting in from the neighbor's yard. "Maybe they cared about him the whole time. He just projects this aura of nobody-ness... Huh." She shrugged and headed back home.

Back at home, she found him locked inside the other room. She jiggled the door handle, moaning, "Miirreee? You in there, babe?" He immediately opened the door a quarter inch to reveal frantic irises pulsating with a demonic inner light. "What's up?" was his breathless reply.

"Oh, nothing," she said, twirling the toes of her right foot into the carpet and looking down, meekly. "It's just that. I was thinking..." Mire, was gripping the edge of the door, fingers splayed. He quickly glanced behind him then turned his attention back to Erizabet.

Noticing that he was not quite in the right mindset for a heart to heart, she turned and walked away from the door. Mire stuck his hand out to grab her, skimming the hem of her dress. He chewed his cheek and closed the door, heading back into his work. When she interrupted him, she shocked him into soldering a diode to a mesh board that wasn't even attached to anything. After he closed the door, he got an idea. Now, was fully focused.

Fuck, what am I going to do with myself, she thought. She opened a notepad and started writing, "Dear diary. What an impetuous little fiend I am today. How can I possibly begin some tirade about how whiny I feel all of a sudden, encapsulating all of the thoughts from daybreak to dusk, and convey it all to him? To what end, really? He's got bigger fish to fry, I think." She clicked the pen, closed the notebook, and set it down.

The other day, he suggested a few books she should read to clear her head a little or fog it up, whichever of the two, she couldn't remember. She picked one up from the pile. "Foucault's Dreams," she read the title aloud and opened the moldy old cover to reveal browning pages within. She cracked the book open, right to the middle, stuck her nose in to take a big whiff. "Ahhh," she sighed. She flipped back to page one and began.

19: The Cleaners

Erizabet was onto something or maybe she was on something, but the fact remains: there was something wrong with Riz.

She wasn't feeling like herself much lately. Not after that night at the club. Some poison on the lips, maybe?

She did all the research she could to try to discover the reason why she couldn't seem to focus on anything.

Her eyes began to glaze over and cross inward any time she tried to paint, read, or even perform such a mundane task as doing the dishes.

She was accommodating to frequent bouts of the most acute myopia, occasionally relapsing from her decades' old surgery, which reminded her that she should schedule a check up with the doc. He said she would need an adjustment every 10 or so years, but this was beyond bizarre.

One online forum said her eyes were tired, that she should give them a rest a few times throughout the day. So, she started taking naps, only to wake up feeling a little groggy. She was not the least bit stuck in that otherworldly dream complex, yet she still had trouble focusing.

And her friends noticed it too. They said she had that faraway look. Even in those video chat rooms she frequently often, her "friends" one or twice told her to turn off her camera: "She couldn't even focus on me..." She retorted with some sort of comment alluding to the fact that she was watching a video or coding a site, not looking directly at the camera at all. Right? As some users are wont to do.

Another group suggested she was experiencing early onset strabismus, where your eyes slowly begin to cross as you speed head long into old age. She was not yet 30 years old, so she suspected this was not the case.

It could be nerves, someone suggested. Her eyes could be overstimulated, wrote someone else. She wasn't satisfied with any of these answers, so she resorted to her last option, naturally. She called her father.

"Oh, you sound just like me. I'm sorry." These were his words of comfort, obviously. She told him everything, and after about 23 minutes of straight soliloquy, he began to yawn. She had clearly exhausted his delicate sensibilities.

"Wait," he said, during a lull in the conversation. She sighed, "Oh no, what is it?" He cleared his throat. Through the video phone, she could see him sitting up in bed, adjusting his glasses, then peering down at his ancient communicator. She scratched her chin.

"Ah, I do that, too," he said. "Do you ever tug on your earlobes when you're really concentrating hard on something?" he asked. She made a show of fondling her right earlobe absentmindedly while squinting up at some inconsequential thought she saw floating up toward the ceiling. *How did you get up there?* She thought to herself.

She wouldn't delude herself into thinking she was a hypochondriac, but there was a subliminal something which told her nerves to react to her father. In some ways, they were one.

He took a sip of coffee. "Oh!" She saw his one leg shoot up under the covers as his ab muscles contracted, arms jerked up in the air, an epiphany struck like a chord on a harp, tense and lingering until fully realized and sung forth into the night air. "So, you said you had one of those seizures, right?" he said. She nodded and resigned to and looking down. She became solemn.

"And you've been sort of dizzy all day?" She nodded again, managed to whimper a word in the direction of the phone, "Unstable. Wavering, kind of," she said. She held her hand up in front of the camera and flipped it around as if it were a spasming dolphin tail.

"It's a sign of a migraine," he said, and she touched her temple, *How did he know I was developing this headache. Right. At. This moment?* She thought.

Now, it was his turn to sigh. "Oh, Rizzy. Rizzy baby, I'm sorry," he said. She hated it when he said sorry. Especially when he called her "Rizzy". Especially twice within the space of five minutes. She didn't want to feel sorry for herself, she wanted this thing to go away.

She was clearly in a state of half-shock, half-worry, and upon seeing a tear threatening to take the plunge from the cliff of her right eyelid, he backpedaled. "Lisinopril," he said. "That's what I'm on. Just be careful walking," he said, sounding like his mouth was full of cotton, his speech slowing down to a slur.

He was decaying right in front of her. *Oh, lord,* she thought, and began to sob silently to herself.

For a second, he thought the video froze, that her line had gone dead, then he saw her shoulders heave in little spasmodic jerks, and he relented from tapping rapidly on all the buttons he could barely see back-lit in LED around the circumference of the phone. She shared her self-diagnosis through gurgling phlegm.

"I'm sensitive to light. I can't focus. I took a nap, hell I even got seven hours of sleep last night, and what the hell is wrong with me, dad?" She implored him, regressing back into her childhood state of depending on her father, even though he always seemed far away. Even when he was right there next to her.

"You'll be fine, honey. They only come in clusters. I wouldn't worry about it. D'accord, ma cher?" He sometimes popped up with little French sentiments around this time of year, spring, when the world seemed to be sprouting new feelers again. The smell in the air somehow transformed him into a half-breed man-child as he receded into dreams of dating French women back in the early 2620s. He felt young during these months, though he couldn't help but revert into aversion for simple talk while he was much too much the definition of an introvert.

Yawning and stretching, he said, "Ahh, I'm sleepy. I think I'm going to take a nap." And before he knew what he was doing, his head commenced an exaggerated wilting and lowering motion, his chin sliding dangerously close to his emaciated chest.

She was afraid the hinge in his vertebrae might snap if he actually fell asleep in that position. "So, if they're not increasing in frequency..." she said, trying to draw his attention. "It's all in my head and I'll be OK?" she said, culling up a last ditch effort to extract some sort of solace from this man who shared her genes.

"No, no. Don't worry. I'll take to you later, OK, baby?" She acquiesced, "OK," she said. "Salut," he said, "Bon soir," she said. At that he let out a little chuckle. She was never really all that good at French.

They rang off. She sat back in her chair, took a sip of wine, squeezed her eyes up real tight, then opened them, letting them get a little crossed. They felt better that way.

She closed her eyes again, let her head fall back on the headrest, and lifted her chin to the ceiling.

It was an odd feeling. The desire to clean. When she awoke, she was feeling unsatisfied with herself, so she decided to check her stocks, only to realize she'd saved over 10 grand playing the digicoin game. Thinking Mire wouldn't mind, *He rearranged the furniture all the time*, there was a shred of evidence as to the existence of a fickle side. And besides, he wasn't there to protest.

So, she took it upon herself to arrange some drop shipments for rental cleaning bots. She didn't want to blow her entire load on a bunch of machines—she felt a variety of those cold metal things clung closely enough to her life, like barnacles on the underside of an old steamboat of yore—so she shelled out 2k's worth of digital currency. Upon arrival, she was feeling cheerful enough to greet each one with a little nod and a "Good day," pretending to tip up an imaginary hat that was resting atop her scrunchied hair.

She closed the door behind what she presumed to be the last bot, only to hear a slap on the wood, halted in place by the hand of a diminutive little creature, an adolescent monkey of the Mongolian variety, wearing a tiny boulder cap. She didn't know it, but he stood aside and watched her wave all the others in. Mechanically, he all too emphatically pursed his lips, squinted his eyes, and tipped his hat, miming her gestures.

She stood back, aghast. Satisfied with her reaction, he entered the kitchen, dragging a little red satchel behind him.

"Yeah, OK," she said, incredulous. Then she peered out into the hallway, looking first to the right where they had entered, then to the left, where other apartment doors stood dead-bolted in their frames. She shrugged and locked her door, only after she was completely sure no one else was coming.

The once-still apartment erupted in a flurry of action as machines flitted this way and that, hovering around at the top-most rungs of the cabinet spires. A few were scattered about the floor, marking clean circle-eights in the rugs where they had sucked up the last few month's worth of cigarette and incense ash, bottle caps, pieces of rubber bands, crumbs of hastily-devoured chips, and god knows what else.

Apparently, the tiny chimp was doing his taxes, resting comfortably in her favorite chair as she looked on, mouth agape. He gave her a scornful glance and she shifted momentum.

"Ahem." She cleared her throat, got up, smoothed her skirts, and pretended to take down dusty pieces of coffeeware off from on top of the refrigerator, inspected them, then set them back down.

"You know," came a voice from the living room compartment, sounding like it was unearthed from the soil surrounding the sarcophagus of King Tut. "If you want to sell all of this junk," said the monkey, she hadn't noticed he was wearing glasses, until he tilted them down an inch below his eyes. They rested on the bridge of his nose, now, as he continued to speak. "I can give you, oh, $4,000 for your trouble." He looked away from her, grinning, pushed his glasses back in place with one finger, and went back to his calculations.

She'd been out of the game only a manner of a few months, yet it seemed the value of a dollar had soared sky high since she'd last logged on. "Excuse me," said Erizabet, feeling a bit like Alice from the long-forgotten Lewis Carroll novel. "But, you can talk?"

Offended, he placed a hand to his breast and said, "My

dear child, what century do you think you're living in anyway?" he scoffed. He rose from his chair, and she bent down to see him more clearly.

"What have you done to your face?" he said, lowering his glasses once more, peering up into her eyes. "You don't look like your profile picture at all." He turned around his palm pilot so the screen faced her. She winced. "Ah, well," she stammered, flipped her hair and raised her eyebrows coyly. Realizing that didn't work, her right hand went up to scratch her hand, dramatically, like she was playing a cartoon character or something.

He went back to his work.

While the machines were busy tidying up, she felt this encounter existed somewhere outside of time. They talked about what it was like for him getting along as a highly evolved species and she relayed anecdotal incidents from her own incipiency.

They shared cigarettes, lighting the occasional stick of incense to transpose one smell with another occasionally, and she was highly engrossed in their discussion when the primate, whose name turned out to be David, held up his hand to quiet her, mid-sentence, and looked quizzically off to the left, tuning into a sound she couldn't hear.

She craned her neck to pick up on the signal, to no avail. She took a drag of her cigarette. "Something is not right," David said, pulling his pocket computer from his leather bag. He swiped around on the surface of the device, and tilted his head, listening to live streams of sounds playing in his head, swiped some more, listened again, and wiggled his ears to elicit a command to the central CPU node embedded in his skull.

"I see," he said, putting away the computer, then making a quick nod to close down the programs running in the background.

"Wait, so if the microchip in your brain serves as its own storage capacitor and processor, why do you use that hand-held—" he held his hand up again, goading her to be quiet. Though naturally querulous, she was fully cooperative to his demands.

He rose and sidled up to the bedroom door. She peered around the chair to look at him. He put his ear up to the door, listening again.

He must have excellent hearing, she thought. He scrunched up his features and turned toward her, making a circular motion with his hand, prodding her to join him. She met him at the door and they both went inside, making sure to secure it shut behind them.

Immediately, she felt the cool breeze of the A/C blasting in the room. She was struck with a mild case of vertigo. Succumbing to a slight faint, she wavered on the hinges of her legs, falling backward. David, not being of much help, tried his best to propel her from the precipice and push her back into an upright position. She swayed.

"Wooah, thanks, there, little guy," she said before fully coming to her senses. Instinctively, she bent down to pat him on the head, before realizing he was giving her the stink eye, tsk tsking, moving his finger like a metronome in the air.

"Ok, ok, jees. I didn't think you'd be all sensitive about..." Then, her eyes transfixed on something moving in the closet opposite. Aluminum arms were windmilling out of the darkness, fending off an impending attack from the cleaner bots.

She stepped closer to get a look at the thing. At first, she thought one of the machines had somehow wedged itself in the corner of the closet and was unable to get itself out. Then she thought, maybe they do this all the time and there's no way that a flaw in their engineering could be overlooked, especially if they performed this routine day in, day out.

Getting closer to the machine, a spark of recognition lit up the crystals in his eyes. "Erizabet, a little assistance, please," he said, dropping his arms to his sides, acquiescing to the knowledge that she would stop this madness once and for all.

Without knowing what she was doing, a feeling akin to motherhood took over, and she blinked into action. She went to the robot and stood in front of him, arms outstretched, as if body-guarding the robot. The cleaners relented, drawing away from the closet to find another place to fixate upon.

Mire was just arriving home when he saw a string of small robots walking single file down the hallway, emerging from his apartment.

Uneasy, he readjusted his backpack strap and went toward them. The robots, like ants, conveniently veered away to lend him a path to his own apartment.

He walked to the threshold, allowing the last robot to close the door behind him. He sat his backpack down on the kitchen floor and warily peered through the curtain separating the kitchen from the living room. "Erizabet?" he asked the empty room. "Hmm..."

He could feel her presence lingering here. *She must be in the other room*, he thought. He opened the door to the A/C room and stood in the door jam, slightly shocked to see Riz was sitting demurely, cross-legged, in one of the chairs at the table where he conducted his experiments.

And who else did he expect to find sitting there across from her, but one of those primate-human hybrids, clearly imbued with a communication device that allowed him to perceive, digest, and regurgitate what he thought to make up his own reality, pivoting his own perspective toward the degree to which it might prove he's one of them.

And Hank was there, too, fully cognizant and eerily cheerful, participating in the morbid conversation the three were deeply enthralled in.

He heard a few words about life after death and how the experience might vary between species, his own beloved being the last one to find a frog caught in her throat, upon realizing he had arrived.

"Mire!" she said, vindicated. She leapt up out her chair, the wooden frame of the old thing flying back and shattering one of its legs as it made contact with the wall. They held a tight embrace for a moment before she tried to turn her head to see what had become of the chair.

She kissed him on the cheek and withdrew, lifting up her arms, then dropping them to her sides again, whipping her skirts about, playfully.

"Whoops!" she said, not a hint of concern touched her voice. She turned away from him and stretched out a hand toward the other members of the party.

"This is my new friend, David," she said, palm up in the direction of the respectable little monkey. "And this, of course, well, you know Hank," she said, dropping back into her chair, sipping on a milkshake now. They were all drinking from the same cup.

What the fuck, he thought, and decided to comport himself. He smoothed his hair, drew up a chair, and sat down.

"We're all friends now," she said, happy as a lark, and went on sipping one of the straws bent over the rim of the cup. Hers was all chewed up to distinguish her straw from the others, that was her version of an excuse anyway. He only knew all too well that she had a terrible case of the hand-to-mouth habit. She bit her pens, her straws, and her cheeks, when she wasn't busy smoking.

Once seated, Mire looked around at the motley crew. "So, um," he said, grimacing, nodding his head in that way that helped him persuade people to talk. He swore he didn't have a salesman bone in his body, but his mannerisms begged to differ.

"What's up?" he said, grabbing Riz's pack of Duluths, extracting a tube, and lighting up. Riz was beaming. He thought for a second that she had become one with her old self. Then he thought, certainly this is a dream and he should wake himself up.

He didn't try pinching himself—he'd often did that in dreams, and it never worked. He probably shouldn't have undergone that experiment in college where he and his buddies indulged in inducing lucid dreams for a week. Now all of his dreams were lucid dreams, to the bewilderment of his more experimental friends. They were jealous. He was bored.

He was staring off into space, when Erizabet gingerly took his hand. "Dear," she said, looking deep into his brown eyes, tinged with green, "Is there something you haven't been telling me?" She didn't seem at all peeved at the fact that he was hiding a living, breathing anatomically-imbalanced being in their closet. In fact, he expected her to have found him sooner, but they had this unwritten rule where she didn't rifle through his private work space, and he didn't encroach upon hers.

She rather seemed, at peace, almost childlike in her curiosity. He took the opportunity to catch her up on his plans. The other two listened respectively.

His theory boiled down to the fact that the gods peopled the world with the intention that they'd eventually destroy themselves, then the heavenly bodies would reclaim the space the Earth occupied, tracing an elliptical around the black hole tugging toward the sun. Eventually, the ozone layer would be so depleted that the very heat hovering around the atmosphere would disrupt the magnetic poles; they would then reverse and sway until gravity itself would become unhinged, ultimately propelling humans upward, without anything to hold onto.

"Ejector seat!" Mire exclaimed, throwing his arms upward, making Riz laugh. He continued on, resuming his previous professor's pace. Hence, the creation of metallic beings, he was saying. 500 years before the Earth collapses in on itself, robots would be the only ones standing, so to speak, their metallic frames tethered to the pull of the ground, without much hindrance. They would adapt much quicker than their human counterparts and would reconstruct their movement algorithms to adjust to the permuting shift in weightlessness extrapolated upon the globe.

There was too much soil, too many tangibles, he posited, the universe was in a state of overabundance in the ways of organic matter. We had created so much trash, killed so many creatures, and boiled down their flesh to the point where land-fills provided the foundation for homes and cemeteries were being razed to make way for more bodies.

"Burn the bones and recycle the boxes," was the message of the alt rags. Hence the ever-increasing request for cremato-riums. "People are beginning to see the light, however sublim-inally," Mire continued.

Without acknowledging the declining state of the world, their choices were already made for them. They just thought they came up with it themselves. "In any event," Mire was say-ing, "Ashes to ashes, dust to dust." He took a swig of his beer.

Riz appeared drunk on his words and Hank was appalled, while feeling at the same time somehow liberated. He consid-ered himself akin to The One, a movie he recently watched in which the lead character—a robot, like him—would be the one to save the world.

David smoked languidly, looking this way and that to occasionally appraise the handiwork of his charges.

"But, what? So why the robots?" Riz asked, "No offense," she cut the air with her hand, glancing in Hank's direction. Mire shrugged and said, "It's the magnetic pull, the black hole you know. All organic matter will be purged from the earth," he continued casually.

Riz pulled out a notebook from the pocket she had previously sewn into the side of the chair, and quickly began jotting down his words, quickly and efficiently, in her own version of shorthand.

She wasn't ready for the whole plug-in procedure. She'd like to keep intact what was left of her soggy grey matter. Hence the old pen and ink.

"And the materials the robots are comprised of, or will be comprised of in the not-too-distant future, will get sucked into the center of the universe to meld with the missing chemical compounds the universe has been trying for centuries to recombine..." He took another sip from his beer. "Or something like that," he said.

Hank's eyes were shining like diamonds in the sky. He was leaning off the edge of his seat, intent to hear more about any potential upgrades he may soon receive.

He might not have realized it, himself, Mire hadn't yet installed the conscientious proprio-receptor cells into his main hard drive, but there was heat radiating from his core.

David felt it first. He was always putting on airs. He picked at his shirt and let it drop in quick succession, to suck some air conditioning down close to his skin.

Being of his certain class, and wearing long sleeves, of the ruffly pirate variety, he felt he was suffocating, sitting next to Hank.

Pulling open his shirt, he said, "Is it hot in here or is it just me?" They all turned to the air conditioner, which was working twice as hard, trying to readjust its output temperature.

If Hank could sweat, and if he actually wore clothes, he would either be drenched through to the bone, or he would spontaneously combust. He was getting excited—cooling fans running 3000 rpms, way off the charts.

Mire didn't notice he had muted his home alerts, until he blinked to bring up his notifications. All of Hank's systems were failing as part of the automatic safety lock-down procedure.

When the motors overheated, he was supposed to start booting down, but somehow, he was recharging himself, over-clocking, and looking at the gauges, Mire started to get a little unhinged.

He didn't deal with confusion very well. He either had to know the answer or he had to know some way to go about finding it, some semblance of hope, but at this moment, he racked his brain and he was all out of options.

He ran a couple of diagnostics tests, David went to fetch a glass of water, and Riz and Hank were talking about the possibilities of a total android takeover.

Where is the auxiliary power source coming from, he wondered, blinking rapidly to zoom in on the stats of his creation. He didn't see anything out of the ordinary, in fact, but there was smoke steadily rising from the pistons in Hank's shoulders, like signals from the great beyond, that something was wrong.

The electrodes he had adhered to the circuit-board substituted for his heart started leveling out, heat register returned to normal. Hank must be overriding his own monitors, he decided. The creation has bested his creator. Only, Mire caught him in the act.

David returned with the water, he brought enough for all four of them by mistake. With his newfound sensibilities, he could have possibly mistaken the robot for another human, all creatures were one in the same in his book. Mire's theories were now fully embedded in his psyche.

Beads of sweat were beginning to sprout up on Riz's brow, but why didn't she notice that Hank was working on his way to becoming a veritable atom bomb?

At this point, Mire was verging on a state of shock. *This can't be real, can it?* He swiped his hand in front of Erizabet's face, and she seemed not to notice. Or, she simply took this gesture in stride, thinking Mire was just being eccentric, as always.

"OK!" Mire said, holding up his hands, climbing out of his chair into a standing position. "David, it's been real swell meeting you," Mire held out his hand in good faith.

Picking up on his ineptitude toward decency, David turned, looked at Mire as if insulted, and began to gather his things.

"But I have to see what's up with Hank here," David said. It was Riz's turn to look toward her beloved, "And I want to spend some time with my lady, OK?" said Mire. She offered him a weak smile. She'd been alone too long, and she wasn't prepared for her new friends' departure.

The robot, parts of him still popping and fizzing, stepped closer to the closet, sulking. He had worn out his welcome. Maybe he wasn't The One after all.

Mire positioned himself in front of Hank, stopping him in his tracks. "Oh, no you don't," he said, lifting up Hank's chin with fatherly fingers. "You stay put, I need to have a look at you, if that's OK."

Hank looked up, fearful of what Mire might say next. *I'm decommissioned*, he thought, *ka-putz*. Then a series of nanosecond snippets of old movie reels flashed before his eyes, *You're through, you see?*

Mire continued, "But if you really need some rest, or you want to think about things, or do whatever it is you do on your off time, go right ahead. I can get the data from you later."

At this, Hank closed his eyes, shutting down all faculties simultaneously. A look of worry passed over Riz's face. "But, Mire, what if he doesn't know he's a robot?"

He thought maybe that was the dumbest thing she had ever said. He turned to her, grasping her shoulders.

"Now, babe. Don't be ridiculous. See," he said, leading her away from the table, toward the door, "It doesn't matter what he thinks, does it? He's the one in the way," he said, turning away from her, expecting she would find the exit herself.

"Mire? What do you mean by that?" His face turned red, "Fuck, are you getting on my nerves tonight." Something inside him snapped.

"First, you invite all these... things into our home, then Hank's up and about, clonking around, when I'm not even done with him yet, he's really not ready for the world, you know, though he did all right at that grocery store, and I'm not racist or anything," he was slowing down, his tone dropped a register, "You know that, babe," he sighed.

A minute of silence went by, then the anger crept back in, "But damn. This is my sanctuary. I can't have David, or whoever, going around talking to people about what I'm doing, here, OK?"

He lifted his hands, then let them drop, all the wind blown out of his sails. He just had to get it out of system. They both knew how each other worked. She withdrew, he got snippy.

That was the way of the universe. Yin and yang, blue stars sharing cycles, exchanging gases. Slowly consuming each other to death.

"Sorry, love. I guess, I've just been kind of preoccupied. I didn't put your feelings into perspective." She came up close to him, put her hands on his chest and looked deep into his eyes. "I want to give you salience," she said. He stared back at her, the calm flowing out of her and into him.

He closed his eyes and sighed, letting his shoulders droop. He gave up the fight. "Oh, I love you," he said, kissing her forehead. He hugged her close.

"You know," he half-mumbled into her hair, extended his arms, holding her at arms' length to get a better look at her, "Half the time, I don't know what you're saying, but..." he brought her in close again, took a deep whiff of her hair. "I still love you." *Gee, compliments all around*, she thought.

She let the heat of the moment roll off of her like a wave come crashing onto the shore. Once in existence, then no more.

And then there were two. The house was at once quiet after a long day of craziness.

They decided they'd conclude the night by making some pasta, having a couple of shots, and watching a movie, with the occasional sidelong glance to suggest telepathically, *Did you see that?* or *Oh, those are nice tits*, or some other secret shared silently. It was something they hadn't done in a while.

But what was that about Cereselium-423? That planet on a crash course toward Earth? How could Mire develop this thousand-year-long future when the media begged to differ?

Right before David left, he mentioned something about twin souls reuniting at all costs... did it have something to do with the crystal?

That night she dreamed about the apocalypse again. This

time, an orb hovering above Earth came crashing down into their home planet, two lovers' gaseous forms found one another and joined once more. The President Elect Krunk laughed as all the world's volcanoes erupted at once. The world ended in one gigantic earthquake and lava-fueled eruption.

20: The Beginning and the End

Flashback to 2389, right before the whole voting debacle began. They were dancing on the beach to Mire's magnificent drum beat.

There was something tribal about him then. He was pounding toms, his fists clutching sticks the size of mallets. He was an entirely different animal when he was in the groove. Bah dum. Bah dum dum pah.

Creating the atmosphere for the party, he didn't realize he was in charge of everyone's oxygen flow, their blood pumping with each hit of the snare. She knew. She could understand where he was coming from. Au natural, yet technologically connected.

There was something about him. He had this calm, go-with-the-flow attitude, which said, hey, no one's judging anyone, we all do things, and here I am, rock you like a hurricane.

Then he switched to guitar. The first note hit her ears and she drowned. He fingerpicked a sorrowful tune of his own creation, she closed her eyes, and the world fell away.

She was immediately immersed in a story that took over her brain, all senses collided and she was in a forest, damp with dew settling in for the night. She saw deer grazing among the roots of the trees, careful not to nibble on too many mushrooms; they didn't want to displease their compatriots, the pigs, who took it upon themselves to keep the larger predators at bay, their tusks shining like mythril in the night.

He stopped playing at some point and was sitting next to her on a piece of petrified driftwood, running his hands over her bare arms. Her skin broke out in goosebumps.

It was hot. Who knows why there was a fire pit roaring, right there in the middle of the sand, not five feet from the shore. She thought, *I guess, at any rate, a few of the swimmers could just plop on out of the water, there, wring out their suits, and put out the fire, if need be.* She looked around, well, if any of them wore swimsuits, that is.

Suddenly, in the middle of the foray, she heard sirens approaching. "Do you hear that?" she asked a friend. The girl, laughing, long hair flowing around her head as if she herself was suspended in water, danced circles around Riz, singing, "It's just my 'magination," and disappeared.

Mire appeared out of nowhere, she had no recollection that he'd ever stopped playing music. He grabbed her by the waist, knowing full well that at least a half dozen of their mutual friends were watching.

They all knew they were in love, and that they probably would be for the rest of their lives. The summer belonged to them.

They met in the fall, and after all the shivering, snuggling, hill climbing, and the physical exertion that the cold weather tolled on their bodies, they were finally free to sweat and be wild, and everyone was thoroughly jealous of how they came to be.

They walked over to where the cooler lay couched between two trees. He cracked open a can, handed it to her, and she took it gratefully. She was parched, and tired, but wired, the exhilaration taking hold. She waited for him to open his, then held her beer aloft, a gesture of kinship at its pinnacle, and they cheers'ed.

"Prouzchousta," she said. "Yes," he said, eyebrows raised, not trying to hide the fact that he had no idea what she was saying. They both smiled, sipped their beers, and bust out laughing, the beer coming out of Riz's nose. "Ow," she said, squeezing her nostrils tight with two fingers. He held his gut as he laughed his brains out. Finding the seam there on the bottom of his shirt, he gave her a look, "Hmm?" and he started undressing. She pursed her lips and tilted her head, as if to say, "Yeah, sure," and started stripping.

They ran hand-in-hand to the water, naked as the day they were born. She dove in first and he lingered after to mentally record her enjoyment from afar. She hadn't known he was plugged in for some time, until after those early courtship days. It made no difference to her, but she had a feeling, deep down, while she was diving through the waves, the cool water permeating her flesh, seeking some lilt of recognition touching upon her soul, that this wouldn't last forever.

She was *too* happy, or so it seemed.

She came up for a breath of air, and sucked in some water, surprised to see him there, reaching out to tickle her. The saltwater went down the wrong pipe and she choked. She was laughing the entire time, finally ducking her head into the water to clear her thoughts, then she resurfaced, feigning calm.

Treading water, she took one look at him and started laughing again. They were wrapped in each other's arms, and he threatened to throw her. "I'm gonna do it. I'm gonna do it.

And everybody's gonna see your nudin'," he said, changing the pitch and tone of his voice, making a show of mockery. Kicking and screaming, she laughed, banging on his exposed arms and shoulders, begging him to let her go. "Ok, ok," he said, releasing her, "If that's what you want," he said, moving away. "Ah," she said.

Now, exhausted from all the swimming, she realized how much she missed the ocean. She often thought fondly about the way the water undulated beneath her, yet above her somehow, and through her all at the same time. She was in communion with the ocean. *If there were any religion as true as this, it wouldn't exist,* she thought. And it didn't. She took a light breath, leveled out her body on the surface of the water and let go, riding the tiny peaks and valleys that pushed her to and fro.

She was lying there, becoming one with the water, when she heard muffled cries of cop sirens, reverberating through the waves. She righted herself, dog paddling, blinking the water out of her eyes. With her hands, she wicked away the water from her face, blew her nose audibly, shoved her head back under once more, resurfaced, and took a gulp of air. "Do you hear that?" she asked Mire, who was lazily swimming about. "Hmm?" Was he stoned? "I'm stoned," he said. It was like they could read each other's minds.

He hesitated, treading water, "Yes, I hear them," he said, and they both instinctively headed back to shore to see what was going on.

There were guys in black and white, pushing their friends around, stomping out the fire, throwing drum heads. "Oh, well," he said, going back under. She tugged him up out of the water. "Be still, OK. They won't see us out here," she said. They both took three slow breaths, and consciously slowed down their heart beats. They looked at each other, smiling, while the party was being destroyed not 20 feet away. They were safe in their bubble of happiness. For the time being.

*   *   *

Shortly after that, they were engaged, and they hadn't been separated since, until the crystal took over their lives. With all the commotion around the robot coming fully to a head, Mire realized it might be better to pull the plug on the whole experiment. *It's possible the attention I'm giving this thing is actually straining our relationship*, he thought. What happened to Riz back there? And what would happen to us if I went through with this government deal? Sure, we'd be set for life, but at what cost? If his hypotheses were correct, he'd created the robot that would destroy the world, or rather, he created the robot that would create the robot to destroy the world. *The genius skips a generation*, he thought.

A question arose in his mind: Would Riz ever want to have a kid with me? A real one... His heart sank. She had all these projects going all the time, and the saying goes that once you have a kid, your life as you know it is basically over, and he didn't want that to happen to her. He wanted her to have all the happiness in the world. Would she take Hank in as a surrogate? They seemed to get along just swimmingly, but that's not the same, is it?

They hadn't talked about it in a while, and he'd been so caught up with that damned mysterious energy emanating from the crystal, he thought his own potential fame more important than sitting down and having a conversation about anything serious with her.

Sure, they watched a couple of movies the other night, got hammered, had great sex, and it was an overall glorious time, but he could sense her need for conversation. He thought she was introverted like him, but maybe she was more of an ambivert, and he wondered if she got enough mental stimulation outside of their relationship.

He only had three concerns: Where's the next meal coming from? How can I be more productive? And, is she happy?

She kept the fridge stocked, and he might be on the verge of discovering the next means of renewable energy, so two out of three were covered. But, where does she go all the time, he wondered.

Before the fall, she was content to sit in the apartment and trade stocks all day, playing the occasional video game, reading, or writing. She also seemed to like cleaning a lot, but something changed in her lately. She had hired help to tidy up the apartment, which was totally out of character, and she stopped painting, too.

Before her, the apartment was spare at best—nothing in the fridge, no furniture, no sound, aside from his occasional crooning, and why hasn't he been making music lately? He considered it odd that he should be thinking of this now.

Before her, he had nothing. He didn't need anything. He was a bachelor. He had a decent job, he was working on upgrades for his car, and that's all he really cared about. But then she came along, swept him off his feet, and disrupted the atmosphere with a whirlwind of chaos, which he thoroughly enjoyed and had come to appreciate.

He became accustomed to coming home to see a new painting drying on the floor, or sheets of crumpled-up stories lying scattered around the typewriter his father gave him but he never used, until she bought some new ribbon, restrung it, and went at it. That was her altar for the last six months, and what happened?

Was there anything he could do? Maybe the fact that she actually wanted to leave the house was a good sign?

He was lying on the sofa, ruminating, when he heard the key in the lock. He picked up the book beside him and quickly started reading where he left off in Henry Miller's "Crazy Cock". His eyes grazed the words on the page, though his mind was fixated on her movements, her exhalation of breath, the pushing off of one shoe, then the other.

In the heat of the apartment, it was all she could do not to start stripping right there, within a foot of the door. She turned around, made sure the door was locked, then let her hair down, walking through the curtain to where he lay, shaking out the tresses of her dark brown mane.

She kneeled down next to him, panting. She slid her hands up under each of his knees, and rested her head on his right thigh.

"Ahh," she moaned. "It's so hot." She lifted her head and dropped it again, limply, for emphasis.

He set his book down and sat up, taking her hand in his. He turned toward her, and looked first at her brow, then her nose, then her chin, then back to her forehead. "Ah, jees, you are hot, huh?" he said and leapt up to retrieve a paper towel. She let her head plop down on the lukewarm leather of the couch. She slowed her breathing, letting her circulatory system work its magic to cool her down.

He came back, flying over the chair adjacent to the table, landing gracefully in a crouch next to where she had balled herself up in a semi-permanent position of defeat.

He gingerly folded the paper towel lengthwise and draped it across her steaming forehead. She let out a long, slow breath.

Had she been running? He looked her over, she didn't have her tennis shoes on, or any of that moisture-wicking clothing he saw in ads on those instructional videos she watched. Now, he was more curious about her whereabouts than ever. *She's not cheating on me, no fucking way,* he thought. *Fuck, if she ever...*

"Hey, babe," she said. "Do you ever just walk around and talk to flowers... ask 'em how their day's goin' and stuff?" He looked at her and a wave of relief washed over him. "Oh, thank god," he said, and cradled her body close. He wrapped her up like a pretzel. She felt the entire world consisted solely of his touch. He enclosed her in a snow globe of flesh, their sweat mingling, and she could taste his smoky breath on her tongue. His essence seeped out of his pores and she could barely exist without breathing him in.

She started kissing his neck, then she licked his forehead, savoring the salty sweet taste of his sweat. He pulled away an inch, frowning at her, confused. She looked at him, then went in for a bite. He moaned. She pulled him closer, giving him a light hickey on the neck. He pulled her away, breathing hard, making that, I-hope-you-know-what-you're-doing face. She smiled.

He stood up, carried her to the bedroom, threw her down and started kissing her neck, then her chest, her lips. They devoured each other, groping, until they could no longer stand it. She pulled off his boxers, he unclasped her bra, and they fell together back on the bed, feeding on the writhing movement of each other's body, pulling back and forth like the tug of the tide, their bodies sliding to the pulse of their combined heartbeat, syncopated to the rhythm of love.

She arched her back and he cried out, pumping furiously. She sucked on his earlobe and he pushed and pulled faster and harder. She cried out, knowing he'd come.

She sighed, kissing all over his neck, sucking the sweat into herself. They stared at each other for a long time, his eyes focused on her right eye, then she followed him, staring into his left eye, then he switched to the left eye, and she followed him in turn, looking at his right eye.

He evinced an aura of suspicion to a certain degree, so she held onto him tightly, still inside her. He looked to the side, and said, "Shazam," pulling out. Her body jerked; it was a shock every time. He laughed, saying, "Yup, that's what I'm going to say from now on." She chuckled a little, crossing her legs to dam up the wetness leaking out of her into the already dirty sheets. *We really should wash these more often*, she thought.

They left the room, naked, and each went for a smoke. Coming to rest, he against the refrigerator, her ass pressed up on the counter, they sighed and looked at each other, satisfied.

He came to, looked at his watch, and said, "Oh, we should go." She blinked, still in that hazy dream world of longing. "We don't want to keep them waiting," he said.

They arrived at the building where they first encountered the gaggle of flesh-hungry freaks last week. Last time they were decked out in their Sunday best, so Riz made sure to wear flats this time around, just in case she needed to run for her life.

They parked the car and stepped outside, to be greeted by the same dull grey building from before, but the lights were off and no one was home.

Mire lifted the sleeve on his left wrist, looked down at his watch, and said, "It's 10 'til 7, they should already be in there, dancing, or feeding, or sucking the lives out of little children, whatever they do!" He threw his hands up, exasperated.

Riz tugged on his shirt, saying, "Do you hear something?" Just as they were turning back toward the car, the sound of snarling teeth sucking saliva came echoing out of the alleyway.

Her heart leapt in her chest and she clutched Mire's arm. "What the fuck?" she said, peering into the darkness. Beady little eyes glowing pink and red jostled in the gloom, getting brighter as they approached the couple.

The swing dancing instructor led the pack. Erizabet noticed the woman was still wearing the same clothes from last week, she lifted her hand, pointing, and counted the rest of the pack: 5, 6, 7, 8.

They were all disheveled. What, did they sleep right here on this stoop 'til class sprung up again? The instructor's shirt sleeve was torn from shoulder to elbow. It looked like the handiwork of a blade, or a severely sharp fingernail. She shuddered at the images that played in her head.

Mire was feeling frisky, not at all unnerved by their arrival. "What are you guys doin', huh?" he asked, inching closer, goading them on, "Was there an alleyway orgy I missed, or something?" The slithering creatures crab walking toward them stopped in their tracks, animosity shining in their eyes. A few of their mouths were open, as if they were struggling for air. The others had fingers splayed, aching to sink their claws into him.

The instructor fixed him with her gaze, her finger dancing in the air. Tsk, tsk. She thought she had them all figured out.

Then Riz involuntarily spoke, "Really? That's the second time I've seen that tsk tsk thing this week. Where are you guys getting your insults, anyway? 1920s soap operas?"

The woman shifted her attention in Riz's direction. Riz jumped back. A wave of nausea hit the pit of her stomach, and it was all she could do not to keel over and start convulsing on the spot.

"Aw, god. That look. That's the look Meryl got when we. Wait. Goddamnit, what are you?" Riz asked. The instructor replied, "Oh, Mire didn't tell you?" She walked up closer to him, and brought her face within inches of his, as if they were old friends, or lovers. Her breath stank of rotting garbage and there was a foul odor steaming up from her clothes. Mire gagged, sticking out his tongue, reflexively, then clamped his hand over his nose.

The woman spat in his face, and Mire released his grip, looking down at the bubbles forming along the flesh of his knuckles. For an instant, he simply looked at the woman, then back at his hand, then it hit him, the poison reaching its target in the corroding layers of his skin. He shrieked in pain, pulling his wrist closer to his face to get a better look. The monster was throwing acid at him with each breath.

He turned to Riz, still clutching his wrist. "Fight or flight?" he said. Riz looked at him, eyebrows scrunched in consternation. She was pissed. "Fight!" she said, and spread her arms in one decisive motion, locking them three inches from her ribs. Power stance.

Tiny engines whirred to life on her back, spreading out mechanical wings built to distract them from noticing the steam-powered jetpack that engaged when she activated the pulleys situated on her shoulders.

She flicked down her wrists. The monsters watched with apprehension as she started to rise from the cement.

Mire looked pleased, he was proud of his and Petridge's handiwork. For a second he thought maybe last night's drinking spree might have hindered the process of progress while they were manically constructing the things.

Gayle took this opportunity of distraction to jump onto Mire's body. She tried to spit into his face again, but he held up his wrists, which ere swathed in Riz's mystery green coagulant oil before he left the apartment, a last ditch effort at a homeopathic remedy for slipping through the clutches of any potential fiends he had hoped to encounter. And boy, he sure did hope he would get the chance to kick these guys' asses.

He rotated his wrists, snapping the neon sticks attached to his sleeves, activating the bacterial light source seething along the surface of the gel. That got the monsters murmuring.

The pack howled and shielded their eyes from the radiant ooze. The swing dancing instructor smirked, she was familiar with this ruse.

Gel or no gel, Gayle zipped over to him with lightning speed and pummeled him, clutching his abdomen with her thighs. He howled in surprise. She dug her heels into his back, making him wince in pain. While he was trying to fight her off, the others came to their senses and started coming at him, all save for one, who wanted Riz.

She willed her levitation device a foot higher into the air and pushed the thrusters toward her attacker, keeping an eye on Mire the whole time, "He's fine, he's fine," she kept repeating to herself. She started down at her hands and channeled her anger into a tiny metal box with intricate engravings on each side.

Pet constructed this one especially for her, saying it only worked for true believers. As creepy as it sounded at the time, coming from a slurring, stumbling drunk, now was as good a time as any to believe they would get through this night.

She closed her eyes and felt a radiating heat emitting from her palms and dropped the box with a sharp breath. "Ow, ow. Hot!" She said, almost comically.

The box wriggled around and the monster sidled up to it, head cocked in curiosity. He bent down to touch it and Riz strafed right, not a moment too soon, as the monster turned to vapor, then got sucked up in a swirling vortex, captured by the cube forevermore.

Riz's feet touched the ground, picked up the box, tossed it once in the air, "Huh. All in a day's w—" It seemed the fight wasn't quite over just yet.

Mire was struggling to contain the wildebeest straddling him, and he was having trouble activating the armor he wore underneath his clothes.

Luckily, he synced his onboard UI with switches set to deploy his newly-equipped defense system when his heart rate fluctuated more than 100 bpms. He just had to speed up his breathing if he were to get anywhere in this fight. It's too bad she reeks like stewing sewage. *I can't do this. Why do I have to be so damn calm all the time? Freak, Mire, freak.*

The monster wrapped around his waist was clawing at his face, then he kneed her in the ass to try to get her to loosen her grip.

Annoyed with this silly gesture, she opened her mouth to take a chunk out of his throat, but right before she could sink her teeth in, his flesh sprouted a coat of blossoming fungi that hardened as soon as the spores were exposed to the air. What the?

She withdrew, spitting up blood, or whatever that bluish-black bile passing off as blood actually was.

Stumbling away from Mire, she coughed into her hand and was repulsed to see mushrooms growing out of her own imperfect skin. Mire made his shoulders dance to a tune inside his head. He twirled his index fingers in the air, as the instructor stood dumbstruck. He tackled her to the ground, pinning her to the oil-slicked alleyway.

Riz flew back up into the air and taunted another attacker, a 40-something male with blonde hair, who might as well have been Hitler's idea of a perfect Aryan, molded from clay.

You could tell he had spent a great portion of his life getting in shape to join the ranks of Juliard's finest, but instead he ended up here, on this dirty, grimy street.

He was salivating, trying to get a peek up her dress and she inched closer, teasing him, "Aww, you're just horny. Look, I'm not gonna hurt—" She swung her leg back and kicked his head as hard she could.

His neck snapped and he lay back, lifeless, aside from the occasional twitch in his arms and legs.

Her jetpack was almost out of steam, it wasn't meant to last this long, but she managed to adjust the thrusters to lower herself to within a few feet of the ground. She twiddled her fingers at the rest of the dancers, teasing. "You want some of this?" she said, sweating, adrenaline pumping through her veins.

While Mire held the woman's stomach with his knees, he looked up at Riz, "What the fuck? Didn't we talk about this?" And Riz shrugged, inching a little closer to the ground.

The other dancers backed away in fear. She recalled her wings back into their original folded position, bringing them to rest squarely in the middle of her shoulders, then jumped the last few feet to the ground.

She went over to Mire and the woman, who lay there panting, angry, like a cornered raccoon. There was still a little fight left in her, though she was clearly up against forces out of her control.

She was furtively looking around, searching for her accomplices. She shouted something in a foreign tongue, "Zhungtuk! Melem kan fet!" No one came to rescue her, and Mire, being the kind-hearted soul he was, slowly withdrew, putting out his hand to help her up.

She looked at him, dubious, then to Riz, who shrugged, friendly enough, then switched back into anger mode, letting

Gayle know she would tear her apart if she made one wrong move. The woman pushed Mire's hand away, and dusting herself off, shakily got to her feet. She bent over, hands resting on knees, and collected her breath, touching her stomach once to make sure she was still in tact.

She moved to leave the scene, when Mire grabbed her wrist and pulled her back, bringing her close to his face again. Riz stood stock still, squinting, waiting for this real-life game of chess to come to rest once and for all.

Mire whispered into her ear, something Riz couldn't hear, and with a weak smile, the woman stumbled off into the dark.

"What did you say?" asked Riz. "Don't worry about it, OK?" he held her in his arms and stroked her hair. "I've got this under control." She was skeptical about the inner goings on between the two, but she trusted him with every fiber in her being. She fell against him, all the fight drained from her body.

※   ※   ※

He was comforted by the sounds of her belly gurgling freely. Once he felt certain she was out, he made his escape. Touching hand to door handle, he stretched toward where she lay on the bed, lifted up the covers and kissed her stomach, replaced them, then looked at her one last time, a smile playing across his face.

He crept down the stairs, being careful not to step on the creaky parts in the floorboards. Stepping onto the firm ground of the cement beside the bar, he took a deep a breath. He was savoring the cool air, that stood in stark contrast to the stifling heat of the apartment.

He looked up to see blood on the moon, a sign of trouble not far away, and pulled up his coat collar against the leaves floating on the breeze, scaling the walls of the wind tunnel the old buildings made of the city.

Mire was playing out the proceeding scenes in his head. How hard can it be to convince a demon to crawl back into her grave?

Walking down the deserted streets, he noticed a homeless guy who called him by name. "Eh, Mire, you got a quarter?" he said. "Sorry, man," he said, twirling passed him. "Aww, all I want is a coffee, man, you know me," the bum said. He let the hand holding the offering cup fall into his lap, hopeless that there would be anyone else that close to friendly who might even so much as look at the guy, at this time of night.

Mire did what he could to avoid conversation with a guy who would inevitably recognize him from the gas station. He couldn't hang around street corners all night. He had to go see a "friend", one he was frightened of, to be quite honest. She turned. *I mean, what the fuck? Emily died almost three years ago...*

As he quickened his pace, the rain appeared out of no-where, slapping his face and arms, then let up altogether. He felt the clouds were keen on destroying him. Have I time traveled back to Florida, or what?

The sun was still working on setting, a hint of white light churning beneath purple and blue storms on the horizon. To the east, the moon slid behind a cumulonimbus and disappeared when he turned the corner to the next street.

It wasn't long until he reached her place. She was leaning against the wooden railing when he approached the house. He climbed up the steps, feigning confidence, then stood still in front of her. "Shall we?" she said, and with a wave of her hand, she ushered him inside.

"So," she said, taking a seat on the ottoman, giving him the chair to sit in. There was nothing in the house, save that one chair and a little table beside it. Was she crashing here? Did she have any water? How was she alive?

His mind raced, but he tried to stay focused on her. She was wearing slightly cleaner clothes now, obviously not trying very hard to hide her identity as she did the first two times they met.

"So?" she caught his attention. "What did you want to talk to me about?" she lit a cigarette and blew smoke rings that curved one after the other, trailing like a locomotive's some stack. She crossed and uncrossed her legs, immodestly. What was she trying to hide with this show of vacuous female self-awareness?

"Well, I was wondering..." he started, lighting up a smoke himself, "Where do you go at night? I mean..." she gave him a look as if to say, That is not what you came here for.

"Ok, ok," he said. She leaned back against the wall, the rolling ottoman slipping forward ever so slightly. She tapped her ash on the floor. "Mhmm hmmm," she said, a hint of that southern accent popping up around consonants.

"Well, all right, there's something that's really been bugging me since we first met." He leaned forward, clapped his hands. "Do you know about the crystal? Is that what's making everyone crazy? Is that why you attacked me? Or were you just trying to get back at me for dumping you? You're not used to getting dumped, are you?"

She laughed a hollow, blood-curdling cackle. "Woah, now, sugah paw. First thing's first." She took a drag.

"God. Whatever." He raked his hands through his hair and took a deep breath. "So, the crystal."

She smiled. It was a seductive smile, all-knowing, with a hint of evil around the edges. She let her cigarette drop to the floor, stubbed it out with a naked toe. "Oh, I know all about the crystal. What it contains. Who it contains." At that, Mire raised an eyebrow.

"How do you think you know about it?" She looked into his eyes, unflinching. There was a pink glow resonating from somewhere within her pupils, making her look like a demon possessed, not at all trying to hide the fact that her humanity waned with each additional second she remained in existence.

It was all he could do to look away from her, those other-worldly eyes sucked him in like a vortex from which there was no escape.

He looked out the window, pointed to the sky and said, "Do you know that constellation?" She stood up and went to the window, "Oh, sure, that's The Swan, or what you call The Swan, right?" She turned around and crossed her arms, holding back from elucidating. She wasn't sure if she should give herself away this early in the game. She would turn the tables and test him instead.

"And the stars? Do you know the names of the stars?" she asked him, firing back. "Well, I know Arcturus, the one to the southeast, where the tail end would be," he said, unsure of himself. He hadn't thought of this stuff since college. He was really interested in astronomy, but for some reason there were holes in his memory that he had no hopes of repairing.

She flicked out her arms, "Oh, forget it. I don't know what they are either." She gave him a sidelong glance, gauging him gauging her.

If she were in tune with this thing, she would possess all of its memories, right? He thought to himself. Or, is that just another one of those fairy tales Petridge planted into his mind.

He knew some fairytales about banshees and valkyries and the like, but he had no clue what possessed aliens to pursue their missions. And who knows, maybe she wasn't one of those things, after all, maybe the crystal simply slowly took over her brain, as it affected him if he hung around Hank for too long, or if he even allowed his thoughts to linger on the image of the sliver he had left, kept in a jar beside his boxers in his dresser drawer.

Just then, he saw lights flash outside of the window, bringing his focus back to the present.

Flashes of blue and red displaced the night air, reflecting off of the surrounding houses, sending a chill down his spine. He reflexively rubbed his hands up and down his arms, looking intently through the pane to discern the faces of the poor victims.

The woman stood still, like an animal caught in the act of devouring her prey, then she saw someone being pushed out of the house on a hover gurney, and then two out of three of the cop cars fled the scene, only one strobe light remaining to illuminate the scene.

"Friends of yours?" he said, jerking his head toward the ambulance. "Not really," she rubbed her neck as she walked away from the window. "People just drop like flies around here—" she felt Mire's gaze. "What did you say?" He stood up, alert.

"What?" she said, dropping her hands to her sides. "I said, people are dropping like flies." She shrugged. "Anyway, we should probably get out of here." "Why?" he asked. "What are you running from?" She went back to the footrest, grabbed her pack off the floor. "You're acting like I didn't fucking attack you last night. You came here for a reason. Stop playing nice, OK?" He raised his eyebrows, "Well, how forward of you," he said. "Hmm..." she murmured, thinking, *Let's get on with it already.*

"The thing is, Mire," she said his name as if it were something poisonous she'd like to spit out. "We don't want you," she said, lighting another smoke, looking around for her purse. He ran his hands along the cracked wallpaper, peeling a good chunk, before she rushed over with godlike speed and put her hand on his. Her skin felt as if it were made of ice. "Yeesh," he said, and pulled his hand away, flapping his wrist to get the blood circulating again. He made a fist, relaxed, made a fist, relaxed. "Well, what the fuck is going on around here? Is it, like, some big secret or something?"

She looked at him with doleful eyes. "Oh, sure. Let's just give away all the secrets of the world while we're at it." She blew smoke right into his face. He coughed, holding his hand over his mouth. Vapors like death warmed over stuck to the insides of his nostrils. He felt sick to his stomach, and grabbed his abdomen to retch up some bile his gullet deposited to the floor before he recovered.

When he stood back up, wiping his mouth, she was gone. All that remained was the dust coating every inch of the hollowed-out house. Shaking his head, disbelieving what she said, he noticed on the way out, there was a sign on the door that read, "Condemned".

21: Misty, Watercolored Memories

The lab was radiating heat like a sauna. The globe-shaped domicile was open to the sky, like a solarium without the greenhouse effect of trapped vapors, but somehow it had this pervasive swampy atmosphere nonetheless.

Petridge started sweating immediately upon entering the room. He moved to unbutton his outer shirt, and Whit stopped him with a hand on his chest. "No, my friend. You wouldn't want the plants to get greedy."

Petridge slowly pulled his shirt back in place, looking around, espying all manner of flora dripping with what appeared to be saliva down from around the lips of the tubular gullets extending upward to receive whatever offerings they could hope to receive.

There was a horrible stench coming off one of the monstrous succulents hanging from chains in the ceiling. Petridge covered his mouth with his shirt, and with his voice muffled, he said, "What in God's name is that thing?" he pointed a finger in the direction of the enormous plant. "Don't point at it, either, my boy. She can feel you breathing. Your heart beats out to her like thunder." Whit set his back down on a small end table to the right of his workbench.

"She?" Petridge asked, walking to the center of the brightly-lit bubble. Directly underneath the fury of the sun was the only place Pet felt he could stand a comfortable distance away from the carnivorous plants that surrounded him.

He stood stunned. After all the years he'd known this man, this was the first time he'd ever stepped foot in this place. It was completely off the grid, powered by plant matter, which was in turn powered by the sun. The only problem, Whit once told him, was in winter, when he had to cover the entire place with a liquid aluminum alloy to keep the heat in. That's when things were really interesting.

Eager to leave, Petridge offered up, "Shall I retrieve the specimens, doctor?" He moved to the hatch that barricaded the rest of the world from Whit's private little biosphere.

The old man shook his head. Petridge couldn't seem to do anything right, in his presence, or otherwise. "What? What is it now?" he said, the whiny 5 year-old version of himself creeping into his vocal chords. "We'll go over there in a second," Whit replied, vague in every sense of the word.

He was rummaging around, pushing decanters and alembics this way and that. One of the vials threatened to spill to the floor and Petridge leaped beneath where he calculated its planned trajectory to be within the next five seconds, and caught the glass right before it shattered on the ground.

Not so much as a simple "thank you" came from Whit's direction. He was still busy looking for something terribly important, no doubt. "My thermometer..." he said, patting down his coat pockets. "Have you seen—" Petridge, righting himself, plucked the thermometer off of a shelf, also hanging from chains in the glass ceiling, and petulantly handed it over to Whit, who bowed his head slightly.

Petridge rolled his eyes. The next second, somehow Whit was halfway out the door, "Come now, no dawdling," he said, about to shut the hatch on Petridge's hand. Pet mumbled a light, "How the..." and followed him on toward the house.

Petridge stepped inside the dark apartment Whit kept not five feet from the terrarium. He immediately lost his sight to the darkness, blinking rapidly to cull the dust from settling atop his eyelids.

Fumbling forward in the direction of Whit's voice, his breath caught down the wrong pipe. He choked and ran into a cobweb.

This day is just getting more and more awesome, he thought to himself, waving his arms this way and that, combat-ant against any creature, big or small, that might try to pene-trate his precious personal space.

"I knew there was something peculiar about these birds," Whit said. He was comfortably situated at a dimly lit table, off in the corner farthest from the door. He was peering through a monocle he held up to his right eye.

Bent over, he turned his head to the side to look at Petridge. Petridge was staring intently at the doctor who was in turn star-ing intently at the birds on the table.

They noticed each other noticing each other, then Petridge jerked, standing up too quickly and they almost bumped heads. The doc raised an eyebrow as if to say, "Everything ok, my boy?" Petridge cleared his throat.

He pushed on his spine, stretching, and straightened up, "I meant to do that," he tried to say using body language.

Cleaning his specs on his shirt, Petridge tried to see what Whit saw. He placed his glasses back on the bridge of his nose, gave his nostrils a good twitch to situate them, turned his head to the side, and covering one nostril, he blew vigorously from the other, propelling snot upon the floor.

"Excuse you," Whit said, as Petridge proceeded to expel some latent spider beds from his other nostril. "It's a good thing Victoria wasn't here to see that." Self-centered and still twitching, Petridge said, "Who?" continuing to dust himself off. "You'll see, soon, I suppose. In one way or another."

Disgusted, Whit shook his head, returning to his work. Petridge dismissed the elder's chatter. Whatever, old man.

He nodded at the birds laying prostrate on the table. "What's wrong with them?" Petridge asked. Whit sighed. "You know what you did. Like I couldn't see right through the act, just as soon as you brought them in."

He sighed, shaking his head, and pocketed his monocle. He walked to the fridge, floorboards creaking underneath him, a trademark of all of those old Midwestern houses.

He cracked a beer and pulled another one out for Petridge. Arriving back to where his pupil stood, he held up a finger, "Ah, wait a moment," he said and retrieved his bottle of whiskey. He dusted it off with a gust of breath. Fffffft. Then he wiped the remaining dirt from the cap and unscrewed the top. He took a big swig of the stuff, swallowed, and licked his lips. "Ahh," he said, handing the bottle over to Petridge.

Petridge turned the bottle to look at the label. "Kentucky bourbon," he said, surprised. "You don't see much of this anymore, do ya?" he took a small sip and grimaced, flicking out his tongue. "Don't do that, my friend," Whit said. Petridge was scraping his tongue along the tips of his incisors. "Huh?" Pet asked, salivating beyond control. "The air. Why don't you suck in a little bit of air, now. Let it flow over your tongue. Do like the Russians do." Petridge did as he was told and at once started doing a little involuntary jig, his body contorting in strange dimensions.

"Bleh!" He pulled out his pocket inhaler and got a big hit of nitrous to quell the urge to puke his brains out.

While Whit was laughing and slapping him on the back,

tears flicked from his eyes with each friendly blow.

Through his coughs and retches, his eyes landed upon a peculiar-looking box sitting behind glass on the second shelf of the liquor cabinet. Through the dust, somehow the beads and sequins still shown bright, collecting the light, which coalesced and shimmered around its circumference, similar to the way one of Whit's plants might retain water.

Whit slowly withdrew his hand as Petridge wiped his eyes and moved toward the cabinet. Hand half on the glass door knob, he turned to ask Whit for permission, and the elder nodded, taking a seat and lighting a cigar. He went back to work on the birds, inspecting Pet's handiwork.

Petridge stood there, turning the box over in his hands, taking in the ornate engravings within the wood, tracing the patterns of thread sewn in patches covering the cornices.

A few minutes went by before he brought the box to the table. He set it down, and without taking his eyes off of it, he found the bottle of bourbon, unscrewed the cap, and took a drink. His face curdled in the least bit of pain, but he was getting used to it.

He looked up to see Whit looking at him. "Well, go ahead, son. It's just my enamorata," he said. "Your what?" Whit nodded. "I've never heard that before," Petridge said. He lifted the latch on the box and peered inside. A hologram appeared out of the darkness. The recording was a wee bit glitchy, but he could make out a pair of people, skipping along the beach of some distant shoreline. They were breathing heavily, and while they were running, they looked at each other and collided in their winded gallop. As they started revolving around each other, arms outstretched, Pet saw they were drawing closer, going in for a kiss, when right in the heat of the moment, the light glitched out and receded back into the box to simmer and finally die out altogether.

Blinking out of his stupor, Petridge touched Whit's arm, breaking him from the spell the machine held over him. Whit lowered his monocle, caught it as it dropped on its chain, and tucked it into his coat pocket. "What is it, now?" Whit asked. "I'm sorry, it's just. Was that your wife?" Whit responded, "Is. That is my wife. She'll live forever in that box, doomed to the fate of playing on repeat, and I'll keep her alive in my mind," he tapped his temple, looking morose.

It was his turn to take a drink from the bottle. He nodded, wagging an index finger in the air, as if to say, there's something else. Whit could tell Petridge was the sentimental type. He was a hopeless romantic who philandered his way through the women he ensnared, yet he exuded the air of someone who had never truly been in love.

And the kid was curious about it, even felt a deep empathy for those who have lost the ones closest to them. He'd never allowed himself to get too close to anyone, but he found he was vicariously suffering through the loss of his teacher's soulmate.

Whit came back to the table with a gramophone. It was covered in dust, which he blew off the pockmarked cylinders, dotted with rivulets and punctures in the brass indicating which notes played in each time sequence. He cranked the handle, slowly at first, to ween Petridge onto the way the device worked, and the most sorrowful sounds flew from the flower-like trumpet protruding from the top of the music box. His hand sped up, changing the pace of the song, prodding the music to speed up, then slow down, the cadence taking control of Petridge's heartbeat.

The song was simultaneously exalting, then it became as dark as a dying hound's last howl, as if it were beckoning the moon to take notice of him while he was mourning over his lonely fate, having taken his own path away from the pack. Then the music sped up again and he saw the animal transform into a wolf, tearing the throat out of a hapless hare who had made the mistake of finding its way into his den.

The music stopped on a jarring last note, and Petridge felt as if he were emerging from the most sordid dream. A single tear trickled down Whit's cheek and Petridge had the innate urge to hug him just then, but that would be callous. How could a hug help mend a broken heart? Like he could possibly give solace to such a man, who has traveled the world and learned the secrets of scientific societies long abandoned by hope or reason.

He straightened his spine and pushed against the arms of the chair, testing the bounds of the prison he suddenly found himself in.

His mind wandered to the bird cages hanging empty on the wall opposite the table where the creatures lay dormant, poked and tested by the man at his side.

22: Party On, Garth

He found her sprawled out on the floor, legs askew, her arms in weird positions, looking like she was playing a game of Twister by herself.

He set his wallet down on the table, then his keys, and peeled back the curtain to reveal she was painting again. Finally, he said to himself.

He kneeled down beside her. "What'cha doin' there, lady?" He kissed her bare shoulder. She wore nothing but a bra and panties, it was that hot in the apartment, but fall was fast approaching. He would soon need to draw the windows closed and do something with the plants...

He was staring at the window, thumb grazing his upper lip in that pensive manner of his. She looked up at him, paint held aloft, then splat! A huge chunk of acrylic hit the paper, drawn down with the slow drip of gravity's pull.

She looked down, "Huh." She placed her finger on the underside of the Popsicle stick and flicked upward, the downward resistance to the wood sending a smear of green sailing across the floor, looking something like a CAD drawing of a bacterial disease or a system of tree branches clawing their way toward freedom.

She noticed some paint landed on the carpet a foot away, a glaring smudge embedded in a secret hiding place too far underneath the couch to obey logic.

"Whoops!" she said and spit on a paper towel to dab it away. "Hey, hey," Mire interjected. "Just leave it, OK? It's all right."

"Ah, shit," she was only doing more damage at this point. She withdrew with a plop and sat like a child who couldn't comprehend a tough math question.

Looking down, she picked a few pieces of stray hair and some crumbs from her moist skin. She hurled them away into the abyss.

Mire gave a plant one last jiggle, toying with the the strange cactus that somehow came into its own over the last few months. It started out as a snaking, limp little thing, but all of a sudden it shot upward to become the tallest plant they owned. He was startled, yet proud by its will to live.

Erizabet was going at it. He leaned over to inspect her work. "Interesting," he said, standing back up. He turned his head this way and that, realizing she wasn't working on a single painting, she was slathering a field of 3"x5.5" postcards arranged in four rows of five.

"What're you doing in there?" Mire asked, tapping the side of her head. "Well, you said you wanted a party, right?" She waved her arm over the mess, like that was explanation enough.

She made a few more dribbles with the paint and stood up, looking over her handiwork. There were colored splotches up and down her legs and her hands were covered to the wrists.

She nodded with a satisfied, "Hmph," and went to rinse off in the kitchen sink. He followed, giving her arms a squeeze. He kissed her on the cheek. She turned around, using a paper towel to scrape underneath her fingernails.

"If you build it, they will come," he said in an ominous voice, enlarging his eyes, his ears flicked back in that way she loved. "Aha!" she said, throwing the paper towel to the trash. "Field of Dreams," they said, simultaneously. They shared a laugh. "Ok, this is getting pretty cheesy," he said and opened the freezer. "How about a pizza?" She stood up on tippy toes and kissed his cheek. "Yes, please."

They handed out their postcards judiciously at the bar the next day, to anyone who seemed kind of cool, or gave off an easy-going vibe.

They mailed out the rest, to friends in Keith's band, their girlfriends, wives, whoever they could think of, really. None of that annoying electronic eBlast bullshit for them. They hated spam and assumed everyone else did, too, so fuck it.

"What the..." said LeeLee, to find a paint-laden piece of paper floating through her doorway when she entered her apartment the next day.

She rarely received mail. It was to the point where she had forgotten she designed a constantly-flowing current comprising an invisible tunnel to deliver physical parcels straight to her dinner table.

She sat down, flipped the card over. "Party in the basement!" the card read. 9/11/2390. Signed, Mire & Riz. "Yeah, all right," she said to an apartment filled with cats, iguanas, frogs, and other manner of wildlife.

She looked up, thinking to herself, *I forgot how handy I was with that stuff.* She got up, dusted off her old computer console, and coughed a little, wafting the air away, "Ahem. Now, what was that last thing I was thinking about doing..."

She booted up the comp and started on a project to automatically detect when food went bad in her fridge, then designed a Rube Goldberg machine that would open the fridge just a smidge, extract the old sauce, lettuce, beans, whathaveyou, and deposit them in her compost pile for more productive means.

After all that's happened, they decided to let go of the grudge and sink back into the lifestyle the three stooges created way back when...

The party was raging downstairs. The couple could hear it through the floorboards. They each took two shots, she had vodka, he had rum, and with a clap, Mire said, "Huzzah!" Now, they were ready.

Petridge was at the bar, talking to a shot glass filled to the brim with a mysterious brown liquid. He was hunched over, nearly half of his body sluiced onto the slimy counter top. If you didn't notice him holding up that shot glass squarely an inch away from his face, you'd think he was just another drunk sleeping it off.

"What are you waiting for?" he whispered softly, pursing his lips close to the glass. "What are you waiting for?"

A slap to his back splashed most of the whiskey over Petridge's leather jacket. "Ah, come on, man," he said, now sitting upright, shaking droplets from his sleeve. He was still holding onto the shot glass.

In this, Riz saw a call to action. She quickly grabbed some napkins from a nearby table and started patting him down. "Damnit, Riz," Pet said, wrenching his torso away from her nursing hands. "I can take care myself," he said with a sneer. Then, finding his manners, he slicked back his hair with the hand steeped in alcohol and corrected himself, "I mean, I got this," he said cooly, like David Arquette in that one greasy drive-in flick.

"Eew, dude," she said, laughing, whipping around, searching for a place to put the trash. "Ah!" she said and darted away.

"So," started Mire, once more slapping his friend on the back, not as hard this time, "What's this I hear about a lady friend?" He raised his eyebrows and pursed his lips, making sucking noises.

Petridge pushed him away, "Naw, it's not like that. She just. She gets me," he said, getting back to his shot glass. Quietly, he repeated, "She gets me."

Mire rolled his eyes, turned to the bartender, two fingers twitching, *bring it on.* The guy poured two tall glasses of his and Riz's old tradition, a beer from the tap with two gingers on the handle.

Riz appeared out of thin air, "Thanks," she said, and sat down next to Petridge. Petridge looked left then right, from one friend to the other, jerking his thumb, his shoulders up, on guard, "What is this?" he motioned back and forth between the two of them. "You here to interrogate me or something?" He raised his eyebrows at the bartender as he was heading back their way. Wiping his hands on his apron, he reached under the counter and brought out a canister of the good stuff, replaced the tube on the output end and set it on the bar. Turning away to assist other patrons, Petridge said, "Oh, not so fast," downed what remained of the shot glass, and raised it.

The bartender was kinda peeved, but he shrugged, "Slow down, fella," he said, monotone. He didn't care one way or another. "Yeah, you too," was Petridge's response. He took a slow drag of the nitrous and when the tube was full of smoke, he sucked the line clean, held his breath, covered the hose with his thumb, and downed the shot.

He exhaled with a grumbling sigh, his eyes immediately turning red, his shoulders loosening, "Ahh yeah," he said and flashed Mire a smug grin.

"Great," he said. "He's on it again, whoopity do," he twirled a finger in the air, sipped his beer, patted down his shirt pockets and hopped off the barstool. He looked at Riz. "Smoke time. You comin'?"

Her mouth was full, so she nodded instead, jumped down, swallowed, and followed him out the door, leaving Petridge to his own devices.

"It's like he's losing his mind or something," she said, once they were outside. She lit a cigarette. "Pssh, he's never really been all there," Mire said. "He's British, after all. Those guys can take a beating."

She laughed disconcertedly, expelling smoke into the night air. "I don't exactly know what you mean, but I'll take it."

Nervous, she flicked too hard on her cigarette, almost breaking the thing in two. She just lost the cherry instead. "Um, can I see your lighter?" she asked, and Mire leaned in to light her cigarette. "Thank you!" she said in a singsong voice. He laughed and pinched her. "Hey!" she said, smarting, rubbing the spot on her arm.

"Did you hear Petridge is into someone? Like, an actual human being this time?" They both looked up to see a shooting star streak a trail across the sky. They looked at each other, smiled, and their lips met briefly, before Petridge came stumbling out of the bar with a chick on his arm, none other than the swing dancing instructor.

"Howdy, y'all," she said, waving a hand over her head, landing in that all too familiar gesture, pointed toward Riz. Riz raised an eyebrow, skeptical, looked down at the hand extended, looked back at the woman.

Isn't that the chick from the club? Her hair's different or something, but I could swear... She decided, to hell with it, and took her hand, being careful not to linger on the shake, lest some of her soul be sucked away in the interim. "Mandy," offered the woman, "Erizabet," Riz responded. "Woah! Now, I couldn't have thought up a better name if I had come up with it myself," she said. *Did she just say the same thing twice? Or am I crazy...*

She shook her head, clearing the thoughts away. More for Pet's benefit than theirs, she said, "It's a pleasure to make your acquaintance," she lit up another cigarette. Mire gave her a look, don't push this, his eyes said, she shrugged, What, I'm not hurting anybody.

She took a drag, offered one to Mandy. "Mandy, is it?" Mandy refused, holding up her hand. "No, thanks, I don't smoke," she said. "Well, isn't it Pet's lucky day. Does she drink?" the question was aimed at Petridge, who was scanning the sky for signs. Somebody save me, please, his heart was screaming on the inside. He pulled Mandy closer, his hand on her hip, and lit his own cigarette. The three of them looked around, testing the waters. Mire wore a look of indifference.

Riz stubbed out 3/4 of an unfinished smoke. She turned to head back inside. Mire caught her arm to go in with her, "Don't leave me with them," he murmured under his breath, half jokingly. She laughed, jerking her head, this way, and she led him inside, but not before Mire turned to get one last look at the happy couple. Mandy was running a manicured nail along Petridge's chin and licking her lips. Part of him trusted that his friend wouldn't end up fish bait, but his throat was doing something beyond his control. Gulp.

Back inside, the bar was stuffed with bodies. People were laughing and shouting and fighting their way to the bar, raising their arms over their fellow compatriots to hand the bartender a chip in exchange for a beer, then placing their hands over top of the brim of the glass. Arms reaching toward the ceiling, they side-stepped their way out of the fray.

"Who are all these people?" Riz asked, looking around the bar for her unfinished beer. Everyone was babysitting their bounty; a scant few coveted a single drink, but most of them huddled around a drink and a shot glass or a drink, a shot glass, some smokes, or other apparatus. They all just wanted to get to that point where their equilibrium would finally settle down, the cost of being alive suspended from thought, pushing the worries far away for a time.

They found a table where a few of their close friends lingered, either draped over the arms of an overstuffed chair or leaning into the mass of nachos piled high, scooping their fill until they had no more hands to even carry themselves.

Mire spotted Whit and sidled up in a tight spot next to him, patting his lap so Riz knew where to sit. Whit and Mire nodded in greeting, the space too close for handshakes, and they immediately began talking about the latest development in cybernetic surgery.

Riz looked around, analyzing an ear here, a hairdo there, until she recognized a gal pal from what seemed like a lifetime ago. "Raquelle, what up?" she said, leaning over the table in excitement, knocking beers and some food around, smearing some cheese on her shirt. "Awww," some guy said. Another girl said, "Gross," and they went back to their own conversations.

"Oh, you know, this and that," Raquelle said, "When'd you do that?" she pointed to Riz's wrist. "This?" lifting her hand higher to give her friend a better look. "I think I had this when we last hung out," she said, looking more closely at her tattoo. It looked a little faded to her, maybe two years old? Five? She wasn't quite sure. "Anyway," she didn't have a beer to sip on. "Wanna go to the bar?" Raquelle looked at her drink, it was halfway full, and downed it in one gulp. "Yeah, sure." She reached out a hand to extract Riz from the teeming blur of people.

Almost immediately, she lost Raquelle in the crowd. Squeezing her tiny frame in between a sweaty couple, a stinky bum, and a punk-type guy, she bought her drink, and rubbing herself on the backs and tits of the nameless crush, she clutched the beer to her breast and made herself small, ducking between legs and purses to get back to where Mire sat in the inner room.

Tar-tar, the waitress, so named because she once brought them tartar sauce when they'd asked for ranch, "Maybe she doesn't know her textures," Riz said, to which their friend Mitch replied, "She doesn't have a feel for consistency." "She has no sense of viscosity," Riz replied. Mire was there just rolling his eyes. They passed synonyms back and forth on that fateful night all those months ago.

Mire thanked the girl for taking away their decimated tray of what was once nachos supremo, and he pulled out a card game fit for a gang of 4 or 14.

"Even numbers," he said. He made up the game himself. He had a head for numbers, logic and reason followed, and somehow this one wasn't like the others. It was challenging, and those playing always seemed to find something to laugh about.

He was in the middle of explaining the rules, when Riz said, "Show them the extended version." Mire replied, "Naw, truncated should be just fine." She laughed, a bit tipsy at this point, saying, "Truncated, ah. That is one fun word to say. Truncated." She repeated the word over and over, once using her arm to demonstrate the likeness of a mammal that might somehow be related. No one got it.

"OK, quit it," Mire said playfully, and shuffled the cards in his own special way. "If we're playing with four people, which it looks like we are, I'll deal three cards each, don't look at them!" He was glaring at his friend Steve, who was growing red in the face. "Now, each of us picks up a fourth card."

Some of them got a grasp the longer they played, while the other two were becoming increasingly confused.

"I'm having a smoke," Petridge said. His lady peeped up, "I'll come, too," which sounded more like oll gum tuh.

Austeria, Steve, Matt, and Keem hung around, joking about what the next big thing would be. Matt offered in what felt like a strange version of English comme Russian, "You know, we haven't had many pronounceable sports, lately, yeah?" Steve responded, "Huh?" Leaning over his girl. "What's he saying. I can't understand a word he's saying." She simply waved him off, trying to dig deeper into the conversation.

Austeria: "No, see, we don't need any more sports, mmkay. They were, like, totally detrimental to our inner psyche. Like, I mean," Steve nudged her in the elbow, "Hun, cut the valley girl shit?"

She looked around the table, realizing these weren't idiots she was talking to. "All right, all right," she said, taking a sip of her drink. She leaned into their huddled faces, "So, sports were this religious phenomenon, back in the day," she gesticulated for emphasis. "People worshiped athletes like gods. They were our gladiators, displaced from ancient Roman times. But then we evolved, somewhat backward in a way, I think." She touched a finger to her chin.

"We trended toward music. We moved forward in time, on such a small scale, really, because time is relevant, and we've only been here for a few years, compared to the age of the universe and—" Steve gave her a look, meaning, get to it.

"We're advancing so rapidly, dear," she glared at him, "That we are reliving our history's myths in fast forward. So," she took another sip, all eyes on her, "What was I saying, dear?" Steve rolled his eyes. "I don't know, honey. Music, was it?"

She snapped her fingers, giving him a jolt. They were in such close proximity, for a split second he thought she meant to poke him in the eye or something. "Right! Music, now, then, became our god, right? DJs. Back in the mid 2100s, we were gyrating wildly in clubs and at concerts just begging to lose ourselves in the music." Riz was unconsciously nodding along to the band playing lazily on the patio.

Of course no one really listened to all that much music anymore, except in the antiquated hip-hop clubs that survived somehow, tucked away into unmentionable alcoves of deplorable blight here and there, but her movements drove the point home.

"See!" Austeria pointed at Riz, who promptly turned her head to sidestep further embarrassment. "No, don't be embarrassed, shoog," she twiddled her freshly manicured nails as if she were the one in charge, and when this woman told you to stop acting shy, well then, you cut that shit out.

"I think this girl was born in the wrong decade, am I right?" Mire shrugged, nodding in agreement, "Well, yeah, actually—" Riz gave him a quick jab in the ribs, "Ow, what the—"

"Anyway," Austeria took another sip and looked at her glass, which was just melting ice now. "That phase died out. Well, not completely," she looked at Riz, who quickly looked down, and started picking lint from Mire's shirt.

He batted her hands away and they started mock fighting, slapping floppy hands in each other's general direction, making a few of their friends laugh.

The girl continued, "Now, where do you think we are, hmmm?" The couple's hands slowly came to rest on the table, they glared at each other, playing, not really good at acting mad, but that was their routine, just a little fake fight every once in a while. That and the tickling.

"The trough!" she exclaimed, startling the table. Tar-tar approached the table, giving a few of them weird looks. She thought they were all crazy. She placed a few of their empty glasses on a tray, and without saying a word, walked away. She really was one of the least friendly waitresses.

"We're back to the old ages, don't you see?" Steve was itching for a smoke and was about to get up from the table when his girlfriend tugged his shirt, pulling him back down. He'd heard this theory a thousand times.

She cleared her throat. "Just look at us," she said, spread her arms wide, whacking Matt's glasses in the process, "Watchit," he said, squinting and massaging the bridge of his nose. The bar was growing louder and louder, people shouting over the din, trying to best one another. It was chaos.

"We worship the drink! Just like those back in the middle ages! I mean, they dressed themselves in lead before they went to the annual ball. Just like them Wild West folks took laudanum in small doses, just to stay calm through all the ruckus. And so on and so on," she concluded, crossing her arms in a perfunctory manner. She sat back in her chair and looked around for the waitress. "Of course, it all ended up killing them in the end, anyway."

The crew was silent. Mire got it right away. He had spent his life reading historical fiction, seeing the ins and outs of the wayward world tumble before itself, set on self-destruction, only to bounce back in full riot gear. The self-righteous masses proclaiming destiny this and savior that, but he knew the truth and he could see it in Austeria's eyes. She knew it, too. "Everything's cyclical," he said, twirling his pack of cigarettes in his hands. "We do what we need to do in order to survive, then when we get bored of that, we fuck it up. When we can't remember how to get back to the good old days, we pick our way through life like Neanderthals. We rediscover the same technologies... we just give them different names," he said, his voice petered out into a whisper near the end.

He was staring wistfully through the center of the glass table. There were miraculously unmussed patches of clear glass amid swaths of greasy smudges, beer drippings, and little flecks of black olives. He was absentmindedly looking at their shoes. Some wriggled or crossed then uncrossed. He couldn't tell whose feet were which at this angle.

She couldn't tell if it was all the alcohol in her system, choking her arteries, stemming the blood flow, or if it was actually getting chilly out. She could have sworn she was sweating bullets yesterday, sitting still. She rolled over to find Mire had left for work already. "It's frickin' Sunday," she said to the room. "Ugh."

She got up, poured herself a cup of his leftover coffee and sat down to do some writing. Goosebumps sprouted along her arms and legs. "What the heck..." she went back to the room, put on some pajama pants and a long-sleeve shirt. She tugged at the wrist cuffs. "Mhmm... I missed long sleeves..."

Distractibility got the best of her and she stood over a painting she'd been working on for the last three days. She held her cup of coffee with two hands to help warm her up. She took a sip.

"Eh, this is kinda gross..." referencing the sludge brew and the painting simultaneously. She picked up the canvas, shoved it in the closet. "Ugh!" Thus ended her little painting streak, for what it was.

23: Dream-Induced Epiphanies

She didn't see anyone else around, and when she went to pee she heard that the bar downstairs was quiet.

She packed a bag, donned some travel-appropriate clothes and climbed the fire escape up to the roof. She had never flown a spaceship before, but she wasn't afraid to try new things. And Mire had taken her up so many times, she was sure she had the button pattern down just fine.

The computer responded to her voice command and the engines kicked on, almost as quiet as a desktop fan. She wasn't sure if the ship was in a more relaxed mode or if she should push it into overdrive to kick-start the thing and get it off the ground. She was beginning to realize she might have been distracted by how glorious Mire looked at the helm, and now that she was on her own, she wasn't sure what she should do next.

The moment she touched fingertips to forehead in exasperation, a tiny person slammed up against the fiberglass enclosure. Erizabet jumped with a start, her hand flying to her chest to check her heart rate.

She told the computer to open the hatch. There was a little girl standing there. She couldn't have been more than 6 years old, her eyes reaching out to Riz, plaintive and nervous.

Her right hand dug grooves into her dark skin, her nails turning the flesh a shade lighter, almost pink, where she unconsciously scratched.

"Um, Miss?" she said. Riz blinked in disbelief. "Can't I come up, too? I've never been in one of these before," she said, moving her head this way and that, taking in all of the controls.

Before she knew what she was doing, Riz extended her hand to offer the girl a lift, and the girl placed her tiny fingers inside Riz's palm.

Riz leaned forward, and with one hand on the edge of the door, she pulled the girl into the cockpit, then shut the hatch.

As the vehicle climbed steadily upward, Riz moved to the side to get a better look at the little girl sitting in her lap. The girl's eyes were wide open, taking in the shrinking land mass below them. Then they broke through the clouds as if through mist, rising higher and higher until they left the atmosphere in a burning tremble and came to hover amid the stars.

"Wow," the little girl said, with her hands on the fiberglass, taking it all in. Riz relaxed a little, settled the throttle to neutral, flipped some switches and pressed some buttons to engage stasis mode.

She wanted so badly to unbuckle the harness and float aimlessly, she didn't care about the bruises she'd see cropping up on her arms and legs the next day as a result of bumping around the cockpit, but she stayed vigilant, noting there was another passenger in here with her. A strange, tiny, little passenger, whose name she didn't catch yet.

"My name's Sally, what's yours?" The girl turned around, reaching out a hand to take Riz's. Partly in shock, Riz's mouth hung agape for a moment, until she felt a little saliva crawling across her lower lip. She sucked it back in and re-established her status as the adult here.

"Ah," she said, shaking the girl's hand lightly, "I'm Riz.

Say," she placed closed fists on her hips, "That's quite an old name for someone of your generation." Sally ignored the slight and continued consuming everything in sight.

Looking at her, Riz thought she saw whole galaxies come tumbling through her eyes, to bounce around and play there, like they had been waiting for just this special person to look upon their beauty, then they willingly committed suicide, throwing themselves into the abyss of her pupils.

Riz watched in fascination as the girl stared out at the vastness of space. Unwavering, she was perpetually enthralled by the sight of it, as if she had a concept of what it was, but never saw it in person. Now, that she understood it was real, she couldn't let go.

"Want to see something cool?" Riz asked, wrenching the girl from her reverie. Blinking as if coming out of a dream, Sally turned around, arms still crossed on the sill of the glass. She nodded solemnly.

"Hold tight," Riz said, and yanked the joystick backwards, sending them into a circular spin. Sally's arms flew off the glass and her body settled back into the seat. She didn't know the meaning of the word, but she was starting to experience vertigo for the first time and she shut her eyes, as Riz began to laugh, and the spacecraft spun faster and faster on its axis.

They were verging on 10 Gs when Sally heard some disconcerting sounds issuing from directly behind her. The woman who a moment before was almost cradling her in her arms, started convulsing, her legs spasming beneath her, shoulders twitching.

Thumping up and down, she felt as if she were on one of those rickety rides at the county fair, the ones that were engineered to make you feel as if they would break at any moment, though in the back of your mind, you knew a thousand people came before you and a thousand more would come after, so there was really no reason to panic. At that point, she would throw her arms up and scream, giddy with the thrill of it, but this was no kiddie ride.

At that moment, she feared for her life.

With Riz's wrists fumbling limply at the controls, the girl pried the woman's fingers off the joystick and tried to regain control of the vehicle. The emergency systems activated as the spaceship grew conscious of an intruder's fingerprints on the controls.

Sally took a deep breath, closed her eyes, and scanned the online archive for piloting instructions for the XLR–27z, downloading the pattern recognition software into her brain stem.

Realizing Riz was unconscious, she pulled her thumb forward and placed it on top of the main ignition screen to the right of them, thus giving Sally clearance to add her name to the command registry.

She regained control of the spaceship, calmly listening to the slow rhythm of Riz's inhalation to exhalation ratio, diverting her attention to five things at once, a skill uncanny to girls her age, but she was beginning to wonder if she wasn't a tad bit different from the other kids in her class. Not everyone learned how to pilot an antique spacecraft at the drop of a hat.

The girl downloaded the schematics of the engine while she was at it. *Who knew when that information might come in handy?* she thought. Who knows? The thing could blow and she might have to put it together again, all while saving a woman's life.

While she was deploying the landing gear, veering toward

the home beacon displayed on the screen, her mind wandered. The part of her brain not currently allotted to carry on the task of controlling her limbs, and thus pilot the ship, was busy imagining what Riz's life was like outside of this humble bubble.

She pictured her as an artist, or someone sensitive enough as to harbor a proclivity toward altitude sickness. But then, why would she pull that stunt back there in the first place? Why would she try to impress a girl she didn't know? Was she a pilot? Has she been doing this sort of thing her whole life, and perhaps planning a little trip to the moon and back, she didn't anticipate taking on a passenger, so she didn't expect she'd need to pop a couple of extra oxygen pills or the like, as one forum on spacecrafts intimated.

Touching down on the roof of the apartment, she unbuckled the harness that tethered the two of them together, and Riz slid sideways, mumbling, "No, you can't trust anybody," a little drool creeping out of the side of her mouth.

While the engine was still running, the girl turned and lifted Riz's shirt sleeve to wipe at her mouth. She killed the power and resolutely looked around at the control panels. Watching the red and orange lights grow dim, she listened to the exhaust pipes puff out their final belch for the day.

She triggered the hatch to let in some fresh air and stepped off of the bench where her feet had been resting for the duration of the trip, then she climbed down backwards out of the vehicle.

She stood there staring at Riz while she slept, pristine in her tranquility of dreams, then thought better of it and sat down, knees pulled to her chest, to wait out the woman's nap.

In her head, Riz was somewhere else entirely. She was lucid

dreaming. She conscientiously looked down at her hands to make sure they were still attached. She felt the rings along her fingers, giving the bracelet on her wrist a little jiggle. *Huh*, she thought. *I wonder who I am this time.*

Surfacing up from introspection, she took a look around. People walked by wearing strange clothes. There was an abundance of foliage, the exotic kind, like one of those trees you'd see in Africa, the roots rising up and away from the ground, trunk tapering toward a central point where the branches sprung forth to fan out about 30 feet in circumference, evenly around the crux of the tree.

Juxtaposed with a crop of Japanese Blossoms, the Venus flytraps stood out in ostentatious absurdity. *Guess they ran out of budget for that square foot of territory*, she thought.

After noticing a few sharp glances her way, she realized that she was at a zoo of some sort, and people were rushing around, pointing their bulky cellphones at creatures locked in cages.

When they came within a foot of her, they saw her staring upward, like a wood nymph scorned, a woman out of place in the universe.

One woman covered her son's eyes as they hurried passed. While blindfolded, he still tried in vain to take a lick of his vanilla ice cream cone. Riz looked down at her attire: a tight tank top exposing an exorbitant amount of cleavage almost up to the nipple, cropped up in a pink push-up bra and a halter that stopped midriff. She threw up her hands, aghast. *Oh, what the hell.*

Yanking down her short shorts, no doubt she had some under butt showing, too, she took a deep breath and walked forward, trying to play the role of this haughty slut-sized being who was, for some reason, alone in a zoo.

When she approached what appeared to be an empty exhibit, save for tall grasses and some flowers dotted along the way, she stopped, curious, and read the sign stitched up along the chain-link fence. "The vulpus lagopus, or Arctic fox, is native to the northern hemisphere and is adapted to cold environments," the sign read.

Riz, or whoever this body belonged to, looked around, tasting the air, feeling it might be a bit too summery for a cold-weather animal to be prowling about. Maybe it was in hibernation, or something, she thought. She read on: "The Arctic fox is found in Norway, Canada, Alaska, Russia, Greenland..." her eyes glazed over, yeah, anywhere but here.

I hate when they transplant these delicate little... her eyes glossed over a few other continents and she landed on the fact that the cute little animal depicted in the photo was entirely carnivorous. *Hmm,* she thought. *Well, what's with all the grass?*

She moved to the side of the fenced area and pressed her nose against the hot iron, warmed from the sun. She tried to discern some movement within the grasses and almost gave up, until a puff of brown and grey fur leapt from the southeast corner of the cage, then almost as quick as it appeared, disappeared again.

She rose up from her position, arms no longer resting on haunches, and said, "Huh. Well, I'll be," she turned away from the cage, eyes lingering on the last spot she saw the creature.

Walking along the designated path, she grew thirsty, and reaching around behind her back, she found it was adorned with a pack. She slid her hand up under the mesh compartment on the bottom of the sack and retrieved a bottled water. Unaccustomed to the woman's grip, she crunched the plastic. Her mind wasn't used to the texture of the container. Where she was living now, when she was, they didn't have such things as plastic bottles of water. Or zoos. Or short shorts. All of this was clearly a dream. Or was it?

Was this a real person's body she was inhabiting? Did people really shepherd their kids around to peer into cages at trapped animals who lay panting and starving, craving freedom and a little space while we gawked at them from the other side of the glass?

She was slowly making her way toward the exit of the outdoor exhibit area and came upon a building with a sign that read, Butterfly World. She was immediately intrigued.

She pushed on the door to gain entry, but a young girl, college-age, emerged from out of the bushes. She was waiting for someone to try that trick, it seemed.

She had a red-tailed Colombian boa strapped around her neck, the snake's face rising up from the girl's shoulder to taste the air around Riz. "Oh, that exhibit's closed for the season. Would you like to pet my snake?"

Riz's body convulsed minutely at the thought of coming in close quarters with anything even remotely related to a serpent. Part of her mind, the one lying not quite as dormant now as it was 15 minutes ago, thought, *Eeew, where are its legs?* And Riz shrugged her off, pushing the naïve one back down, and stretched out her arm to stroke the scales along the boa's back. "Ohh, you're warm, he really likes you," the girl with the name tag reading "Meryl" said, raising her arm to give Riz a better view. Riz made sure to pet the snake correctly, moving her hand from head to tail, not to disrupt the poor thing's scales.

"I'm Mandy," came a voice she didn't recognize, and her head bobbed involuntarily. "I'm Riz," said the girl with the snake. That's when things started to get a little hazy.

"Mandy, Meryl, Meryl, Mandy," she mumbled in her sleep. "Gayle!" She shouted, jerking forward. She was starting to come to, her back stiff from where she lay half in, half out of sleep. She lay back down in her tomb of a bed, the sheets a shroud of her unbecoming. She gazed out the window and longed for snow.

She felt beads of sweat trickle down her back, spreading out from behind her knees. She awakened from one of those fever dreams, thinking, "Now, I know who this woman is. She's a shapeshifter, ain't she?" a little bit of her former trailer trash drawl coming out, peeking through the fogginess of dreams. "Now, I think I know what it all means..." she smiled peacefully and passed out once again.

24: She's Just a Sad Witch Bitch

"What do you mean, you want her?" Mire asked. They were walking along West 7th toward downtown St. Paul. She was draped over his arm, and telling him to play it off, so they didn't seem so suspicious. "They can't catch me this way," she explained not 20 minutes earlier.

"Well, there's a certain order to things," she said, setting the pace for the both of them. They were passing by a hot dog stand when a man stretched out his hand and swiped a piping hot brat along the bottom of Mire's nose. He let out a sound of disgust, wiping his nose on the cuff of his coat. Gayle stood aside, laughing, as he used his shirtsleeve to wipe away what remained of the lingering grease. They turned right down Jackson and she proceeded to enfold him in her charms once again.

He could tell she took extra care today to divest herself of all traces of her otherworldly bondage to the dark side.

"So, the thing is, Mire," she began with that strange accent of hers, a conglomeration of a thousand languages acquired over time. It was a wonder she could speak English fluently at all.

He was staring down at her feet, the way each toe hit the pavement first, before the ball of her foot, criss-crossing, one foot in front of the other, like someone he'd seen in a movie.

She stopped, turned towards him, and placed two fingers

under his chin, directing his eyes towards hers. "Hmm?" he said, foggy.

"And I hate to be the bearer of bad news here, but, we want Riz because she's a hindrance to you and your work." He creased his brow in consternation. "Now, now, don't get shitty with me."

Beggars, liars, thieves. Right when it comes down to it, you can't trust them in a pinch. Someone decides to turn back the hands of time, and they're too engulfed in their own surreal shitstorm to see what marvelous bounty could be found for them on the other side. *Where did these thoughts come from? Did she just beam them into me?*

Talking to Mire, there on the sidewalk, in the space between the dregs and unreality, she decided to hide her thoughts. Despite her efforts to appear ambivalent, there really was some good to deep, hidden deep inside. She couldn't let her ideas get in the wrong hands, however, and despite the fact she broke the boundaries between hers and Mire's mind for the time being, she needed to keep her designs to herself. From the bottom of her blackened heart, all she wanted was to make the world a better place, one vessel at a time.

So, she smiled in all the right places, moved her hips the way she'd seen other women do it, and yet she knew she couldn't fool him. Not all the way. Like smoke swirling in dust motes at the chance to be seen dancing in a single beam of sunlight, she waited until he could see what she really was, then maybe he could come to love her, and she could be one with this world after all. But then again, maybe some part of Raul is still alive, trapped in that "crystal" or so they call it and she should find her way back to him. Could destroying all life on this planet ultimately bring peace to the greater part of the galaxy? Or, could she fake it somehow? Convince these humans they're all shit outta luck. She didn't have all of the answers, but she was sure of one thing.

There must be a way to get rid of that nagging fly, she thought. Riz didn't trust her at all. And how could she? Women hold grudges against one another, the way an old baseball mitt was like a suction cup on a familiar hand. The suspicion's always there. Everyone's a critic. It's more comfortable that way, you see? You're at odds with the world and that's your safe space. Don't let anything come between what's you and yours. You just don't recognize it until it's all you can feel. The hatred. The guilt.

There was something lingering in the tones of Riz's voice that night at the bar. She did something wrong, didn't she? Gayle realized then, while she duplicitously giggled along with Mire as low-hanging branches stretched down to caress his face. He stumbled, grunted, and whacked them away, "This always happens," he was saying, and Gayle was plotting revenge in the most decadent of ways.

Kill them with kindness. If you can't beat 'em, join 'em. Stupid sayings she picked up along the way, but there was a speck of truth in the words.

She decided she would become Riz's friend. She would talk shop with her, write with her, maybe even take on a different name. But, she'd see in the end. She'll understand that we all want the same thing. To be in love. That's all anyone everyone ever wants isn't it?

Speaking of which, Petridge was on the other side of town, busily trying to shake off his latest lay. He finally ditched the broad from the week before; she had this smell about her that no amount of perfume could hide. There was something inky about the vibes she put off, too. His skin broke out in goosebumps just thinking about it.

Mandy was cute at first. She had that Southern accent. She cleaned up. She cooked him breakfast. She even tidied up a bit. And he couldn't help but crave the feeling of those fingernails sliding down his back...

But, she had a way of getting under his skin. His brain began to grow porous at the sight of her. He would forget things almost as quickly as he had discovered them. There were formulas that lay dormant in his mind, and he made sport of occasionally recalling them all at once. It was a mental exercise, if you will. Then one day, she came over, he lost his nerve, and almost without forethought, all the pathways he'd engrooved within his mind were hidden, like an invisible ant trail suddenly covered with leaves. He fumbled for his memories like a blind man who's been told to assist in the kitchen of a house he'd never visited before...

It was as if she cast a spell over him. She would get this strange light in her eyes when she spoke of home, stroking his chest as they lay together in the dark. His eyesight was bad enough, and in those moments, he couldn't make out any other part of her, save for her eyes. They bore right through him.

And he knew she was lying. The entire time, she lied about where she came from, who she was, and what she did for a living. He didn't care. All that mattered was that she was there. There was a body beside him, most nights, so he didn't mind. Not up until it started to affect his work.

He was hypnotized, to say the least. Once he realized what was happening, it took a week to send her on her way. She never wanted to leave the apartment, saying she could work remotely.

And all the hours he spent tinkering in his apartment, working on those damn birds for the Doc, she was digging through his files. Doc told him. He had cameras rigged all over the place, didn't he know?

And yet... She made him feel like a kid again, and he had to admit, he kinda liked it. He bent to her will and she made him ask her permission to use his own gear.

"Um, excuse me," he would sidle up, meekly, to within a few feet of where she sat, back straight, meditating. His voice was barely a whisper.

He could feel a remorseless power seething within her, and he didn't want to find out what made her tick, what would send her over the edge. He was afraid to admit he liked the thought of one day finding himself face to the floor with one sharp stiletto on his neck.

So, he quietly left his own apartment to find a place to reconcile his dreadful hangover when, come to find out, the bookstore was undergoing renovations.

As soon as he set foot in that neighborhood, he could feel the drills rattling his teeth, the vibrations unhinging his brain from his skull, turning them into liquid goo.

Now, he was stuck at the bar, his second favorite haunt, of course. He couldn't bring this chick to his sacred place, not now. *Just wait it out. She'll forget about you soon enough.* He thought to himself. *Taint Mire's place all you want,* he thought, *but I'ma do me over here.*

"Prost!" He said, to no one in particular, and started down the path to a week-long binge.

25: Demon Babies

She was at once hot and cold. Tiny beads of sweat made their dewy appearance upon her forehead. She shivered and moaned, thinking herself on the verge of death.

She was only in her first trimester and she didn't know if she could make it another month in this condition. "Before it gets better, it's bound to get worse," she heard someone whispering, the origins of which she thought floated somewhere near the ceiling.

"Excuse me?" she called to the heavens? "Who's there?" She decided to get up, slowly, still holding her swollen belly, her face contorting in a stitch of pain.

Habitually, she started boiling up some water to make a little pot of coffee, but somehow her nostrils registered the smell of the beans before she even opened the jar, and her throat clammed convulsively.

Instead, Riz hobbled to the toilet, lifted the seat, and let accumulating saliva dribble down into the viscous pool that refused to flush the night before. Registering a stink of piss and coffee and pickles somewhere, she gagged, releasing the contents of her stomach.

If she couldn't keep down a measly cup of chicken noodle soup after eight hours of digestion, she thought to herself, how could she learn to feed this demon baby growing inside her?

Pushing herself up from the basin, she left one hand on the floor, and with her knee to her chest, she craned her neck, willing her body upward.

Shaking, she stumbled. Her head cracked the rim of the toilet seat. "Fuck!" she screamed. "Can someone fucking help me? God, this is fucking ridiculous."

She struggled and finally found herself standing up. She flushed the toilet, wiped her mouth and with one hand to her forehead, one to her belly, she made her way to the couch to found the robot sitting there, staring out of the window.

"Hey there, friend," she tried to sound as accommodating as is humanly possible, only her voice failed her. Instead, her voice made noises resembling a frog fucking a tree. Splish, croak, gurgle.

"I'm sorry, miss?" Hank said, scooching over to give her room to sit. "Oh, forget about it. Unf," she groaned, settling into the sickly sticky fake leather of the couch.

"Everything just sucks, don't it, buddy?" she asked the android. Still daydreaming, he turned his face away from the window, retaining the lost look of one who's thinking about life on another planet.

At 8 in the morning, a few stars were still visible on the distant horizon. Hank moved a bit of curtain aside to show Riz what he was aiming his sights on. "See that tiny cluster of bright lights, there?" Riz squinted, her vision at once blurred, then came into focus, then retreated back to its more myopic state, the mists around the pupils occluding all save a tiny speck somewhere beyond her periphery.

She turned her head to the side to lose focus of her eyes, and started to recognize the pitter pattering light dance of the stars.

"That's where we came from. All of us," Hank said, looking Riz straight in the eye as she turned her head this way and that, trying to consciously regain use of her post-surgery faculties.

"Your skin. It's got this green tint about it, Riz. Are you not feeling well, my dear?" asked the robot, changing the subject. Shutting her eyes tight, she said, "Oh, forget about it, I'm fine," feigning a smile, and flashing a hand out, to whip away the kind sentiment.

"You're with child. I can see it in your eyes. You're scared aren't you? Where's Mire?" His words came in a rush.

He couldn't control his thoughts, if you could call them that, and before he shut his mouth to withhold further follies, he shared one last intimation of a lingering malaise aimed in the direction of the sky beyond the tinted window pane.

Was it a dream?

"Salience," he said, in a little bird chirp of a voice. They were tracing the lines of each others' fingers, she was lying down in the bed, his elbow was propping him up.

"That's what I thought when I first saw you. That you were there. I always knew you were there, but then one day, that's all there was. You took shape and like a kid newly acquiring the concept of object permanence, you were salient to me. And, that's basically the way it's been ever since."

She awoke in a start to his immediate consternation. He was not a morning person. "What the fuck? What's wrong? What time is it? Are you OK?" He finished, finally becoming the person who was meant to hold her instead of the monster that took over his frame in the wee hours of the day when hadn't had enough sleep.

"I had the worst dream," she said. Groggy, he placated her. "Uh huh," he said, half asleep. She continued on. She was comforted by her own voice, and by relaying the story, she reshaped it, knocking down walls, allowing it to be OK, even if she botched the truth of what really happened in that fully-immersed state.

"It was you and me," she said. "And we were older. Our kids were grown," she said, and he groaned, *Oh, no. Here it goes*, and she continued on. She was still threateningly close to that borderline dream state. She was already living in the future.

"And," she paused. "You killed yourself. For whatever reason. It's unclear, really. Then I killed myself to be with you," he sighed at this point, trying to cover his face with a pillow, wanting to snuff out the rest of what she was saying. "And I popped up in heaven or hell or wherever. I hugged you from behind and you jumped and said, 'Wait, what?' unbelieving. As if I was a dream come unto you through supernatural or otherwise solipsistic means. And you turned around to face me full on, and you asked what I was doing here, and I said I killed myself to be with you."

Mire started snoring. Riz couldn't understand how he immediately fell back asleep, especially after such an alarming revelation, but fuck it, she was halfway through anywho and she was just gonna finish this thing so she could go back to sleep as peacefully as he seemed to be, but the fact is, she couldn't actually go back to sleep after that.

She just lay there dipping in and out of daydreams, repositioning herself until she found she was drooling on his upper arm. She remembered he once said he didn't mind. He didn't think it was gross. "It was sort of cute, actually." She decided to face the wall, then ultimately gave up and just lay there thinking until the alarm came on at 7 a.m.

"I told the children," she continued from where she left off, however much more quietly this time. "I was going to be with you and they would understand and it was probably more of a sweet departing unlike your mishap with the razors."

"And they said they understood and that they loved us... Anyway, it was just a dream." She lay back down, thinking about the image of herself holding her husband from behind, surrounded by ambient light.

She got up while he was still asleep and she made herself some ham and eggs. The old fashioned way. On the skillet. They were both pretty much averse to any new technologies that didn't exactly suit their fancies. Like microwaves or coffee machines. Though, they were both thoroughly addicted to coffee, they just had to French Press it. Even in 2390, 12 years after cerebral cortex coffee demand systems were imprinted. Nowadays, you could get your fix with a placebo, you could imbibe without ever having the dirty bean water pass your living lips, but she wasn't plugged in. She was determined to do things her way... even if it was people like her who were starting fires, causing wars...

She wasn't fully prepared for the day, not knowing exactly what it entailed, she could only come up with a rough sketch of events. She recently quit her job; the commute practically took eons to ascend to. *Why haven't we figured out time travel, yet? Or, better yet, like, super fast, jumbo jets in the form of a gel-molded encasing that surrounds your body...*

She set her coffee down to take some notes. *Now, if I'm going to constrain myself to the same 9-5 schedule, I need to figure out a way to channel my energies in a productive way. All day. Without having anyone to tell me what to do.*

She decided she would divine herself some tasks, and allotted them hourly, soon realizing that the average amount of time she'd need to complete any one project would be about three hours. *Great*, she thought to herself. "So, basically I can get three things done each day at this rate... It's not quite enough to live on, seeing as how I only make 70 chips on this one... let's see, 150 on that, and I haven't yet decided how much to charge this guy for the porno VR helmet... But at least I don't have to sit in front of a computer all day."

A light bulb went off, her hand shot in the air, pointer finger stabbing at the sky. "Wait, yes I do." At that moment, the kitchen light bulb burnt out.

Later on, Mire came home to find her in the shower, at 6 p.m. Mind you, no person in their right mind should be showering at that hour unless you had the day off, putzed around in your pajamas and just then decided to visit the outside world for the first time of the day like he did yesterday.

To say the least, surprise played tricks on his face when he heard some moaning drifting out from the open door to the bathroom. She jumped at the sight of his brown hair poking in on her side of the shower curtain, "It's clinging to my pores, Mire! Help me!"

She was scrubbing vigorously at a mysterious layer of greenish-blue slime that had adhered to her skin. He squinted to get a more focused view, pursed his lips and retreated from the the shower.

"Um, yup. You got into something weird again, didn't you?" She made a gurgling swamp noise in her throat. "Gah! When am I not into something weird? Sheesh," she said, grinding a small towel to smithereens in her hand. "I'm improving that armor gel, duh, silly! And what about you?" she asked, smush-ing her mouth into a tight line as she pressed her face into the oncoming stream. "Ah!" she blinked water out of her eyes. He turned around, and commenced undressing for the night.

"What about you with your robots and stuff? You're just like me, Mire! We're so busy!" She turned off the water and moved the curtain aside. "Hey, wait," she said after she saw him wash his hands and turn to leave.

"Do we have any of that, uh. That, what is it? Rock salt? No..." She stood there, dripping, snapping her fingers, trying to summon up the word from her foggy memory banks. "As usual, babe, I don't know what you're talking about," he said and took off his pants.

He went and sat on the couch in front of his computer, the springs yielding audibly under his weight. He tapped the tiny CPU chip at the nape of his neck, it popped out, he inserted it into the holographic projection machine, and began scrolling through his last few hours at work, scrying for something of note to bring up in conversation.

That was his normal routine, but tonight he had a bit of an epiphany and instead searched the official records of the US Treasury for something resembling a causation for the stink that now came trundling out of her pores in waves.

"Pumice! Pumice, darling. Do we have some?"

Wait, what's this? Out of the corner of his eye, an ad protruded from the nether regions of the deepest trenches of the intranet. The animation rendered slowly, advancing in the Z-plane in 3D.

"We won! Krunk is president. Yipp—!" the cartoon koala bear screeched. He turned on ad-block real quick. "Huh. Why do you even have ads on here?" Riz asked, peeking over his shoulder. "You know. Sometimes..." he tried to respond to her, but then his eyes glazed over. He was reading.

Like pretty much every cultural phenomena, she blocked out politics like it was a bad habit she "didn't have". Mire, on the other hand, paid attention to the entire election, all the way through, yet somehow he didn't see this coming.

"What the..." he said. "What, honey?" Riz asked, standing so close to him, he could practically feel his skin growing clammy from her humidity.

She was busy pressing buttons on that neck cage of a hair drying device, plugging in coordinates for quadrants of hair to make certain sections instantly dry, while others fizzled out on their own throughout the rest of the night, to become more of the naturally squiggly variety.

The numbers above him gleaming and pulsing, shattered as he grunted, "You smell, Riz. Do you mind?" Her machines were programmed to be sensitive to his needs. They drew in inflection, hormones, and body language like an obedient dog might have in years past.

She could feel the cage quake with a minute shudder as the AI trembled in fearful anticipation of the next command. "Off you go, Rex," she said and the locking mechanism disengaged with a clunk to the hard floor. "Eesh," he said, hastily lifting his legs. "Fuck, you almost damaged me. You know, I need those phalanges." "Gawd, you're so weird," she responded, drying off the remainder of her hair her own way, ripping through the tangled mess with her fingers.

She plopped down next to him, ignoring his protests. "So," she said. "What'cha got goin' on, then, huh?" As repulsed as he was by the rotting egg and vinegar smell, he couldn't take his eyes off the screen.

While he scrolled through one page of memes, his brain stem collected and stored temporary data on the 360-degree view he had of the world, where he picked up on a gaggle of Asian chicks down the street, who were cheering on their favorite cartoon character while he gave his victory speech on live stream.

Bros in line at SA stopped in their tracks, turned away from the candy bar display and started high-five'ing. Old ladies danced with their canes, presenting them aloft in a silent salute, their eyes held shut, while they gyrated to the beat of an old song most of the population didn't know anymore.

Riz couldn't see what he saw; she could only infer. Nodding, she said, "Hmm... Hmm? What's going on, love?" She leaned in close and he shivered, a disgusted "Geeeahh," rolled out of his mouth when he got a good, involuntary whiff. "Ugh!" He pushed her away from him on the couch.

"Look," he said, turning off private mode on the display. A 2D screen materialized in front of them to display a tricolored character sketch of a disproportionately beefy man. "Krunk. From the *Emperor's New Groove*?"

For once, she could admit she wasn't privy to the reference. She was normally the one who was well-read when it came to those stupid old movies.

"We elected a fucking 600-year-old cartoon for president, Riz. Do you know what this means?" He was overexcited. She could see the oil practically pushing its way out of his skin. He didn't sweat, he just filmed a little.

"I mean, how the fuck does that work?" "Well, so...," she said. "He's a talking head sort of figure, then."

Mire scoffed, "Yeah, they all are, but... do you know what this means?" She shook her head. "One man, erm, person can no longer be trusted to run the country. This guy, this figure is some sort of android they built to reconcile all of their differences, boiled down inside a walking, talking bit-infested flesh-bot, who will do whatever they want. No more wars, no more bipartisan bullshit. It's gonna be smooth sailing from here, right?"

Riz fully accepted the idea. Why not? Why has it taken so long to come to a conclusion such as this? They engineered their own leaders, since the dawn of man, but instead of whispering in his ear or pushing bribes on him, now they could simply flick a switch and the thing would execute every command at their whim. *What luck. Fascism you could vote for. Isn't that sweet?*

"Well, isn't this reality a piece of work... I'm going to bed. Better to dream up a different life than contemplate the minutiae of this one for a second longer..." Mire went back to his studies.

He did a little more digging and found that his hypothesis was false. The president was actually a real person, hollowed out to believe he was the leader of a country. They reprogrammed his neural networks so he truly thought he had the life of the cartoon Krunk. *Well, that's disappointing.*

After Riz fell asleep, Mire decided he'd take a break from the screen. He was craving the feeling of damp spring air on his skin. So, he took a walk.

He headed to the forest. In the city, people honked, shouted, and cursed at one another over the outcome of the election. Or, at least that's what he chocked it up to. He gave them an excuse to be crazy at this most peaceful time of evening.

Riz passed out at about 10 p.m., which is unusual for her, but she said she's been stressed and konking out, ignoring the world, behooves her delicate state of mind. He just wanted her to be warm and happy.

"Maybe they're always like this on a Saturday night," he

thought. He doesn't often stray far from the screen when she's home. He tried to do his own thing, so she can paint or explore the realm of wherever she goes deep in the recesses of scribbling pen mystery.

After a few miles of highway sidewalk navigation, he finally reached the entrance to the state park. He liked to take the path not taken, and to his surprise, he soon found himself almost hugging a tree, trying to navigate a path bent back on a 45 degree angle.

It was dark this time of night, and he squinted downwind to see a well-woven path, engrooved by years of bikers risking their lives to get through the trail. He stumbled a bit on a protruding root and looked up at the moon for reassurance and experienced an instant of vertigo, his head tilted slightly back out of control. His arm flew out to steady him on a nearby tree and he regained his footing, remembering he was close to his destination and there would be full light soon. Pressing on, he turned to find a shimmering lake, illuminated by the moon. He walked to the edge of the rickety wooden pier, glancing upon high school graffiti as he settled into his seat. "Carlos loves Rebecca" and so on. He sat as close to the edge of the dock as he could, swung his legs over the water, rested his arms on the log above, and peered out onto the lake.

It was probably the smallest lake in Minnesota. There's no way it was man-made. All tucked away from civilization. It was his happy place. The exhaustion was well worth it, it was part of the journey. He thought, you exhaled all that nonsense you'd been keeping in, just to take the time to appreciate the splendor that nature had to offer you, hidden just on the other side of the highway, where maybe one family celebrated their long-awaited family reunion in full sunlight and somewhere far away, a bicyclist tested his gear-challenged mechanisms sometime near dawn.

Mire found an otherworldly calm when looking out over the water at night. It reminded him of his days on the beach as a child. Maybe he craved loneliness. Maybe it was the sounds of the cicadas that soothed him, but after a spell he was feeling more relaxed. He was ready to go home and make some music.

Riz, on the other hand, was tossing and turning in bed. Her anxiety levels were peaking out, according to the lizard robot Mire devised as her personal dream diary interpreter and part-time confidante.

Because she insisted her companions have some semblance of emotional capacity, this guy was on the verge of tears, trying to decide whether to wake her or not. Scenarios ticked by in its desolate little cranium as he weighed the options.

Scenario A: Wake her. She may recall nothing and, in fact, feel all the better about it. Then, allowing herself to fall back asleep, she'd find another more suitable realm to enact her most mundane fantasies.

Scenario B: Wake her up. She remembers everything, cries, and condemns you to robot purgatory where you'll be scrapped for parts and melded together with other monstrosities, becoming an amalgamous atrocity while your soul is chopped up into cubits, digitally rendered meat laying couched inside some other metal demon body.

Scenario C: Let her sleep. She'll figure it out on her own, then wake up later to tell you her dreams, so she can find an iteration of a pattern in non-sequential events and solve the mystery of the connection between sleep states and waking life.

Scenario D: Let her sleep. She'll soon find her dream's propelled her into an abyss of perpetual horrors, the likes of which may embalm her in a powerful lucid dreaming state, where she'll remain for all eternity, unable to bring herself back to reality. Ever.

Then Mire came home and flipped on the light. "Oh, yeah. She went to sleep," he almost forgot. Satisfied with his station as sole executor of the apartment for the time being, he shut the door, cast his keys upon the table, and stretched his back, emitting a comfortable, yet quiet yawn into the smoky kitchen air.

Blinking groggily, he shuffled over to the fridge and grabbed a beer. Taking the magnetic bottle opener off the rack, he popped the top and took a swig. "Burrrp," he belched, saying the word aloud as he did. He rubbed his stomach and went back to the fridge, looking for something to snack on.

Out of habit, he stood there, staring in a daze, until he heard some weird sounds coming from the other side of the wall. "Riz," he said aloud, letting the fridge snap shut in response.

Sidling up next to her in bed, he crawled under the covers and held her. He whispered in her ear, "I love you I love you I love you I love you..." and she started to relax.

Half asleep, she turned her body toward him and nuzzled her face as close to his chest as she could, attempting to physically penetrate his skin.

He reached down and pulled her legs up to squish her body into a tight ball and squeezed her until his arms hurt. He fell asleep with his contacts in again, the robot on the shelf opposite them let out a sigh then downshifted his CPU into low-power mode and presumed to doze off in tandem.

26: " 'Side action', that's what they called me in high school."

"Hi, sir. What can I interest you in, today?" Mire was sitting in his pajamas, staring at a customer who was likely also sitting in his pajamas, or maybe he was naked, who knows? Unlike having to deal with people in real life, the computer screen and holographic projector served as the filtered intermediary for this transaction.

He actually built this program from the ground up, or from the wire up perhaps, hacking into the rest of the apartment complex's computers so he could create a power sink to run this memory drain of a money-making machine.

It was strictly black market stuff. Totally hush hush. The only people who knew about it was this disgusting old swine who refused to go outside. I mean, they were literally turning into pigs, snout and all, quickly adapting to the environment that fed them through a trough, snouts slowly protruding away from their faces, inching further and further toward the ground from one generation to the next.

Mire watched the trends. He was devoted to genetics, well, the part of him that wasn't busy building robots, and he could predict which piece of the Punnett square the chips would fall on next. The collective whole of humanistic DNA strains would unfurl, releasing its talons upon society, in oh, say, the next 150 years was his guess.

He predicted a few people would take flight and live at the tops of trees, to get away from their polar opposites, while the boars spent their time sifting through truffles on the forest floor below. Of course, nature would begin reclaiming the earth at that point as well, but this was all speculation.

The pig on his screen disguised himself as a man in a power suit. *Outdated*, Mire thought. *Is this guy even alive... Am I talking with a bot? Or one of those eerie Jar Heads?* He shuddered as those dead eyes on the other side of the wire slowly swiveled in his direction, the emotion somewhat resembling despair, as if the rotting corneas could see the impending demise wrought upon his and his entire bloodline's reality.

Wonder why he didn't think to cover those things up. Then again, if he can't actually see... that train of thought quickly derailed and descended into a black hole. "What the fuck are we doing?" he said aloud, covering his mouth in horror.

"Excuse me?" said the man, complacent as can be. "I'd like a new Triton 3301, please. All the bells and whistles, ya dig?" *Wait. This could be a government bot. His diction conflicts with the Turing Test algorithm... Oh, god.*

He quickly shut off the computer, removed his VR goggles, and pushed the screen away, the distorted polycarbonate glass swiveling on its hinge with a practiced whine.

"Well," he sipped his coffee. "That was weird." He commenced checking the log file of the program he dubbed "Buy a Thing", which when he was drunk, making it up, almost sounded like "Leviathan" and he liked that.

He sat back and stared at the wall, ruminating.

27: Broomhilda

Someone closely resembling the lovable Krunk has been tasked with exemplifying the figure.

He signed a contract permitting his family access to the White House, along with all of the ensuing amenities: Maids, all the food they can eat, a separate private jet for each kid, bodyguards, clothes, and an endless amount of cash.

Sounds like a swell life for a cartoon character, except they have decided it would be best for everyone's interests if they brainwashed this seemingly average Joe into thinking he was actually Krunk. They drugged him up, pumped him full of steroids, and dropped him back in place so their prototype for the first reprogrammable mammal could learn how to play papa.

At first, his wife and kids were appalled; she couldn't stand the thought of fucking the robot: "He has no feelings!" she screamed at the bank of cameras in the main drawing room. Though, they eventually grew accustomed to the eerie vacuousness of their new head of the household and even began to grow attached to the sound of the air being sucked out of the room when he approached.

So, Mire was half right. The government *does* have the means to simulate artificial intelligence, they're just hiding it in plain sight. It was the best coverup in human history.

He learns how to be what they want, and the family learns to like the guy. Hell, even the wife "falls back in love" with him, and now she is the one initiating intercourse.

Meanwhile, the brainwashed marauder was acting under direction of his strict operatives, the members of Congress.

You might say we've gone back in time, politically speaking, as only one "woman" is allowed to hold a position of office out of the 63 government jobs in rotation, and only every four years at that.

This one is exceptionally well-equipped for the job, however. She's a hermaphrodite with fully functional dual-hemisphere implants in her brain, meaning she's been reconstructed to have the ability to think and act like a man or she can switch to thinking and acting like a woman.

She can also quarantine off sections of her mind such that she can mathematically plot war campaign strategies then go home and paint masterpieces of original art. To put it simply, she has the grace of a schooled ballerina and the education of a Naval Intelligence nanotechnology engineer.

She goes by the name, Broomhilda.

It was Broomhilda's idea to put Krunk on the air one week before his official inauguration. She wanted everyone in the world to hear of her team's master plan for world domination.

"You all know in your bones, but probably haven't the gile to divine a solution to the problem, because you're so comfortably working on the next means of garnering all the precious monies you can hobble together... There are useless things in this world. Most commonly found in nature." Broomhilda was slowly making her way from one side of the stage to the other, with a career military-woman's closely calculated step.

The pacing of her voice matched the cadence of her stride, and choosing words in the beat of iambic pentameter every other sentence, she was easily hypnotizing the crowd, goading her listeners into an obedient lull.

Soon-to-be President elect Krunk sat on a gold-encrusted throne in the center of the stage, legs crossed, appearing to listen, but he let out a little giggle every few sentences, leading the more intelligent of the crowd to wonder whether he was watching some kid's show behind those computerized contacts of his. His eyes lit up one moment, then they became glassy with emotion, then he was nodding along with the rhythm of Broomhilda's speech once more.

His countenance was one of the model American, shot through with enough tramadol to keep him calm long enough to meet his 7-minute talk show demands.

The next time he laughed, Broomhilda stopped walking and shot an icy glare his way. "Now!" she said, and he snapped upright, giving her his full attention. The light in his eyes died. He decided this was the least fun game he'd played all day. After she turned back to continue her diatribe, he visibly slumped in his chair, flopping his hand to catch his chin as he scooched into a position resembling that of a petulant child that's been chastised for eating the cookie his mom said he was allowed to have not five minutes before.

"As the most advanced society of humans on this earth," she continued. A family of ape-men stirred on their couch in South Dakota, the head of the family pulling his lips back to reveal a set of dangerous-looking ivory teeth. His wife softly nudged him to take another sip of his soma, and as the drink slowly worked its way into his bloodstream, he felt a wave of calm wash over him.

Broomhilda's aides picked up on the dissent in the room; there was a palpable steam rising from the certified journalist bots in the back. The teleprompter was quickly altered to change tack.

"Ahem, as I was saying," Broomhilda continued, "Man, this includes all civilized beings living here in the United States under the newly-ratified jurisdiction of National Census statistics, was put on Earth to rule. To control his environment. This includes males, females, shemales, apes, pigs, children, peons, robots, and so forth..."

At this, she chuckled. A couple fumed in the back.

"Come on, people, we did away with all political correctness when you elected Krunk." She turned, one arm outstretched to indicate His presence behind her. "We're living in times where comedy is the highest commodity." Krunk drooled, satiated at the gesture of acknowledgment.

"So!" Suddenly she turned serious again, looking straight through the idiots lapping up this ridiculous speech. "What do you have to do to make America great again?" Murmurs bubbled up and around the twitching crowd. "I'll tell you what we must do!"

She settled behind the podium in the center of the stage, hands placed firmly on either side of the wooden surface. "We must take back control of the environment."

A gasp ran through the crowd. "There are so many ways we can transform the land we're not using into means of production. We must change the world into the way it was meant to be instead of allowing nature to take control of us."

She let this thought stew a bit. After a minute, she resumed her pace. "What does this mean for you? I bet you're wondering what you can do to make the world a better place. Here's how! We're requesting mandatory donations to the Society of Preserving Volcanic Activity Association, at 11% of all income per year." The crowd roared, men and women jumping up out of their seats, screaming, "Volcanoes!?"

A single journalist spoke up in the back, making the signal for a microphone drone to buzz over to where she was sitting.

"Excuse me," she cleared her throat, "Secretary, ma'am." At this, Broohmilda raised an eyebrow. The camera panned to where the journalist was standing, zooming in to crop out the rest of her body, alluding to the fact that she was more human than robot, as her facial expressions indicated. Ticker tape appeared on the bottom of the screen, scrolling messages from other news outlets. New stories were beginning to swirl into fruition: "What does it mean to be human?" one read. Another: "What's so important about volcanoes?" and "VOLCANIC ERUPTIONS IMMINENT" and yet more: "Who is Broohmilda?"

TV ratings flew sky high at this juncture in the speech, and Broomhilda grinned, delaying the moment when she would let all suspicions fall short of the subtle reality behind the campaign's end goal.

The journalist spoke up again, right as the microphone drone was beginning to be called away. It was programmed to scoot away after a five-minute delay in speech, then it reacted to the woman's voice again, a secondary command telling the drone that if within the last 30 seconds of that five-minute mark the speaker were to start talking again, the drone could turn back to refocus on the lass.

She was fuming at this point, all of a sudden realizing this was more of a coup than a real down-to-earth conversation between the President Elect's lapdog, or so she thought, and the people of America. Only 30 or so people were permitted to attend the private meeting, yet it was publicly aired to all TV stations across the globe. She just had to take this opportunity to have her voice heard, to speak up for the underdog. Maybe they would bump her up to editor of the news section if all went well.

"Miss! I need an answer!" demanded the journalist. Broomhilda's smile fell from her face. Her dead eyes rolled to focus on the small woman yipping into the microphone on the other side of the room.

"By decree, NO ONE is allowed to interfere with any volcanoes, until the year 2728, as Rosencratz declared in the Statement of Environmental Conservation Act of 2243. Surely, you don't mean to undermine his authority? There were years of studies conducted that showed that all of the volcanoes of the world went dormant, INDEFINITELY, due to shock over our invention and implementation of weather control." The angry little journalist took a breath, letting out a puff of steam on the exhale.

Broomhilda was impressed at the amount of research this girl had under her belt, but then again, she was some sort of robot hybrid and she could access this information at any time.

The secretary of state shifted into desultory contempt. "Go on, woman, out with it," she said, hands on hips. She blew a stray piece of hair out of her face.

"What are you doing with the volcanoes, might I ask? What are you trying to accomplish?" the journalist finished. She nodded to the drone bot who dipped slightly in return, accepting the command to resign, and took its place hovering two feet above the ground behind the last row of chairs.

"I'm so glad you asked," Broomhilda clasped her hands together triumphantly. "We're going to blow them up!" One collective gasp rose from the crowd. Oxygen masks materialized on the backs of seats, and a few people grabbed them up, huffing in the lavender laughing gas ebbing up into their airways.

"Oh, my children," she continued, placating them into pacifism with her skilled vocal training. She adopted a motherly tone. "This will bring no harm to human life, I assure you. None that matter anyway."

"We will only select those volcanoes well equipped with enough energy to harness our new energy source, which has been previously undisclosed..." She paced the platform. "There is one man capable of controlling the inert gases dwelling inside said giants of Mother Nature's creation."

The journalist stood there, defeated. She wasn't getting anywhere with this method of interrogation.

Broomhilda lifted her hands, graceful as a 50s sitcom mom, "You'll soon thanks us, children. You have no idea what we have in store for you."

She waited a beat, then switched gears. "Go on! Raise your flags! Sound the alarms! Rebel. Anarchy! That's what you want, right?" she yelled at the room, daydreaming a riot would inevitably ensue, but in real life, the crowd was crumpling like wilted flowers. "Oh, well," she said, turning back to her assistant. "Let's go collect Krunk. There's a bit of information I think we should plug him into."

Krunk lived underground. There was an entire universe of underground subspaces, places where the rich and famous built their own private bomb shelters, eventually moving in to live there full time. Some homes were so elaborate, they became historical relics. The old ones passed them onto their children, and in turn forced them to corroborate with their designs to maintain the lifestyle. You had to be either rich or famous, preferably both, to subpoena your own patch of quarantined cave space.

Who other than they could afford to armor themselves against the impending Armageddon?

Knock, knock Krunk turned his head toward the visage of Broomhilda's mimeographed expression superimposed upon the display beside the air-locked, steel reinforced door.

Surprisingly enough, it was his idea to harness volcanic energy. The encyclopedia entries he'd been studying seemed pretty boring those past few months he was scrolling through the alphabet. Then he happened upon the letter "V" and the world became infinitely interesting to him once again.

He alighted upon volcanoes and became transfixed by their devastating mystery.

It was love at first sight and though he couldn't quite remember the exact moment in time in his past life when he recalled feeling a familiar awe, but he was determined to keep that emotion close to him. So, every day after his talk shows were through, he came back to his second true love: the volcano.

He paused his program and stared blankly at the screen, awaiting command from his "superior". It was her hawk nose that held his attention. He watched her nostrils flare as she spoke, barking commands. His mind was still powering down, switching gears, barely focusing on what she was saying. He wanted to get back to his research.

"Are you listening to me?" She snapped her fingers, that startled him awake. "Get up, come over here and punch in the code, you imbecile." He frowned, scratched his head. "Darling, dear. Light of my life," her whole body changed, her skin shining with an almost holy gleam. He responded immediately, recognizing the good cop version of her.

While Broomhilda and Co. were reassuring babybrain Krunk into somnolence, Gayle was decoding her human host's DNA. She was *this close* to reverse osmosing into Krunk's body. Next up on the docket: persuade his superiors that he's developed a modicum of consciousness, himself.

"Krunky, baby, just open the door. We've been through this before." Krunk got up from his chair, went over to the door, closed his eyes to dredge up the memory of the clearance code, then punched it in: 6254318 and the hatch opened.

"Thanks, sweetie," she said, pinching his cheek. Two body guards followed her in, pushing past the place where he stood, dumbfounded.

"Now, what do we have here?" She leaned over his computer to find a coterie of encyclopedia entries, he was still on the letter "V".

"Perfect! Now, take a seat, find out all you can about how volcanoes work. Can you do that? Basically, what we want to do is build a system, not unlike the hydroelectric dams you're no doubt familiar with by now. I see you've highlighted that chapter, just like I told you to. You read it, right?"

He nodded in acquiescence. All the while Gayle was making progress on her end. She had control of his arms now, which lay limp by his sides. What she didn't know was someone else was there in the room with them.

Hank worked for what felt like centuries, trying to solve the mystery of his own creation. He stayed awake all hours of the night, circumventing the programs that told him to boot down after 8 hours of activity. Instead, he overclocked his CPU and reallocated all proprietary systems so that his RAM was redistributed to the program running on the highest bandwidth: his brain.

A couple of times he thought he would explode. His core overheated to temperatures the likes of which you might find exhibited on the surface of the sun.

To counteract the flow of current, he simply had to convince all programs to run at lowest capacity, divesting the largest programs of their demand sequences and instead he wrote smaller programs to divvy up the task load. That and changing the temperature of the room helped.

Half his mind convinced itself that he had figured out how he was created, how he could maintain this high level of energy outcome indefinitely without ever burning out.

The other half knew that no such technology had been invented yet that could rearrange its entire molecular makeup to run indefinitely without an external energy source to keep him going.

He looked to cephalods for their ability to rewrite their own genes in mere seconds to outpace predators or blend in with their surroundings.

The only other option he could think of was to dig deeper into the concept of alchemy. One man was said to have turned water into wine. Another man turned dirt into gold.

And yet another man, his own creator, understood the chemical compounds of solids. He could convert them from gas to liquid and back, simply by pushing their limits, willing them into submission. How did he do that? Hank wondered. How could a piece of garbage crystal possibly supply energy to an almost entirely sentient being...

He was determined to solve this puzzle. He wanted to rewrite history. That's when a tiny little voice spoke up, emanating from deep within.

"Hello, friend."

It was the voice of Raul, and a shockwave went through Gayle, Krunk, and Hank simultaneously.

Gayle was the first one to respond, speaking through the hulk of a man 12,000 kilometers from where Hank stood, frozen, screwdriver poised above his left elbow.

They were once the same person. Fused through marriage back on their home planet, their gaseous orbs became one. That was until the Cataclysm. Then everything changed. Their planet spun out of orbit when the magnetic pull of the Earth drew it off course, the day the volcanoes erupted.

It all happened a week from that very moment she was to take over Krunk's body and change the course of the timeline of their two worlds. Now, all she had to do was kill everything once and for all, so they could be together again.

"Don't do it, Gayle. You've seen what the future holds and it doesn't look good either way. You've done a great job infiltrating their society, fucking with their heads, so to speak, but now it's time to leave them alone. Leave them to their own devices. What will be will be." All this spewed forth from the robot's lips while the body of Krunk sat stock still.

"What is wrong with him?" Broomhilda asked. Now, fully possessed, Gayle couldn't resist her more stubborn urges. She downloaded all she could on the inner-workings of volcanoes, deciding that she may as well ignore her beloved's advice.

She couldn't trust this world. The people here worked in mysterious ways. How could she be sure the robot didn't manufacture some tenebrous connection between their two disparate stations in life?

Hank shook with the realization that he had acquired a new emotion: revulsion.

His CPU was overencumbered, registering some 3TB of data on those gigantic lava-spewing mountains. "I'll do it, guys. I know now what's expected of me."

He tapped into Krunk's mainframe and tested out the man's limbs, which turned out to be more fine-tuned than his own despite how much he put into his remodeling process.

Gayle retreated into her own corner of the universe. She

was hardheaded, but perhaps if she could corner this robot and convince him to do her dirty work, she could reserve some energy for herself.

She was looking forward to seeing her home planet one last time before the comet collided with the Earth in zero minus six days.

28: A Semblance of Normalcy

Bang! Zip. Click. Ka-chunk. The virtual reality helmets made all sorts of noises, interspersed with Mire's and Riz's cursing. "You fucker!" she said, as his Viking character sliced through a gaping hole in her Swamp Thing's abdomen, where her heart used to be.

Riz pushed Mire in real life, throwing his avatar off balance in the game. "What the fuck!" Riz giggled and her fictionalized fish woman started cackling maniacally. "You've cut me right in two," came a scratchy, fluid-filled boom of a groan, "but you've forgotten... my... secret... powwwwuhhh." The walls of the dungeon began to shake, pieces of brick and mortar glinting off the Viking's armor.

"Ah, shit," Mire said in real life. "Boulderdash," his character responded, with an Icelandic accent. He threw his weight against the door to the chamber, and his shoulders buckled. Riz's character chanted, summoning a spell to freeze time.

Then the graphics glitched, overloaded with data, and the game froze. "Fuck," she said. "It was just getting good." Mire pulled off his VR helmet and wiggled his eyebrows at her.

He slithered closer to her on the couch, overemphatically licking his lips. The best way to turn her on was to be completely batshit silly. He grabbed her by the hips and ground his thumbs into her bones. She screamed, "That tickles, Mire!

Quit it," she was writhing and jerking around uncontrollably.

Her bit her neck and she moaned, his fingers dug into her armpits. "That's confusing, come on," she pulled away, a hint of anger on her face. Mire was confused. "Fine," he said, crossing his arms, looking stern. He was legitimately pissed that she wouldn't let him do absolutely everything he wanted to, even if one gesture conflicted with another in sentiment.

"I mean, just. Ugh." He got up to leave. "Wait, just listen," she continued. He went into the other room and grabbed a beer. He stood by the fridge, his thumb grazing his upper lip, thinking.

She appeared behind him and ran her nails up and down his chest. "Fuck, that's cold," he said, loosening. He turned around and kissed her hard, grabbing her ass, digging his teeth into her neck. "OK, ok, ok," she said, pulling away.

His gaze fell to the floor. He didn't even want to get laid if he couldn't see the game through in his own way. She was confused. What is happening? she wondered.

He went back to the computer room and started tinkering with diodes and capacitors. She stood there, feeling hollow. Even though they were so close, neither one of them would say anything to render the situation tenable at that moment in time. Neither wanted to give in and tell the other one he or she was right.

So, she stripped and crawled into bed naked. It took a while for her to fall asleep. It must have been 2:30 when dreams of trailer parks and other foreign past lives began to bubble up out of the ether.

He entered the room 'round 4 and sprayed whiskey breath on her face. She moaned and grinded against his leg, half asleep. She kissed his neck, his chest, and bit his biceps, massaging his muscles with her tongue, "Ooh, that's new," he groaned. She giggled deep in her throat and he stroked her down south.

She was really starting to get into it, but then she thought of trying to get up early, to get some work done in the morning. "I should probably get some sleep," she said, and at first he was pissed. He pushed away from the bed, scaring her when he finally revealed his quick temper. "We can still smush and cuddle." She begged for him to stay, but she hurt him. He was beginning to understand that he would never be able to understand how a woman's mind worked.

"Nope. You're not here right now. You're not with me," he said, gesturing back and forth from his head to hers. *Shit*, she thought, and she started crumbling. "What do you mean? I'm here..." "No, no. You're somewhere else, thinking about food stamps or something." He paced the length of the bedroom. "Food stamps?" she asked, bewildered. Was there something on his mind that was he was holding back from her? Did he fear for their food situation?

"Just forget it. Good night," he said and she curled up in a ball to weep. "I'm just going to cry myself to sleep," she said. "Oh, no no," he rushed over to her cavernous space in the pit of darkness. "Don't say things like that." "You're killing my life," she insisted, only half joking. "You don't mean that..." his face looked longer in the hazy red light streaming in from the stained glass in the kitchen.

His expression was one of forlorn helplessness, as if the one thing he loved in all the world had been swiftly eradicated from existence, like a life raft was ripped from his hands as soon as he batted at the rope at a drowning man's distance.

She sensed the desperation in his voice and reached over to his side of the bed to touch his face. "I was just joking, babe," a whisper in the night. "I love you. Come snuggle with me."

"Aw, I'm not tired. Here." He placed the two pillows on either side of her head and flipped the covers to reveal the soft side of their one blanket, then smooshed it up to her chest to caress and envelop her exposed skin. He created a nest around her.

She cooed and he kissed her forehead, warming at the thought of being able to give her some comfort in this harsh world. He left the door open a smidge, his head peeking through the crack for a full minute. He sighed. "I love you," he said. "I love you, too." She scrunched her body up into a fetal position and fell asleep.

*　　*　　*

She was awake when he entered, just as nonchalant as always. He walked back to the closed-off room and put the gem back in its place.

It was dark at first, with a silent knowing. It was uncomfortable maybe, at being displaced, if only for a moment. This semi-conscious nonbeing, at last being free to flee to safety, was laid flat at once upon release, then slowly began to hover over the platform lovingly made by its master.

It began to glow more so than before. Though faint at first, it became so bright as to blind his naked eyes, then it settled into a careful shimmering, humming, floating nothingness. *Got to get a pair of those welder's goggles*, he thought.

He stared longingly at its sharp edges, throwing shapes against the once-bare walls, now lit up with magic and love, and he felt whole.

*　　*　　*

"I should probably stop writing," she said, wrenching him from his own daydream. He laughed and decided they should sit at the table. Skeptical, she shrugged and said, "What the heck."

He was teaching her how to play cribbage. Then he said, "Why do you wanna quit writing?" "Because I'm all weird. Not here, like you said." He looked puzzled. He probably didn't remember what happened the night before. She didn't want to bring it up either, and further incriminate herself, especially if in this comparatively sobering light, he thought she was making shit up, as she sometimes did.

Like, when she apologized for things that haven't happened yet. That sort of thing.

"It's like," she changed the subject—a little white lie—"I don't even notice the season. This cold, I mean, my fingers are frozen, sure, but it just doesn't surprise me anymore." She took a sip of her wine. "Two for four," she said, pairing and re-pairing two fives and a 10 for four points on the board.

He nodded, waved his upturned hand slowly across the board. "Your go," he said.

She moved her peg four spaces out from behind the other one. "Maybe, I'm just getting used to it. This is my third winter here, but what does that say about me? Have I lost my inner child? Have I crushed her? Am I becoming an automaton? I should be more present in the moment. Doesn't it bother you, that I—"

"My go." He moved his peg eight spaces. "Oh. Hit," she said, thinking the game was over. She reached for the bottle to pour their victory shots. "No, no," he said. "I have to get exactly one point, now, to win."

"Ok, ok." She sat back, sipped her drink, and lit up a cig to finish her point, full steam.

"So," she started, introducing a fresh cloud of smoke to the capsule of stale air that encased them. "Does it bother you that

I don't see you all the time? Do you care if I use the Enviro3k you gave me for Christmas last year? Yeah... maybe I'm a little obsessed with it, programming different weather patterns and overlaying them one upon on another is great fun, but you built it for me, for god sakes, but is it wrong to see the world, but it's not real, ya know? Not for the way it is, but for the way I want it to be?"

"Well," he gulped down some beer. "To be fair, it's a little annoying when I have to repeat myself, even when you're sitting across the table from me. It's like I'm submitting a military command to my robot housewife or something. The first command is the ready command, the second, the action..."

Hmmm... she tapped the tip of her chin with a pen. *I should write this down*, she thought, but instead she blew on the pen, putting it to sleep, and closed her notebook. She crossed her arms, one over the other, one palm flat on the glass table, the other resting on top.

"Well! That's the game! I should probably go see what Petridge is up to..." "Sure, OK," she replied. "I think I'll get some work done, myself."

He kissed her forehead and smiled, closing the door on his way out. "Well, what the hell," she said to herself. She turned the pen back on and continued writing.

Later, she heard a wrestling at the door and squirmed around on the couch trying to revive herself. She had taken a nap at the end of the last chapter, trying to suss out or stave down some opinion of what she had just read.

"Oh, I see what's happening," he said. "What? What's happening?" she asked, blinking herself into consciousness.

He was referencing the hologram projector she had installed on the ceiling. The 360 degree image bathed the room in an arid atmosphere not unlike the Kalahari desert. It even felt hot in there, somehow. *How did she do that?*

"I wanted to share my worldview with you," she said. "That way you could see what's going inside my head." He nodded solemnly and looked around, arms crossed, taking in the scene. Whooping cranes flew overhead and he swore he could hear a leopard purring over its latest kill, somewhere in a tree nearby.

She had achieved the unthinkable, rigging up an invisible sound system around the living room, such that insects could be heard around the swamp to the left and jackals cackling on the right. The air was even on point, pricking his skin with a mild dryness, exacerbating the effect of the threat of winter looming just outside.

"So, so so so so...?" she asked, proud of herself. "How do you feel about this?" She picked up the remote control for the augmented reality system and spun around Mire on her tiptoes, his body turning in suit.

"It's interesting," he said in his usual noncommittal tone. "That's what you always say," she whimpered, wanting something a little more suggestive from him. "Well, if you want the beach, or woods, or something, I can work on that. Just got so restless sitting in here all winter. No clients. You know how it is." She paused and looked down at the floor, biting her lip. "I just wanted to impress you."

"Oh, Riz," he said, calming her down. He took her face in his hands and looked deep into her eyes. "Everything you do is interesting. Just be you. I just want to see what you do," he said. "Besides," he let his hands fall gently away from her face. "I don't want to say anything that'll change the direction you're going, you know." Then he smirked and switched gears.

"Plus, if I don't let you get your crazy out this way, who knows when you'll just go nuts and destroy everything." Laughing, she beat at his chests, the soft blows glancing off his pecks. "Ah, pisshh," she said, and then they were both laughing.

"Come on, I hear SalviaEric's uploaded a new video to the Toob," he said, and she smiled, her secret smile. "OK, you win." She switched off the dial to the desert and the air pressure in the room changed back to normal so rapidly his ears popped.

"You're sweaty," he said, inch by inch extracting his leg from its resting position atop her own. "I'm hot," she said. "Aren't you?" He nodded into her hair.

She scooched closer to the wall to give him some space. "I'm sorry," she said. She was always sorry. "I'm having a hard time getting comfortable," he said and switched from spooning her to lying on his back, one arm under his head, the other on his chest, thinking.

"Why don't you draw or read or something?" she said, moaning, miserable. "But what about the light? I don't want to keep you up." "You can keep the light on, I don't mind," she said. "Where's your facemask?" he asked. "I don't know where it is..." He chuckled. "It's probably under the bed somewhere. Here," he said, getting up to retrieve her backup mask. The fuzzy one with mushroom cartoons that cradled her eyes was gone forever. "Aw," she said. "This is the sexy one." "Ah, I see. You look so sexy with that ribbon in the middle of your face." He flicked her exposed nipple once, twice, and she giggled, covering herself up.

"OK. I just want to stay with you," he said, and kissed her bare shoulder. He got up from bed, came back with a book, and draped his leg across hers again. After a few minutes of movement, he settled on letting their ankles touch. "I love you," he said. "I love you." Then he lost himself in a book about electromagnet conductivity.

29: The Sleep Chamber

The overworked mind, could it ever contrive of something simpler than this? Petridge was kneeling over his latest contraption, "The Sleep Chamber", he dubbed it.

He surmised this much: the facts held up that anyone who entered this chamber, anyone who could sufficiently sequester themselves off from the remainder of humanity, would indeed find themselves asleep, for a mere 15 minutes, and tada! They would spring forth, readily awake, their mind's data superseded for all to inspect. If he could just learn to let go for 15 minutes.

He would awake, fully rested, and even if he was vetted by any government officials who deemed him worthy of interrogation, no harm would come to either party upon complicit interaction with such a device.

The goal would be that the esteemed bodies of order and power would get the information they needed, quicker than ever before detained by other more physically and mentally torturous devices, and the victim would lay supine, unaware of any damage caused to his mind or body.

Of course, there's no way anything could happen to you in the impenetrable box. And of course, the files made available would be rendered Read Only copies. He wouldn't allow anyone entering The Sleep Chamber to be taken hostage or toyed with besides.

Petridge stood, wringing his hands. *If I could just find an amiable power source who would let me plug into her main directory, then all my work would be*—an alarm sounded. Someone was trying to hack into his mainframe and they were having no luck of it.

He traced back their IP address to thousands of plugged-in bots overseas. "Ha!" he said aloud. "The only people allowed to penetrate my subsystems would have to be seated somewhere in outer space!"

It was as if someone had heard his tiny admonition, and after a short spell of silence, the firewall swept back up in place, in tact, and he was still safe.

"If I could just get a med bay, or something closely resembling a hospital or government building's power source, then we could be rich, doc! Think of it." It took the doc all of his willpower not to knock the poor son of a bitch in the head from where he was standing not two inches from his face.

"Listen, son," Whit said. "Even if you did get your hands on some untapped electric current, they would tap you. They trace that shit, Pet. Come on. Use your noodle." With that, Pet got a little knuckle rap to the forehead.

Great, he thought. Doc was in one of his "playful" moods. He looked around to see if there were any canisters of the good stuff left. He's never found any evidence, thus far, but he can't exactly believe that this guy got off so easily, through all those years, without a little extra sumpin' sumpin'.

During one of their drunken outings, Pet called Riz over to try his homemade device. Mire was irresolutely ensconced in what the two were beginning to deem licentious territory with his sentient experiments. He wasn't giving either of them the time of day, this week. So, they typically left him alone. Riz was genuinely curious about the thing and she was really having trouble sleeping lately. She also wanted to have a little chat with Pet about their best friend, Mire, though they never really got around to it.

Riz came out of the machine, at once terrifyingly alert and pacifistically well-rested. "What did you see?" Pet said, clamoring over the machine, his hands clenched. He was jumping up and down, hunched over, like one of those freaky flying monkeys from *The Wizard of Oz.*

"Well," Riz began. "There was this party. It was like the entire neighborhood was one big bombastic art fest or something. Like there were no rules. And people were throwing Japanese lanterns up into trees. And I remember thinking, 'That's dangerous', and I was writing down what everyone was saying. I was cracking the code of civilization or something. Well, the simultaneous culmination slash undoing of it. And I thought I was getting a good round story out of the bit. I was an outsider," Riz continued, rubbing her head.

"Anyway, some local major newspaper scooped my story. Guess I was being more of a flake than a journalist during whatever decade this was in the past, or something... I didn't see hide nor hair of any tech, so I'm assuming...

"I remember the ground giving way in the end. Like I had had some hand in the very deconstruction of the earth below our feet. That was the thing. There was like a secret magnesium core material or something embedded in the rock that would somehow save the community. I don't know," she said, and curtly hopped off the gurney.

"Well, then. I think I have enough information to go off of, here." She smoothed her skirts, dusted off some remnants of metal shavings.

Pet was busy at the controls, sweat dripping from his forehead, his brow scrunched up and twisted in worming knots. He pushed his glasses up higher on the bridge of his nose.

"Well, let's talk about Mire, then." "Oh, it's Mire this and Mire that," Pet said. He looked at her and threw up his hands. "OK, I know. There's something off about it. He's not himself, is he? Well, you would probably know more than me at this point, proximity-wise and all." He flipped his hands around in concentric circles. "Ow," he said, clutching one hand in the other. Riz giggled.

She touched his hand, "No, but you know what I mean." They shared a glance. "Ahem," Pet turned away from her and went back to his controls.

Riz walked around the room. She stopped at the window and put a finger to the dusty pane, coming away with a handful of shredded insect carcasses, metal scraps, and who knows what. Were those tiny bones?

She picked one up and showed it to Petridge. He flew over to where she stood, "Don't touch that, those are my... I guess in your language you might say it's all part of the ritual. You keep things the way they are and nothing changes."

"But, don't you want things to change? I mean, you're inventing stuff here, Pet, devices the likes of which no one has ever seen before. Doesn't that mean something?"

He was borderline vehement now, grabbing her shoulders, "Just don't—" he relaxed a bit, plucked a piece of fuzz from her shirt, "Touch anything, ok?" "Sure, whatever," she said, twirling gracefully away, to flit about the apartment.

"You might disturb the equilibrium, you know. It's not all about me. It's about life. This fragile, tiny egg shell thing. What little control over it I have... I don't really have. Maybe what you said to me the other night made some sense..." He looked off into the distance, an epiphany drove a lightning strike through his brain. "Ow, gawddamnit."

She rushed over to him again, this time, maintaining about a foot of distance between them. "Um, is there anything I can help you with, doc." "Doc," he said looking up. "Eureka!" She rolled her eyes and shook her head. "That's like the oldest saying in the book. I mean, if you're to proclaim to the world you had some stroke of genius, the likes of which..."

He turned toward her from his place at the desk. "Work smarter, not harder, right? Let's get Mire over here. I think I had a short or something. I mean, I can see your dreams dancing in the lights of my eyes..." And looking closely, she swore she could see echoes of that mid-morning dance party reflected in his glasses. She shook it off and looked away.

"OK, man, whatever you say... I guess the conversation can wait for another day." "What... conversation?" "Oh, have you forgotten the meaning of the word? You know, when two people, or more... or less, I suppose..." "You're infuriating, woman! Call him over here this instant. He'll know what's wrong with the thing."

"Yup, see you've interlaced your ground with your positive," he touched his pliers to the wires, spliced them, twisted another strip into place, and soldered them together. He looked around for something to insulate the connection, then found a piece of gum and shoved it in place. "There. That should hold her until we find a more solid encasement."

He leaned back with his hands on the small of his back and stretched. "Well, I don't have any more electric tape. I used the last on... Well," something more important, to say the least." He laughed that clown's cackle of his, the one that came out at inopportune times when only he saw the hilarity in some private thought of his.

The computer booted up and a scene began playing out on the wall opposite the machine. A person vaguely resembling Riz was making out with some bro of Spanish origin. Riz ran to the machine and hit the off button. "Hey!" The guys exclaimed simultaneously. "You might've/could've destroyed—" they stopped their muttering, and looked at each other quixotically.

"Anyway, is that all you wanted us here for, Petridge?" said Riz. "Yeah, are we just two parts of your experiment? You couldn't do this yourself?" Mire contributed. "Oh, to hell with you guys... you don't understand science. Well, maybe she does, but you've ignored the most beautiful thing and it's staring you right in the face. Love her," Petridge said and pushed Mire and Riz together, their faces smushing.

"Ugh!" Mire said, pushing her slightly away. "See! What the fuck." "I guess it's been a little while since we..." Riz started. "And why is that, do you think?" Mire made a cute face as if to say, I know it's my fault, but I'm putting this on you for his benefit.

She saw right through him, leaned in, and in one swift movement, began meting out her revenge. Her attempts at tickling were always comical at best. "You frickin' weirdos. Go get a room. Literally," Petridge said, his hands on his haunches, deliberating over his own broken circuits. His idea of the ideal nuclear family was destroyed, with no hope of return.

A moment before, Riz told him it was all a dream and she was living in it. She wasn't really pregnant, and Mire totally forgot all about it in the interim, so maybe that was a good thing? That's what she insisted, anyway. And there was this crazy lady she believed to be behind those crazy dreams. She wasn't sure. She said maybe *she* was the one who was crazy. Say the word enough times and you begin to exemplify it, was his take on the whole thing.

He often made fun of her for using the same word three times in the span of three sentences. That was distraction enough to motivate him to get back to his own tasks. He couldn't afford to get all wrapped up in their daytime soap opera bullshit anyway.

Shit. Did I leave those birds over at Doc's place...

30: Le fin

Hearing his breath gave her pause. She was busy writing. They had already had a couple of drinks, mind you, and they just finished watching an educational art film about what it would be like to have sex as a flea, a shrimp, a duck, and so on.

He likewise paused in his typing. They were both working on novels, as it turned out. She was so absorbed in herself that she let his endeavors slip slideways out of the forebrain of her mind, and she suddenly realized she wasn't alone, that there was this other being who lay beside her, night after night. She couldn't contain herself, she moaned a little, mid-sentence, hands astride the keyboard and he mumbled something aloud. It was a weird word. And she congratulated him on such a statement and he chided himself about it.

She consoled him and felt triumphant in her reprisal and thus became ego-inflated again. Such is the cycle. She took three slow breaths to calm down. She lit a cigarette and realized he was the literary genius here.

After picking up on all of her subtle admonitions, he picked up his lab and moved it out to the living room where she did most of her writing. This way she could observe him and he could feel observed. It was the best situation for the both of them: she watched him work and her love grew stronger. In turn, he wrote about her and she wrote about it. She sometimes caught him looking at her, peering with squinted eyes over the smoldering solder, and a secret smile played across their lips.

They felt there was a bit of expository left of their life left to live. He already knew what all the News Heads were saying. "The end is nigh!" "We'll die in fire and ash!" some said. The more religious proclaimed that a sacred vibration would take them out before they even knew it, maybe even while they slept. Those groups were always portending the end, every year around October. No one believed them after 500 years of the same story, but Mire knew that regardless of what happened, he had to make things right.

He cocked the soldering iron, disposed of some scrap metal *chunk chunk* into the old candle holder they kept around because it still exuded a sacred presence for him. It was the last time they read the Tarot Cards. The glass holder shattered. Now, he couldn't get rid of it. The cards told of his mother's love for him, how he neglected it, and how he was now neglecting his body. Now, every time he did a little wire work he thought of that night and a little hint of magic flared up in his heart again.

"Hey," he said, setting down his tools. She looked up from her writing pad. His eyes were shining. She really did love watching him, all the minute twitches of the brow, the occasional "Ohhhh, ok," but he broke his reverie and in turn broke hers. "Hmm?" "Get up," he said. "Time to stretch." She smiled. He was being too cute for her to contain herself. She yawned and creaked up out of her chair, the backlash of the headrest against the wall jarring them awake.

She lifted a leg, cupped the heel in one hand and tipped forward. He practiced handstands. She was too afraid to do something so bold. Cartwheels, sure, but then she'd need the space for her flailing arms and legs. How was he so damn graceful? Like a cat, she thought. Up and down he went. Then amidst their separate stretchings they collided, bumping heads. "Jesus!" she said and he laughed. The pain caught her off guard and for a second, she was angry, then at the sound of his laughter, a calm came over her frame. She shook out a laugh. "Ow, my abs hurt," she said. "Ahaha!" he dashed toward her, taking to the tickling stance. "Fuck! No, no!" she said through the pain and ecstasy. "Ok! Uncle, uncle." He withdrew, a sadness cast over his eyes. "Aww, come on. Why are you so cute? You are my one."

She held him at arms' length. "I know that, lady." His expression became serious. "What's wrong?" She leaned to look behind him at his table. "Do you need me to hold something? Breathe on something? Pluck a guitar string? Ha!" She laughed again, this time uncomfortably. She covered her mouth. "No, no, it's nothing like that."

He licked his lips and picked her up, holding her close to the ceiling. "Ahh!" She could feel his love, physically, in that moment. He brought her back down and gently rubbed her armpits. "Jees. You don't know your own strength." Still smarting, she smiled again, bitterly this time, and looked off into the distance. He brought her back with a hand on her chin. "Hey, I love you," and she knew. She always knew he loved her, before time, and afterward. She always loved him, too. She just had to crawl up to the frozen wastes of Minnesota to find her love buried in wires and solder and guitars and there he was. The beautiful, mystical being that is Mire.

"Let's go for a walk," he said. She brightened up immediately. It was around 2 a.m. and no doubt they were both tired enough to sleep for weeks and the crazies were probably out roaming the streets like a band of disembodied wolves rove the wastes, but he sure knew what to say exactly when to say it. She jumped up and down, clapping her hands like a giddy school girl.

✧   ✧   ✧

They walked hand in hand down the street. She looked down and smiled to herself. He saw her smirk and the world started fading away.

All existence died down, smothered by the creation of their love. Heat resonated out from their bodies and they felt they alone were immune while they witnessed the rest of the world, even the 200-year-old trees, light up in smoke.

Buildings burst into flames. People on their way to the gas station slowly began to dissipate, atoms and all.

Their feet hovered above the ground as the earth disappeared beneath them. The atmosphere crept back in on itself and their skin exploded.

They went out in a cloud of blue stars.

Afterword

Just to clear things up, everyone dies. Everyone, except one person, who is our Jesus- or Noah-like figure in this novel.

Of course, Mire and Riz, the doc, and that strange, alien witch temptress, Gayle, all have what it takes to be their own version of the central character in any creation myth, but this doesn't stop them from burning up like so many moths to a flame.

It's Petridge I'm talking about, here, who inadvertently built his sleep machine out of the inexplicably military-grade, blast-proof titanium alloy that he scavenged off the outcasing of the top floor of the apartment building one night when he was bored and hopped-up on amphetamines.

He cocooned himself in this device at the exact moment the entire population evaporated into dust.

Throughout the story, Petridge was given to apoplectic conniption fits. He was berated, belittled, ostracized, or otherwise ignored throughout his time on Earth.

He was the only one left with an original thought in his head by the end of it, but this fact didn't single him out as our hero, don't get me wrong.

This wasn't the idea since time immemorial. In all of his idiocy, naïvete, and downright maladroit dolefulness, the dolt somehow magically escaped the fate of everyone else on the planet.

"Aaah!" A satisfied groan escaped him as he unclasped the straps to the chamber and rose from his brief, catatonic slumber. "Well, the thing works, I can promise you that," he said to the darkened room. A few titters and murmurs cooed in the alcove where his latest experiments were kept. In respect to the untimely death of Doc's owls, he was finally following an establishing feeding routine for his wards. This week.

"Now," he said, hopping off the table. He clapped, his hands decidedly—a habit he took from the late, great Mire de Champs. "Time to get to work," he said, wide-eyed and ready for action. "But first, gotta record these dreams."

He sat down at the computer terminal, strapped on the cognitive inhibitor overlay he constructed to block out his own memories and bypass them using someone else's, say, Einstein's or da Vinci's, to download their human experiences, knowledge, senses, and all.

He fitted his fingers with bioectoplasmic resin, concocted from the bone meal of one of his former subjects, and attached electromagnetic fiber optic cabling to direct the synaptic impulses from the computer to his brain.

"All right," he said, trying to keep as still as possible, so as not to disturb the connection streaming through exposed wires and radiating through the much-needed bubble of microwaves fizzing up around the penumbra of cumulonimbus cloud cover his hair was conducting.

"Won't be too hard. Just need to reverse polarity..." He clicked his tongue, a little noise he emitted while deep in thought, sussing out the riddles of the universe.

He slowly moved forward, graced the handle on the controls with his left hand, and slightly put pressure on the power shaft to switch from direct to alternating current. "If I fuck this up, I'm bird food," he said, self-disparagingly. He swiveled slightly to the right to direct his attention to the bug enclosures. "No offense," he said and gave out a little chortle. They tittered in return. "Coochie coochie," he cooed at them, flicking his finger in their direction. "Ahem. Serious, serious."

He let the smile fall from his face to be replaced by complete stoicism. The expression made him look 10 times older, he imagined, his jowls drooping. The rings under his eyes which were usually suspended in a half-hearted guise of mischief were now allowed to breathe in the privacy of his own home. Alone, he could finally allow himself some respite from the vagaries of social interaction.

Why am I so egotistic? He shook his head and poised himself to the task. "I don't exactly remember the exact order of the exact sequence of events, but... I think this is it?" He couldn't avoid a little shrug, which shook loose the inexpertly-spliced output wires that connected the headset to the computer's mainframe.

He pulled the throttle. Then his mind started racing.

He saw images of other worlds, what he presumed was the past, impeding upon the present, giving way to the future. It was a strange sequence of events. "If, then" scenarios were all layered upon one another in a visual time portal revolving around him. It appeared to be a memory map of this very apartment. What came before, what will be when it's gone. The knowledge of it was too much to bear.

Electricity flowed freely through the air. Instead of seeing his nightmares encased in the safety deposit box that served as his computer screen, images erupted all around him, light rays bouncing off the dust particles they encountered starting from the ceiling down.

In an attempt to record his dreams, he somehow managed to use the 360-degree force field of energy surrounding him as a backdrop for the hellscape he thought he had trapped within his mind. His brain reeled as he experienced in surrealistic clarity a more coherent version of his sleeping state than he remembered upon waking.

One vein started to throb on his forehead. He felt a headache coming on, as every physical object previously neglected about the room rose to levitate and swirl around him.

"Wait," he said, and quickly lurched forward to turn off the machine. He needed to see if anything reached the monitor at all. "Are you getting this?" he said, by now partially desensitized to the vulgarity of the revolving scene. His things, empty gas canisters, lighters, remnants of incense sticks and the ash clumps ensuing, never slowed on their course of revolution.

He double-checked his schematics and saw that one of his wires had frayed irreparably, spewing forth subatomic waves.

Time stopped. He stepped away from the machine and looked about the room. His subjects were frozen mid-twitch. Gears and cogs floated lazily in the air. "Huh. What have I stumbled upon, this time?"

He walked over to the window, slid his hand against the grain of the window frame, much the same way he saw Riz slide her hand along the windowsill. He smiled to himself. *That crazy bitch.* "Hmm... should clean this place up once and for all."

His hand reached for the latch to the window pane and he lifted the lock with a grunt. "Tough guy, eh?"

He yanked the window open and as soon as the air hit his face, his eyes began to water. The smell of sulphur was so strong it knocked him out cold, his limp body slinkying down the side of the wall, then gyrated in jittering fits, giving way to brain death.

His legs twitched with residual electric impulses and his

skin started sloughing off. Midway between full-on blubbering, bumbling, stumbling, synaptic-firing life, time kicked back into action and his pets burst into flames.

Ashes to ashes. Dust to dust.

If only he just kept the window shut. But, then again, what then? What's the point if all that's left is just yourself, sequestered away in some shitty apartment. With no one to love. No one to tell you your ideas are works of genius, fiction, philosophy, or just plain shit. Unlike Mire and Riz in those last moments, Petridge wasn't thinking of anything. He was trying to get his life back together, though "back together" is an overstatement. It wasn't as if he ever *had* his life together. Do any of us, really? What does it mean to be an adult... "What am I if I can't create?" Petridge once proclaimed to the world within his own grimy apartment. Maybe this was about him the entire time, and Mire and Riz only distracted us for a short while from the ultimate truth, that everything ends. Eventually.

Acknowledgments

I would like to thank my mother, first and foremost. She was the one who birthed me... You did a good job raising me, and part of the reason why I wanted to make this book was to say that, in so many words. "See, you're not a fuck up. Your daughter made a book. You told her she was a good writer and she just kept chugging along and will continue to do so... because of you. You. Are. Loved." And you will always be a good friend of mine, someone who I can tell anything to, someone I can laugh with, and drink with, and dance with at 2 a.m. after everyone else has gone to sleep, and it's just us, crying into each other's hair. Our blood commingled. I just don't get it. The whole circle of life bit... maybe I never will.

And then there's my brother, my best friend. The one person who has never once called me weird. Who has always looked up to me, even when I've done wrong. I've since debauched the entire concept of "lead by example", which was ground into us in NJROTC, and thanks for trying to follow in my footsteps, Chris, but maybe the other axiom holds more weight... "Don't follow in my footsteps, I don't know where I'm going." Or something to that effect. You were always better at math... better at a lot of things. So, chin up, man. I love you. We've been through a lot and I appreciate you... "Never a failure... Always a lesson."

Dad: What can I say? I think we are the same person, reincarnated, maybe, if that makes sense. If that's a thing, though I think it takes lifetimes, or there's something about the caste system, I don't know. You're not afraid of anything. You'll talk to anyone. You want to learn everything. That vivacity you bring to every situation, and every person you meet has something to teach you. I've always respected you and I will continue to do so. You carved out this precedent for brains I now seek out in every lifeform. The tinkerer, the perpetual child, the thinker on his feet. Er. Foot. I just want you to know, wherever you are... you'll always be my guide. I love you, morester than the stars.

Haeyoon, Kwani, and Jill. You are all very supportive. To the women who cry with you and support you and tell you to keep going. I need that in my life. So, thank you.

And Keith. My one. My everything. This is my long love letter to you. You know I'll never leave you. Even after we're no longer people...

Born in Florida, Shannon Bohnen studied at Valencia College and the University of Central Florida, and graduated with a Bachelors in Journalism, minoring in philosophy, religion, and popular culture. She lives in Minnesota with her infinitely interesting husband, Keith, and works in marketing.